Praise for Lindsay McKenna

"The believable and real romance between Tara and Harper is enhanced by the addition of highly dimensional supporting characters, and a minor mystery subplot increases the tension by a notch. This is a fine addition to a strong series."—*Publishers Weekly* on *Lone Rider*

"Captivating sensuality."—*Publishers Weekly* on *Wind River Wrangler*, a Publishers Marketplace Buzz Books 2016 selection

"Moving and real . . . impossible to put down."—*Publishers Weekly*, starred review on *Wind River Rancher*

"Cowboy who is also a former Special Forces operator? Check. Woman on the run from her past? Check. This contemporary Western wraps together suspense and romance in a rugged Wyoming package."—Amazon.com's Omnivoracious, "9 Romances I Can't Wait to Read" on *Wind River Wrangler*

"Set against the stunning beauty of Wyoming's Grand Tetons, *Wind River Wrangler* is Lindsay McKenna at her finest! A *tour de force* of heart-stopping drama, gut-wrenching emotion, and the searing joy of two wounded souls learning to love again."—International bestselling author Merline Lovelace

"McKenna does a beautiful job of illustrating difficult topics through the development of well-formed, sympathetic characters."—*Publishers Weekly* on *Wolf Haven* (starred review)

**Books by *New York Times* bestselling author
Lindsay McKenna**

WIND RIVER WRANGLER

WIND RIVER RANCHER

WIND RIVER COWBOY

WRANGLER'S CHALLENGE

KASSIE'S COWBOY (novella included in
CHRISTMAS WITH MY COWBOY)

LONE RIDER

WIND RIVER LAWMAN

HOME TO WIND RIVER

Published by Kensington Publishing Corporation

HOME TO
WIND RIVER

LINDSAY
McKENNA

ZEBRA BOOKS
KENSINGTON PUBLISHING CORP.
www.kensingtonbooks.com

ZEBRA BOOKS are published by

Kensington Publishing Corp.
119 West 40th Street
New York, NY 10018

All Kensington titles, imprints, and distributed lines are available at special quantity discounts for bulk purchases for sales promotion, premiums, fund-raising, educational, or institutional use.

Special book excerpts or customized printings can also be created to fit specific needs. For details, write or phone the office of the Kensington Sales Manager: Attn.: Sales Department. Kensington Publishing Corp., 119 West 40th Street, New York, NY 10018. Phone: 1-800-221-2647.

Zebra and the Z logo Reg. U.S. Pat. & TM Off.

First Printing: January 2019
ISBN-13: 978-1-4201-4750-6
ISBN-10: 1-4201-4750-1

ISBN-13: 978-1-4201-4751-3 (eBook)
ISBN-10: 1-4201-4751-X (eBook)

10 9 8 7 6 5 4 3 2 1

Printed in the United States of America

*To Rosalie, her family, Bonnie, and her employees
(Patty among these terrific folks), who make
Cork and Catch the BEST restaurant,
with the freshest seafood in Arizona!
I love the family atmosphere there!
Customers ARE family.
It's a love fest between people who come to
Cottonwood, AZ (central Arizona and sixteen miles
south of Sedona/Red Rock country),
for the freshest meat, seafood and veggies EVER.
I've traveled the world, gone to many starred
restaurants. And our Arizona gem, Cork and Catch,
in a town of ten thousand people here in Cottonwood,
is where I go to eat. If you're in my neck of the woods?
Drop in and see Rosalie and her family.
You'll never want to leave. Me? I'm the lucky one ;-)
www.corkandcatch.com*

Chapter One

How was Jake Murdoch, her foreman, going to react to the news?

Maud Whitcomb, owner of the Wind River Ranch, pushed her fingers through her dark hair that was threaded with silver. Sitting in her large office, she waited with anticipation. Jake was an ex-recon Marine with severe PTSD he dealt with day in and day out. As the foreman for their hundred-thousand-acre ranch for the last three years, he'd proved himself invaluable despite his war wounds. She was pretty sure he wouldn't be happy.

Jake's symptoms made him a loner, boarded up like Fort Knox, and he liked living alone in the huge cedar log cabin a mile from the main ranch area. Dragging in steadying breath, Maud heard heavy footsteps echoing outside her open office door. It was early June and, for once, there was bright sunshine and a blue sky in western Wyoming.

She saw Jake's shadow first and then him. He was six-foot, two-inches tall, a solid two hundred pounds of hard muscle. His shoulders were almost as broad as the doorway he stood within. At thirty years old, any woman worth her salt would turn her head to appreciate his raw good looks and powerful physique. His temperament, however, was open to question. He was known as "Bear" around the ranch. Bear as in grizzly bear. He was terse, not PC, completely honest and didn't brook idiots for more than two seconds.

Swiftly glancing up at him as he entered, Maud watched him take off his dark brown Stetson and saw his expression was set; any emotion he felt was hiding behind what he called his game face.

"Jake. Come on in," she said, waving a hand toward a wooden chair in front of her desk. "How's your mom doing?"

Grunting, Jake hung up his Stetson on a nearby hat tree and turned, boots thunking across the highly polished oak floor.

Maud girded herself. He wasn't happy. At all. "Coffee?" It was nine a.m., and usually by this time he was out on the range, managing their wranglers. He probably wanted to be out with his hardworking crew rather than in here with her. But they had to talk.

"Yeah, coffee's good," he said, making a beeline for the service on the other side of the room. He poured two cups, black, and turned. Setting one in front of her, he sat down and took a quick sip of the steaming brew. "You know my mother broke her thigh bone a couple of days ago. I just finished talking to her surgeon before coming here, and they said she pulled through the operation with flying colors. She's resting in her room right now."

"That's great to hear," Maud said, relief in her tone as she sipped the coffee. "I know they call it breaking a hip, but in reality, people break their femur or thigh bone."

Shaking his head, Jake muttered, "Yeah. Bad anatomy, if you ask me."

"So? What's her prognosis?"

She saw him grimace and set the coffee down in front of him. "The surgeon says she's going to need eight to ten weeks of care. She lives alone in Casper. And she's fighting having a caregiver in her home twenty-four hours a day."

Managing a sour smile, Maud said, "Like mother, like son. Right?" She saw worry in Jake's forest-green eyes. He had been close to both his parents; his father had died at the age of fifty-five of a sudden and unexpected heart attack. For the last ten years, his mother had been on her own. Now, at sixty-five, she had a broken bone and needed help. Jake's expression turned dark, and she saw him wrestling with the whole situation.

"I'm afraid you're right, Maud."

"So? What do you want to do about it?" She leaned back in her squeaky leather chair, holding his narrowing gaze. "How can we gather the wagons and help you out?" Maud made a point of being there for the people who worked for them. Jake had not asked for anything. He never did. Her experience with her wrangler vets, however, had taught her early on that those with PTSD, man or woman, never asked for help, never asked for support, and she knew it came from the shame that they had been broken by combat. "Well?" she prodded, arching a brow.

Jake squirmed. "Mom asked if I could come home and help her for those two months." Mouth quirking, he mumbled, "I told her I couldn't, that we had fifty grass leases with fifty different ranchers coming here, bringing in their herds by truck, in the next two weeks. I told her the Wyoming grass was thick, rich and nutritious, that the cattle would fatten up far more quickly on these lands than being put into a livestock pen. That I couldn't leave because our work triples from June through September."

"How did Jenna take the news?" Maud heard the pain in Jake's low, deep tone. He was a man who hated showing any emotions, but they were plainly written all over him now. Some of it Maud attributed to their strong relationship. Jake could let his guard down around her, one of the few people in his life he did trust.

"She was disappointed but understood." His black brows fell and he looked away. "She needs help. I don't know what to do. That's why I'm here." He gave her a hopeful look. "You're the go-to gal for ideas, Maud. I'm hopin' you can come up with a fix."

"I think I have one, Jake, but I don't know how you will react to it. Here's my plan. I talked to Steve last night and he's in agreement with me. I hope you will be, too." She straightened, resting her elbows on the desk, her hands clasped, her full attention on her foreman. "We both feel Jenna could be brought by ambulance to the ranch. The foreman's house is two stories, has three bedrooms, three baths, and is large enough for you to take care of your mom as well as an in-house caregiver." She saw his brows raise momentarily. "I know you'd rather live alone, but honestly, your cabin is the second largest on the ranch, next to where we live. It has plenty of room for you, your mom and a hired caregiver."

She took a breath, watching his face go from hard and unreadable to something akin to discomfort, coupled with relief. Jake had a set of good parents, that she knew. And he'd been very close to both of them. As well, Jake had protective instincts toward women. His mother was no exception to that rule. Maud knew he wanted desperately to support and care for her, but he hadn't thought outside the box on how to do it. That was her job.

"Now," she said firmly, "before you say no, I talked to Dr. Taylor Douglas, our PA, physician's assistant, in town. She said I needed to find someone with a medical background, preferably a registered nurse, who could take care of Jenna: help her walk, be there to assist her with the mandatory exercises, as well as cook and clean for you. Taylor put the word out in Wind River for such a person. I haven't gotten any bites on this yet, but I'll keep at it. Your mom and the caregiver could have the two bedrooms on the first floor. You have the master bedroom upstairs. If I find a caretaker for Jenna, would this work for you? It would be for a minimum of two months."

Jake rolled his shoulders, scowling in thought. "Maybe. But I can't afford to hire a caregiver for Jenna."

"No worries," Maud answered briskly. "Your mother is on Medicare and our umbrella insurance on the ranch will cover a full-time caregiver until she doesn't need one anymore. I'll pay for the caregiver because you're so important to the daily work that goes on around here, Jake. I'd do it for any of our wranglers. We meant it when we said they were family, and that's what you do for your family." Opening her hands, she added, "We're grateful to have made money and we aren't taking it with us. Your mom will have the best of care and we'll cover any additional expenses. How does that sound?"

"You've always been more than fair with us vets," he said, his voice low with emotion. "And I appreciate it, Maud."

"So? Is that a yes? Can we move ahead with this idea? Are you okay with it?"

Rubbing his stubbled jaw, Jake studied the fifty-five-year-old woman. "I don't like takin' handouts, Maud."

"This isn't a handout. Our insurance covers it. You've earned this, Jake."

He made a low, growling sound and stared hard at her. "I've never been in a position like this before. I like living alone, but I want to help my mom, too. I guess my uneasiness with havin' two women underfoot for two months or so isn't gonna kill me."

Giving him a half grin, Maud said, "No, it won't. And you can always hide up on the second floor if you're feeling overwhelmed with estrogen in your household." She heard him chuckle and saw his shoulders drop, indicating he was relaxed at last. Jake wasn't the kind of person she could trap and put in a corner. He had to come to this decision entirely on his own. And he was an honorable man, if nothing else. Jake would never knowingly hurt someone. At least, as a civilian. What he did as a recon Marine was different, and although he never talked about it, she knew enough to realize he'd been in harm's way all the time. It wouldn't surprise her that he'd killed the enemy either. She knew the burden of killing another human being through some of her other wranglers. It stayed with them the rest of their lives.

"I'll probably make the second floor my home."

"If I can find a caregiver, she'll do the cooking for the three of you. That won't be so bad, will it?"

"No, that sounds kinda good, to tell you the truth. And she'll housekeep, instead of me doing it. I like that part of it, too."

"I thought you might." She allowed the humor to come through in her voice and Jake gave her a slight grin. "It's only two months."

"But they're the busiest months of our year, Maud. I won't be around that much."

"And that's why a caregiver is essential. You won't have time to drive Jenna to her rehab exercises in Wind River, or to see an ortho doctor if necessary."

"Well," he said, straightening, "if you can find a caregiver, then we're set?"

"Yes." Maud looked at the bright red landline phone on her desk. "I'm calling Kassie and her husband, Travis. They're plugged in with everyone in town. Maybe one of them can give me some leads."

Rising, he said, "If there's such a person around Wind

River, Kassie will know. She's gossip central at her café," and he grinned a little.

"I'll let you know," Maud promised. "Once we hire someone, we can get Jenna out of the Casper hospital and over here to heal up."

Walking to the hat rack, he gripped the edge of his Stetson. "That sounds like a good plan, Maud." Settling it on his head, he turned, giving her a grateful smile. "I don't think outside the box like you do."

"Oh," she laughed, standing and walking around the desk and heading toward where he stood, "yes, you do! Every day around here, I see you thinking of ways to do something that needs to be fixed." She slid her hand on his shoulder, patting him in a motherly fashion. "All humans are good at something. Your skill set happens to be in ranching, Jake. Mine is about seeing patterns and putting dots together," and she chuckled with him. Jake rarely smiled. When he did? She saw the kindness and sensitivity he held protectively away from the world. Allowing her hand to fall to her side, she walked him to the door. "I'll be in touch by cell phone once I get something."

He nodded. "Thanks, Maud. I honestly don't know how I landed at your ranch, but I have to be the luckiest bastard in the world to have you as my boss."

"Get outta here, Murdoch. You got a shitload of eighteen-wheelers on your plate with these leases trucking in the beef right now."

He gave her a sour grin, opened the door and thunked down the wooden stairs.

Maud watched him climb into the white, dusty-looking Ford pickup with the name of their ranch in big red letters on each door. Turning, she felt lighter. Jake had never been in this kind of situation before, and she hadn't been sure how he was going to react to it. His care and love for his mother was heartwarming. He was such a gruff person, hardly letting anyone near him or his vulnerability. Maud sensed Jake's life was going to take a turn for the better. She didn't know how, as she walked to her desk, sat down and dialed up Kassie's Café, but she knew it was going to happen.

Lily Thompson was working in the no-kill animal shelter run by Maud and Steve Whitcomb, when Suzy, her boss, who manned the front desk, stuck her head around the door.

"Lily! Maud Whitcomb is on the line for you!"

"What?" She knew Maud was the owner of this large shelter, but in the two weeks since she was hired, she hadn't met the woman personally. She closed the cage on a black Lab with a gray muzzle, after giving him a bowl of fresh water. "Hold on. . . ." and she hurried across the spotlessly clean concrete floor, wrapping the hose she'd used and hanging it on the wall. Rubbing her hands down her jeans, she asked breathlessly, "What does she want?"

Suzy, who was in her early twenties, shrugged dramatically. "I don't know."

Squeezing out the door, they walked down the hall toward the reception area. "Does she always call her employees?" Lily wondered.

"No . . . not usually," Suzy responded, giving her a concerned look.

"Oh, dear," she muttered. "I wonder if I've done something wrong."

"I doubt that! All the animals love you. Some of them love you to death!"

Wincing inwardly at the word, Lily nodded and picked up the phone. "Hello? This is Lily Thompson." Her heart was pounding in her chest and she curled her fingers into her damp palm. Was she going to get fired? God, she hoped not.

"Lily, this is Maud. I just got done speaking to Kassie, and she mentioned you were an RN. Is that true?"

"Yes, ma'am, it is." She gulped, unsure of where this was going.

"Suzy told me you have a part-time job there, fifteen hours a week?"

"Yes, ma'am, I do. I love it." Inwardly, she was praying the owner wasn't going to tell her to leave. It would devastate her in ways most people wouldn't understand. This was the first real job she'd been able to find since receiving an honorable medical discharge from the Army due to her extreme PTSD symptoms.

"Are you looking for full-time work?"

"Well . . . uh . . . that would depend. I really love animals." *Because they give me peace. They accept me for who I am now. Not who I used to be*, but she didn't divulge that.

"Can you drive out to our ranch? I'd love to talk to you face-to-face about a job possibility. I assume you're looking for full-time work?"

Was she ever! Licking her lower lip, Lily said, "Yes, ma'am, I am. But I can't work in a hospital or anything like that." Lily had to be honest about her skills and how much she'd been harmed by her time in Afghanistan.

"This is a job in a home, as a caregiver for a sixty-five-year-old woman who has broken her femur. You would cook three meals a day and do some light housework besides helping the woman with exercise and walking to strengthen herself once more. It should last around two months, full-time. Are you still interested?"

"Maybe," she answered tentatively. "Could you tell me more?"

"Come out to the Wind River Ranch. We'll talk. Can you make it at one p.m.?"

"Yes, ma'am. I'm done today at noon. I know where your ranch is located and can drive out there. I'll be on time, I promise."

"Great. Just come to the office. That's where I'll be."

Lily hung up, her heart pounding even harder. *A job. A real job.* A caregiver. Well, she could do that.

Suzy glowed as Lily told her about the call. "You said you wanted another job, that this one wouldn't pay your monthly bills."

Lily smoothed out her jeans, some damp spots of water on them from watering all the cats and dogs in the shelter that morning. "I did."

"Kassie's a good go-to person to find a job. You must have told her you were looking for another one."

"Yes, I'd love to find something full-time. I don't want to leave the shelter," she said, looking around the small but homey office. "I love the animals."

"It's only a two-month job, Lily."

"It's better than nothing. And it sounds like something I can manage. I always enjoy helping animals and people."

Suzy sat down. "Hey, good luck on it. Maud's a really nice person. You'll instantly feel at ease with her. She has a heart of gold, so don't sweat the interview. Okay?"

Easier said than done. Nodding, Lily picked up her jacket and pulled it on. It might be June 2, but it was only forty-five degrees outside despite the blue sky and sunshine. "I'll see you tomorrow morning at six a.m.," she promised Suzy, lifting her hand in farewell as she pushed the outer door open.

Outdoors, she halted and looked around. It was something she did without thinking about it. There were a lot of things she thought about since being in the Army, since that village was attacked . . . Resolutely, Lily compressed her lips and walked doggedly toward her dark blue pickup.

Her parents had bought it for her when she returned home, wanting, in some way, to help her adjust to civilian life. It was used but in good condition, and as she climbed in, her heart warmed at their helping her after the Army released her.

To her right was the Wilson Range, rising out of the flat plain west of the one-hundred-mile, oblong-shaped Wind River Valley. It was covered with snow on its blue granite flanks, then surrounded with thick evergreens from ten thousand feet downward and flowing onto the flat of the valley. The shelter had been built on the southern end of the town. The parking lot was gravel, with a wooden corral around it except for the entrance and exit points. The tires made crunching sounds as she backed out and headed toward the ribbon of two-lane asphalt that went through the valley.

Since discovering this small town nestled between the Salt River Range to the east and the Wilson Range on the west, she'd found some level of peace. Her money was running out, although she knew her parents would give her more if she asked. They'd done so much already, trying to help her with her devastating PTSD symptoms.

Driving slowly through town, she parked at Kassie's Café. Kassie had given her a back room in the large restaurant, free, until she could find a job. She, like Maud Whitcomb, was partial to military vets and had married one, Travis Grant.

Lily left the pickup and walked around to a side door. The little apartment had a bathroom with a tub, which she loved to soak in. Water always calmed her. The bedroom had a queen-size bed and a purple comforter that was cozy and warm for the freezing nights that occurred even in June around here. There was also a small kitchenette. She discovered either Kassie or one of her women vet waitresses had thoughtfully put a bowl of fresh fruit on the table for her. When she opened the fridge, she found three complete meals wrapped in Saran wrap.

Lily didn't know how she'd managed to luck out, but Kassie and Travis had been saviors to her. She'd come here two weeks ago, low on money, low on morale and questioning whether she'd done the right thing by leaving her home in Blackfoot, Idaho. She was looking for a job that had low stress, something that would pay her a salary she could live on.

As a vet with PTSD, her career as an RN was pretty much over. She didn't have the ability to stand the stress of working in a busy hospital. Or even a doctor's office. Sometimes, crowds of people, noise and the combination of the two, made her mind blank out and she was paralyzed for moments, unable to think or react.

During her therapy, after breaking emotionally over what she'd witnessed in an Afghan village, her therapist gently told her she would never be the same person again. Lily found those words disheartening, but Major Ann Dawson had shown her the strength that was still within her, helped her to understand how she could call upon it to heal. That, too, was a part of her.

The first three months after her breakdown out in the field had been the hardest. They'd put her on medications that made her feel out of her body. Her mind didn't work, and she was in some kind of cottony cocoon she couldn't wrestle out of.

Only after the medication was slowly withdrawn and she started with therapy sessions with Major Dawson had she started to come alive once more. And as she recounted the horrific attack by the Taliban at dawn, the murdering of innocent men, women and children, she broke down and wept until she had no more tears to shed.

But the pain, the anguish of watching people systematically beheaded with swords, stabbed with knives, shot in the head, still peppered her dreams nightly. Dawson had urged her to remember, not push away what she'd experienced. It had been so hard. It was still hard, but her emotional reaction to it had diminished in intensity. Her therapist said that with time, it would lose its grip on her, and Lily believed her. She just wished it would hurry up and happen. Unfortunately, the therapist told her it would be many years before it slowly took place.

Lily went to the kitchen counter and made a pot of coffee. If she took certain antianxiety meds, she'd calm down. But they interfered so much with her ability to feel connected to life that she finally refused to take them anymore. Lily would rather suffer and feel alive than be anesthetized and slog through the day feeling robotically removed from everything. Truly, the meds had turned her into a zombie.

Because Kassie had given her this space to live until she could get back on her feet, Lily wanted to help where she could. The dishwasher room, where dirty plates and flatware were cleaned, was too loud and jarring to her sensitive nervous system. Noise could bring on a flashback of that dawn morning in the village. And getting a flashback made her curl into a knot, her head buried against her drawn-up knees, arms tightly wrapped around them, unable to do anything but remember to breathe in and out until it passed. It could take an hour, but then the rest of the day or a sleepless night followed.

She felt helpless. Alone. Broken. Too fragile to live in this rough-and-tumble world civilians easily dealt with day in and day out. At one time, she could do it, too. But no longer. Major Dawson had told her to find a low-stress job, doing something that made her look forward to working daily. The shelter in Wind River was perfect for her. Dogs barking didn't bring on a nasty reaction within her. The dogs and cats loved her, and she wallowed in their unselfish adoration, lapping it up like the starving emotional being she'd become. These last two weeks had been heaven for her because she was the only human with all the animals. Things always went better when there wasn't a crowd of people around her.

She sat down at the table that had two chairs around it and ate a tuna sandwich she'd made last night. Luckily, she'd slept well, a rare thing but so welcome. Major Dawson had told her that over time, years, the anxiety, the hypervigilance, the nightmares and those dreaded flashbacks would begin to ease. Lily took it as a good-luck sign that Wind River was a place of healing for her. In the last two weeks, she'd had seven nights of solid, unbroken sleep. A new record! Attributing it to her beloved dogs and cats, she remembered her caring therapist telling her she would find an inner strength that would support her healing. It would be a journey that would consume her life to come, but a worthy one.

Well, she'd found it. Kassie and Travis Grant were her guardian angels. Just as Maud Whitcomb had been, by hiring her part-time at the animal shelter. Yes, this place, the kindness of so many people who lived here, was the medication she needed to get her feet solidly under her. Tonight, she'd call her mom and dad in Idaho and let them know what had transpired. Idaho Falls was about six hours north of where she lived now, but sometimes it seemed like half a continent away. Other times, a six-hour trip by pickup home to see them would be easy for her to accomplish.

Sitting and munching on her sandwich, she went over her short talk with Maud. She'd never been a personal caregiver but liked the idea of helping a sixty-five-year-old woman rehabilitate. After all, she'd worked in orthopedics while going through her last two years before receiving her RN degree. Maybe that would help her get the job. But it was only for two months. Then she'd be back to square one. Still, it felt hopeful, and she had to try.

Fear was something she had rarely felt until after joining the Army. Then it had been a daily companion after her breakdown. She felt the emotions rising in her, felt her stomach shrinking, as if a hand had grabbed it and was squeezing it until it was painful. Fear of rejection. Yes, that was it. Shame and humiliation were the two biggest feelings in her life. Ashamed that she couldn't *take it*. Some of the male vets in her hospital ward due to their own PTSD had called her weak. Fragile. Even though they themselves were in as bad shape emotionally as she was. How many times at night, in her bed, had she cried, face pressed deep into the pillow to stop the sounds? Lily had lost count. Crying helped relieve the pressure within her. Better out than in. Crying was healthy, and she saw the difference in her state of mind since giving herself permission to do just that.

Humiliation haunted her daily, reminding her that she couldn't take real life, the natural stress everyone around her could deal with without blinking an eye. She couldn't handle a crowd on a sidewalk, or be squeezed into a theater, or be comfortable in a department store. Instead, walks around the hospital grounds, green grass, trees, colorful flower beds, birds singing, all combined to ramp down the anxiety that savaged her. Lily understood what fragile meant because that was how far she'd sunk into her own wounded being. There was so much she could no longer handle.

Frowning, she wondered what Maud would think of her. Because she wouldn't lie about what had happened to her, and how it affected her daily. If she lost the job, so be it. Lily wasn't about to put herself into a position where there was high stress, loud noises or too much hustle and bustle. In an hour, she'd find out a lot more. The fear grew in her, making her feel hyper with anxiety.

Chapter Two

"Come in," Maud called, rising from her desk as she heard a tentative knock on her office door. She saw Lily Thompson open it, allowing the chilly June air to mix with the heat inside. Giving her a welcoming smile, she held out her hand once she was inside and had closed the door. "I'm Maud Whitcomb. Thanks for coming out for this interview, Lily."

"Yes, ma'am," she murmured, releasing the woman's firm grip.

"You can hang your coat on that rack, if you'd like. May I get you some coffee or tea?"

"I'd love a cup of coffee. It's cold out there. I guess I'm used to the milder spring in Idaho Falls, where I come from." She hung up her dark purple nylon-and-down-filled coat on one of the hooks. Smoothing her hands along her black wool pants, she stood, unsure.

"Have a seat in one of the chairs in front of my desk," Maud invited, pouring them both a cup of coffee.

Noting two chairs, one at each corner of Maud's huge oak desk, Lily sat. Nodding her thanks as Maud gave her the cup, the ceramic mug warmed her chilled fingers. "Thank you."

Maud sat down, facing her. "I'm a pretty casual person, Lily. You can see I'm wearing jeans and cowboy boots. I'm not much for getting gussied up."

"It's a nice way to be. My folks aren't much for fashion dress either." She looked down at the pink cable knit sweater she wore with a white, long-sleeved blouse beneath it. "I guess I'm not either."

"That's okay," Maud said, "because I prefer people who don't wear masks or pretend to be something they aren't." She held up the résumé Lily had faxed over to her. "I've read this, and I'm impressed."

Heartened, she took a nervous sip of the hot coffee and set it on the edge of the desk, then clasped her hands in her lap. "That's good to hear. Could you tell me a little more about this job, ma'am?"

"First, don't call me *ma'am*. I know you're a military vet, but around here, no saluting and no *ma'am*s. Okay?" and her grin widened.

"That sounds good, but it's tough to leave years of being in the Army behind me. I'm still adjusting to being back in the civilian world."

"Well, if you don't know it yet, our ranch hires only military vets. My husband and I believe in supporting vets because they've paid the ultimate sacrifice to keep our country free. We're here to support you." Maud saw relief come to Lily's beautiful turquoise-colored eyes. She had an oval face, her short sable hair making her look much younger than the twenty-seven or so years the résumé reflected. Her shoulders dropped, too, indicating she was less stressed than before. "You are truly welcome here," she added sincerely.

"Thank you. It's a real change from what I'm used to." Lily frowned and then said, "Maud, I know I'm not whole anymore due to my PTSD, but I can work. I put in my résumé that I received an honorable medical discharge."

"Yes, I saw that," she murmured gently. "And I know you have a part-time job at our animal shelter."

"Yes, and I love it. I'm so glad you don't euthanize animals."

"Makes two of us. Suzy is the boss there and she'd already told me about you a week ago, very enthused over how caring you were, how the animals loved you so much. For me, the best validation a person can get is when animals adore you."

"I love to help others," Lily admitted quietly. "It doesn't matter whether they're human or animal. My joy is stopping suffering and helping others get to a better place and space."

"And that's why you became an RN?"

Nodding, she said, "I hate to see someone hurting. It tears my heart out. I wanted a career where I could help relieve pain, not cause it."

Maud felt her heart expand with compassion for the young woman sitting tensely in front of her. She understood she needed a job, money, to eat and find a new life. "All worthy ideals," she agreed. "Can you tell me a little about your medical discharge? Are you able to function in a job now?"

"I suffered an emotional breakdown after witnessing the slaughter of Afghan men, women and children," she offered softly. Twisting her hands in her lap, she forced out, "I–I'd never seen such things in my life . . ." Taking a deep breath, she went on. "When I got home, I thought being here would help me get well, but it didn't. My poor parents didn't know what or how to deal with me. I realized I had to get out on my own and find my own way, a job where I could function. I found out quickly I couldn't handle big crowds, stress or a lot of noise."

"Most vets I know have the same issues you do." Maud smiled a little. "They hold wrangling jobs here on the ranch and it helps to subdue their symptoms. Some are cooks, others do landscaping, the rest do ranch work."

"That's so good to hear."

"Do you think caring for Jenna Murdoch would stress you out, Lily?"

"No. I'm fine with up to three people in a room. The dogs and cats at your shelter calm me. I love my job there. And I think I can be fine around Jenna, too. If I can't, I'll be the first to tell you, and you can get someone else to replace me." Lily wasn't going to whitewash her emotional wounding.

"My gut tells me you'll do just fine, Lily. I'm well acquainted with the challenges you face every day. Thank you for your honesty. I cherish that in people. I don't think caring for Jenna will be a stress on you. From what Jake, her son, tells me, she's very easy to get along with. May I tell you about the job?"

"Please . . ."

Maud heard the relief in her tone. "My foreman, Jake Murdoch's mother, just broke her hip. Well, actually, she broke her left femur, to be medically correct."

"Yes, they call it a hip, but it's actually a femur fracture of some kind," Lily agreed.

"Correct. Jenna Murdoch is sixty-five years old, a recently retired high school teacher who lives over in Casper, on the eastern side of the state. We've just swung into grass lease season, so Jake can't take off two months from his job to drive home to help his mother. The surgeon said Jenna will have to undergo rehabilitation, and someone who is medically qualified needs to work with her. I suggested to Jake yesterday that if we could find the right person, Jenna could be brought here to his house. He lives a mile away from the main ranch area. He has a two-story cedar log cabin. There are two bedrooms on the first floor and his room is on the second floor. I figure Jenna could be in one of the rooms downstairs because she won't be able to climb stairs at all."

"That's correct," Lily said. "There's a very detailed, daily rehab she'll have to go through and someone does have to be there to help her. And she wouldn't be able to climb stairs for a minimum of six weeks, if everything goes well."

Nodding, Maud said, "We figure the caregiver could live in the house as well. You could have the other bedroom on the first floor."

Brows raising, Lily said, "You mean, I'd live there for the duration of Jenna's rehab?"

"Yes, and I'd like to know if you'd mind making three meals a day for the three of you, plus doing light housekeeping."

"Oh. I thought I'd be going back to my place at Kassie's every night."

"Well, I suppose you could, but it would be rent-free if you stayed at the cabin for the duration."

"I'd like that. It makes sense to stay at Mr. Murdoch's home to take care of his mother."

"Good. I see here on your résumé that you were trained in orthopedics as an RN?"

"Yes, I was."

"So, you're familiar with Jenna's type of injury?"

"Absolutely."

"And can you drive Jenna to Taylor Douglas's office when she needs to see a doctor?"

"I can drive with no issues at all. I love to drive. I find it calms me."

"Interesting. Jake has a rocking chair in the two first-floor bedrooms. He also has one up in his suite."

"That's nice to hear. The rocking motion calms me, too."

"Good. Does this sound like something you'd like to take on?" Maud picked up a photo and stood, handing it to Lily. "This is Jenna Murdoch."

Studying the photo, she saw a black-haired woman with silver among the strands, smiling, her green eyes sparkling. Jenna was wearing a summer frock of white with a bright red scarf around her neck and shoulders. "She sure doesn't look sixty-five," Lily said, looking up, smiling.

"Good genes?"

"Really. She looks very nice, Maud."

"She is. I met her a year ago, when she came for a visit and stayed with her son for two weeks. She's very athletic, loves hiking and being out in nature."

"All the things I love. That's good to hear. I'm sure fracturing her femur has put her into a depression of sorts."

"She's not too happy about it," Maud admitted dryly. She took the photo back from Lily. "Now, as to the salary, we'd like to offer you three thousand dollars a month." Lily's eyes widened. "Our ranch insurance covers that amount. Are you comfortable with that salary?"

Gulping, Lily croaked, "Why . . . yes!"

Suppressing her smile, Maud said, "I'm sure it will help you. If Jenna requires more than two months, would you be willing to stay on, Lily?"

"Absolutely. But I need to keep my job at the shelter, too. It's fifteen hours a week. I love animals and I don't want to quit. I don't believe Jenna needs twenty-four-hour care. Maybe the first couple of weeks will require more time, but I'm sure I'll be able to do the fifteen hours a week at the shelter."

"Wonderful," Maud replied, adding, "I want to get Jake in here to meet you, Lily. You'll be living under his roof and he might have some questions for you. And you can certainly ask him about his mother, too."

"That's fine. I'd like to meet him."

* * *

Lily got up to move around while waiting for Jake Murdoch to arrive. Maud had excused herself and would return when she found him.

Her anxiety had amped up during the interview. Often, she would silently predict things would go badly, that she wouldn't get a job or the interviewer wouldn't like her. She crossed her arms, walking slowly around the office, stopping to look at the many photos in frames hanging from the gleaming gold and red cedar logs. The floor shone with the same colors, the sunlight glancing through a window, scattering the golden light across it. Her mind was frantic, running on hyperspeed, as it did when she was caught up in anxiety. Trying to appear relaxed, measuring her footsteps, she wished she was outdoors, on a trail, where her symptoms settled down and sometimes left her completely, which was a godsend.

So far, she'd won Maud over, convinced her that she could take care of Jenna Murdoch. But what about her son? What was he like? Would he hate her on sight? Be disgusted with her because she had PTSD? It was true, she was underweight. When anxiety hit, she lost her appetite. Since returning home from the Army, Lily had forced herself to eat. She'd gained ten pounds in those two months home. Her clothes still hung on her, though. Now, she wished they fit a little better. What would Jake see in her when he walked into this office? Fear took chunks out of the confidence that had been built during Maud's kind interview. Now, she felt like an animal in the sights of a much larger predator. Her anxiety heightened. When this happened, she had to devote so much time and inner resources to controlling the monster inside her, not allowing it out to kill her.

Lily knew from her therapy that it was the hormone

cortisol soaking into her bloodstream that caused this hyperalertness, this feeling of dread that she was being stalked by something that was going to destroy her. Ordinarily, her therapist told her, cortisol played a key part in helping a human survive during a life-and-death event. But in PTSD, the hormone never shut off, so a person remained in this heightened state of awareness, their hearing amping up, looking for real or imagined shadows stalking them. That left her exhausted from an episode, and it took a while to start to relax again.

The door opened and closed. Lily was down at the end of the long, rectangular room and turned on her heel, her heart thudding heavily in her chest. Her arms were crossed, and she tried to remain calm, which was virtually impossible, so much cortisol flooding into her.

The man standing inside the office was huge. Or at least he appeared that way as her gaze swept over him. A pair of leather gloves was stuck in his pocket, and he wore a blue chambray shirt, the sleeves rolled up to show his hard, muscular lower arms. She could tell he worked hard. The way he stood, those broad shoulders pulled back with pride, his wide chest stretching the cotton fabric across it, relayed nothing but a sense of not-so-subtle power.

Her throat grew dry as she lifted her lashes, meeting his forest-green eyes, which were large, hard with intelligence, missing nothing. Lily felt momentarily stripped as his gaze swept her up and down, as if sizing her up. She liked his mouth and his strong-looking nose, softened by broad cheekbones. Those black eyebrows lay straight over those X-raylike eyes. Shaken by his stature, the power swirling around him, she wanted to take a step back but forced herself to remain where she was.

"Ah, thanks for coming so quickly, Jake," Maud said to him, entering the office behind him. She headed for her desk. "Lily Thompson, meet Jenna's son, Jake Murdoch. Jake, this is Lily, who I feel will be the perfect person to help your mother in her recovery."

Paralyzed for a moment, she watched him move toward her with a boneless male grace. As his callused hand moved forward, she stared down at the squareness of it, his long fingers, short-cut nails, the many small white scars. As their eyes met, she saw the hardness leave them. In its place was a softened gaze laced with what she was sure was curiosity. That one change broke her paralysis and she stepped toward him. Without thinking, simply reacting, she slid her much smaller hand into his. Ripples of pleasure surrounded her damp fingers as she felt him squeeze them gently. There was another look in his eyes as she stared up at him, something she couldn't interpret, but she swore she felt it in his handshake.

"Ms. Thompson, nice to meet you," he said, releasing her hand almost reluctantly.

Gulping unsteadily, she quickly reclaimed her hand, which sizzled as if it had been in a warm mitten, the tingles still bubbling up through her skin where he'd touched her. "Call me Lily?" She watched his eyes thaw, sending a tremor through her chest. It was the oddest feeling, but it was a warm sensation that filled her with something she hadn't felt in a long, long time. Happiness.

"Call me Jake."

"Come and take a seat," Maud urged the two of them, gesturing to the chairs in front of her desk. "Jake, I think Lily is a good fit. I told her about Jenna and showed her a photo of her. She has orthopedic RN experience and that's exactly what your mother needs."

He grunted and walked at Lily's side. "That's good to hear." He halted and moved Lily's chair out for her, inviting her to sit down.

Trying to swallow her shock over his gentlemanly gesture, Lily couldn't quite reconcile his weathered, unreadable face. He wasn't pretty-boy handsome. That square face and nose and chin all spelled toughness. Murmuring a thank-you, she sat down. Jake took the chair at the opposite corner of the large desk. Forcing herself to move her gaze from the foreman, she found herself shaky inside, but it wasn't from fear. Lily didn't know what her reaction to him was all about. Maud looked pleased as she clasped her hands on the desk.

"Let me share with you our talk, Jake." She launched into it with enthusiasm.

Lily sat with her hands in her lap, feeling how damp they were becoming. She had thought she already had the job, but Jake was the unknown factor. She knew she wasn't a glamorous or beautiful woman. Was Jake a Neanderthal? Stuck on the way a woman looked? She had mouse-brown hair and never liked wearing makeup because it made her skin stretch and feel weird. As an RN, there was no using fingernail polish or long nails because they could harbor bacteria beneath them, ready to infect a sick patient or infant. For a moment, she unclasped her hands and turned them palm up, studying her long, slender fingers. Jake had thick calluses across his palms. She had none. Her skin was soft in comparison. But their jobs were different, so Lily didn't see that as a negative.

"That's it in a nutshell," Maud told Jake. "Do you have any questions for Lily?"

He turned, studying her. "Have you ever taken care of older people?"

It was a fair question. Lily said, "Well . . . over in Afghanistan. We frequently went out to the villages around our firebase, and I took care of patients from newborn babies to eighty-year-old women." She saw his eyes flicker with an undefined emotion.

"You were in Afghanistan?"

"Yes."

"How long?"

"Three different deployments in Helmand Province."
Again, she saw his eyes narrow slightly.

"That's where she got her PTSD," Maud said. She
handed Jake her résumé.

Fear nibbled in her chest as she watched Jake take her
résumé, his full attention on it. Literally, Lily could feel a
shift of energy around him.

Maud had mentioned that Jake was a recon Marine.
Lily knew they lived behind enemy lines, their lives always
in danger. And she was sure Jake's focus was finely honed
like a razor blade as a result. Anyone not focused wouldn't
be sitting here. Instead, they'd be dead.

"Helmand is a hellhole to this day, riddled with Taliban," he muttered, glancing in her direction, giving her a
look of admiration as well as respect.

"Yes," she answered softly, "it is." She watched as he
flipped to the second page. That contained her hospitaliza-
tion, her honorable medical discharge and that PTSD had
been the reason for her separating from the Army. She saw
his lips thin and compress. What did that mean? She used
to be able to sense other people quite well, read them,
which was helpful when working with her patients. Her
symptoms had dulled that skill, and right now, Lily wished
she had it fully online. Would it ever return?

Jake handed the résumé to Maud. He studied Lily. "My
mother is a pretty easygoing lady, unlike her son. And she's
not demanding."

"Unlike her son," Maud said, giving him an evil grin,
teasing.

One corner of Jake's mouth barely lifted. "Guilty, but
then, that's what foremen do: manage. And not everyone
likes to be managed."

"True," Maud agreed. "I feel very good about pairing Lily with Jenna. Do you, Jake?"

Instantly, Lily's heart banged hard in her chest. Her fingers tightened momentarily, and she forced herself to relax. Staring at his harsh profile, Lily found herself really wanting this job.

"You a good cook?"

Lily was taken aback. Was that what was important to Jake? Was he satisfied she could take good care of his mother? "I haven't poisoned anyone yet." She saw a faint lift of the corners of his mouth. She got the sense he rarely smiled. And if then, only grudgingly. Why? So many questions and no answers.

Maud chuckled, rocking back in her chair. "Well, I can see this is a marriage made in reality."

Jake raised a brow, holding Lily's gaze. "My mother has a huge garden where she lives. We don't have any here because we don't get a ninety-day growing season, but she loves a lot of vegetables in her meals."

"That's good to know. I'm kind of a garbage can myself," Lily admitted. "I'll eat anything that doesn't move first. It sounds like Jenna is something like that?"

"Yeah, she is. But she likes things that are fresh, not canned."

"With your help, I can make a list of her likes and dislikes. Yours too, Jake." Lily was intimidated by him when it came to her care of Jenna, but she'd speak up and be forthright. For a moment, she thought he was amused, but that look quickly dissolved.

"Good enough," Jake growled. He stood up. "She's hired, Maud." He looked over at Lily. "Do you have an apartment in Wind River?"

"No. Kassie and Travis Grant were allowing me to stay in the apartment behind the café until I could get a job."

Nodding, he said, "Then you'll need to move things into

my house. First, I'd like you to drive with me to the cabin to check it out. Then," he looked at the watch on his hairy wrist, "I've got to get out and work with my wranglers. I'll give you a key to the house and you can get your gear and move in. There are two bedrooms on the first floor. You choose one and the other will be for Jenna."

He was brusque, no nonsense, and Lily liked that about him. "Sounds good." She stood up and gave Maud a grateful look.

"Skedaddle, you two kids," she said, making a shooing gesture.

Jake moved to the door and opened it for Lily. "You can follow me in your car."

"I have a truck."

"Even better," and he pulled the door open and eased the screen door aside for her.

Lily couldn't get over how tall a bulwark Jake was physically. As she slipped past him after waving goodbye to Maud, she wondered if he had a woman in his life. Of course that was a silly thought, and she quickly banished it as she took the stairs to the sidewalk. Jake was too good-looking, the right age and a man of authority. Many women were drawn to men for those reasons.

The morning sun was bright, casting fingers of sunlight against all the log buildings in the area. She saw wranglers on horses trotting by. There were several barns and corrals farther down from the office. The place was like a beehive. Off in the distance, she saw what she thought was a herd of buffalo.

Jake joined her on the sidewalk. "I'm in the parking lot," he said, waving in that direction.

"So am I." She watched as he walked on the outside of her, closest to the asphalt two-lane road. Squelching a smile, Lily said nothing, but the gentlemanlike behavior shouldn't surprise her. All the cowboys she'd ever met were just like Jake Murdoch. She noticed he had a wide, dark brown leather belt around his narrow waist and a Buck knife. On the other side, he had a much longer knife in a scabbard. Leather gloves stuck out of his back pocket. The bright red kerchief around his thick neck was partly hidden by the chambray shirt he wore. He automatically shortened his leggy stride for her benefit. She wasn't a short person, but at five-foot-seven, Lily would have had to race to keep up with him. She appreciated his thoughtfulness toward her.

"You're a little thing."

Startled, she lifted her chin, meeting his gaze. "Me? No, I'm not."

He made a sound of disagreement.

"Are you saying that because you don't think I could lift or help your mother?"

"No, I think you can manage her just fine."

Her brows dipped. Then why had he said that? Lily cautioned herself not to let whatever came to mind fly out of her mouth before she gave it serious thought. "Then why did you say that about me?"

He stepped into the parking lot and halted, placing his hands on his hips as he stared down at her. "Just a fact," he admitted. "You feel fragile to me."

Her heart sank as she put a few feet between where they stood. The morning breeze was chilly. She knew he'd read her medical issues. "There are times when I feel that way."

Jake's mouth thinned and he looked away for a moment. Turning his head, he met her eyes. "PTSD does that to a person. I have it, too."

She almost laughed but didn't because this was such a serious topic in their lives. "You don't look like anything or anyone could knock you over, PTSD or not." She saw amusement for sure, this time, in his green gaze. It made her feel more trusting of him, though she didn't know why.

"My wranglers call me Bear."

She laughed a little. "Seriously? That's a good nick-name for you. You're like a mountain!"

"Well, it's not exactly a nickname without reason," he cautioned her. "I'm pretty gruff and not PC at all, and you're going to have to get used to that."

"I was in the military. I know the type."

"I like your pluck, Lily. I'm sure Jenna will, too. Where's your truck parked?"

She allowed his compliment to soak into her, desperate to be welcomed by Jake instead of being considered a petri dish to be studied. "Over there, the blue one," and she gestured toward it.

Two wranglers galloped by on horseback, and both lifted a hand to Jake, who returned the greeting.

The place was busy!

"We're parked next to each another," he said, brows raising.

It was a huge parking lot and at least fifteen trucks were there. Lily fell into step with him. "What are the chances?"

Jake grunted but said nothing. He was looking around, keeping an eye on his wranglers and the duties they were carrying out.

Lily's pickup was older, and she pulled the driver's side door open. She saw Jake giving the truck a once-over. It had some scratches, the paint dulled by sun, weather and years. The truck next to hers looked like a brand-new Dodge Ram three-quarter-ton truck. It was huge, like its owner. After she slid in, Jake gently closed the door.

"Follow me," he said.

Lily smiled nervously, her hand trembling as she took the key out of her purse. Follow Jake Murdoch, eh? Those words were heavy with many meanings, she realized as the truck purred to life. *Follow me.*

Well, okay, she would. But she wasn't a yes woman. Her

pluck, as he put it, was real. She might be suffering PTSD, but she was no pushover.

As she watched Jake ease his massive truck out ahead of hers, she followed at a reasonable distance. Lily got the sense Jake was curious about her. And he saw her as fragile. Well, that was true, but she'd never allow it to interfere with helping Jenna or caring for her. She wondered if Jake realized that. Over time, he would, and yes, she'd have to prove herself.

Would Jake be sufficiently impressed with her skills and abilities working with his mother? That was the important question, and not one Lily could answer.

Chapter Three

June 2

Jake tried to squash the burning need that unexpectedly surfaced within him. *Hell!* Why did Lily Thompson look so helpless and vulnerable? What was it in him that had him pulverized the moment he drowned in her wide blue eyes? No good would come of his reaction; he needed to focus on Jenna. Not Lily. He'd expected Maud might find some middle-aged woman, married, who lived in the area, to take care of his mother. Not an attractive young woman who seemed at one moment as fragile as glass and the next plucky. He'd absorbed her résumé, curiosity driving him. Very sure PTSD had all its claws into her, it would explain her porcelain skin, which looked this side of pale. Despite that, she stood straight and proud, and she wasn't afraid to give as good as she got.

So? Why did he want to see her as someone to be protected when she clearly was able to handle her symptoms and still do a credible job for his mother? Rubbing his chest while he scowled, he kept the truck moving at a slow speed, even though they were on an asphalt road. He noticed Lily wasn't driving too close to him, which was smart.

Jenna, he was sure, would love her. But then, his mother loved everyone. He didn't. There were reasons for that, too, but he didn't want to dig into them. Let the past remain buried in the past. Rounding a curve was a hill covered with evergreens. At the base was the two-story cedar log house. His house. He never called it a home because, frankly, he didn't spend a lot of time there, especially from May through September. It was pretty sterile inside, he'd been told by Maud on more than one occasion, who'd hinted it could have a cozy, lived-in look. He wasn't very homey, he supposed.

The two-story cabin stood out far enough away from the tree line, free of any brush that might turn it into a blaze during a wildfire. In front of the cabin, a hundred feet away, was a huge, spring-fed pond. There were a few white-and-black-granite boulders near one side of the shore, the area surrounded by lush Wyoming grass that was shooting up now that winter had finally released its grip on the area. He checked his watch as he turned into the driveway, the sunlight glanced across the long, oval valley. The sky was a light blue, free of clouds. It would be a bright, sunny day, something rare for this area nine months of every year.

Getting out of his truck, he watched Lily park her vehicle next to his. The graveled area was off to one side of the cabin, with spots for ten more vehicles, if needed. He sometimes held meetings with his senior wranglers on busy days, sharing a timetable and discussing which teams would be assigned to the jobs that demanded their time that day. He tried to ignore Lily's silky hair, those fine golden strands intermixed with darker, umber-colored ones across her broad forehead. She had slightly arched brows, a slender body and her manner was refined, like the rest of her. He didn't want to be so damned curious about her, about her past and why she was here in Wind River.

Maybe the PTSD was making a tumbleweed of her, as it had him. Maud and Steve Whitcomb had anchored him to the ranch three years ago, and he'd been grateful to them for a chance to turn his miserable life around.

Lily pulled her jacket tighter about herself as she rounded the end of her truck, then coming to where he was standing.

"This is a *huge* cabin!" she said, gesturing to it.

"Yeah, far more room than I'll ever need. Let's go inside. I have a meeting with some of my wranglers in twenty minutes and I have to be on time."

"Sure, of course."

He shortened his stride as he moved to the three cedar steps, the entryway at least twenty feet wide, with a log railing porch on either side of it. A wraparound walkway went around the entire cabin, a swing at one end, a couple of log chairs at another point. Moving to the door, he used the key and pushed it open for her.

"Here," he said, "you're going to need this key." He tried to ignore the warmth of her palm as he placed the key in it. There was pleasure, warm and soft, to his fingertips brushing her flesh. For a moment, her pupils grew larger, a sign he knew meant she enjoyed the contact.

"Thanks."

"Go on in," he urged. Lily was not a voluptuous woman. Rather, she had a sturdy, medium-boned frame, her breasts hidden beneath her down jacket, and her hips as well. She had long legs and there was a nice sway to her as she walked into the foyer and then turned, waiting for him. That didn't take away from the fact that he was inexplicably attracted to her. Maybe because she was a vet? They had a strong, common bond. He watched her expression turn to awe as she looked around the airy space that showed a curved cedar staircase leading down to the first floor, where they stood.

"This," she breathed, "is so beautiful!" and she turned, smiling up at him. "I feel like I'm in some kind of wonderful fairy tale! I've seen photos of places like this in magazines."

"Steve Whitcomb is an internationally renowned architect," Jake told her. "He designed the foreman's house long before I came here. It's a fancy place. I'm pretty plain and simple."

Laughing, Lily said, "What? A one-room log cabin would be more suitable for you?"

He managed a slight shrug. "Something like that. I want you to snoop around and check out the two bedrooms over there," and he pointed to the other side of the living room, toward a wide cedar hall. "Go get your clothes and anything else and choose one of those two rooms as your own. I'll be home about eighteen hundred . . . I mean six tonight."

"I don't mind if you talk Zulu time with me."

"My mother will. She gets confused when I drop into military language."

"I'd better curb my military terms then, too. Thanks for letting me know." She tilted her head. "It's not going to take me long to move my clothes in here. That's all I brought with me from home. I'll look at the two rooms and decide which one would be best for Jenna. Would you like me to cook you something for tonight?"

Jake warmed to the idea. He was in a hurry, pushed by a schedule, and didn't have the time he wanted to go in-depth with Lily. "That would be nice if you're up to it."

"I'm not helpless."

"I'm beginning to realize that."

Lily snorted, giving him a keen look but remaining

silent, the challenging glint in her eyes telling him she was a helluva lot stronger than what he saw.

Jake settled the Stetson on his head. He went to the granite kitchen counter, pulled out a notepad from the nearby wall phone and wrote down his cell phone number. "Here," he said, handing it to her. "If you need anything, call me. Cell reception is spotty in certain areas of the ranch, so if you don't get me, call Maud and I'm sure she can help you. I'll see you tonight."

Jake didn't want to leave, but it was best under the circumstances. He had five different ranchers hauling hundreds of cattle via semitrucks up here and they were going to arrive at designated times during the afternoon. It was going to be a busy day, without any breaks.

"Okay, I will. See you later," she called.

As he thunked across the cedar decking to the steps, Jake wondered what the hell he was going to do. He honestly liked Lily's spunky attitude, and he'd seen it in other military women, too. They weren't simpering puppets to be manipulated by men. No, they were fiercely independent, confident and spoke their minds. At least, the ones he knew and worked with were like that, and he respected them as equals.

As he headed to his truck, he worried about her pallor. For her height, which he guessed was around five seven or eight, she was underweight. Something told him her PTSD and resulting medical discharge had a lot to do with her loss of weight. They had a lot to talk about. His mother hadn't been around him and knew nothing of the nightmarish symptoms he had weekly. And she needed to be brought up to speed because she'd be living under his roof for a minimum of two months. He was no stranger to flashbacks, which were slowly receding. Nowadays, it was the nightmares that haunted him. He'd wake himself, screaming, remembering the dangers he'd managed to survive.

His mother had no idea about his grappling with these damning symptoms. And God only knew what Lily was wrestling with. He could just picture the two of them screaming themselves awake at night, jolting his poor mother out of her badly needed sleep, scaring the literal hell out of her. Mouth twitching, Jake knew he had to level with his mother somewhat, prepare her for that likelihood.

Lily had been in Helmand Province, one of the most dangerous places in the country, poisoned with Taliban. It was the hellhole of all the provinces. Something had happened to her while she was there. What?

Opening the door to his Ram truck, he swung his bulk into the cab. He knew either Lily had had her PTSD symptoms come on over time or something tragic or horrifying had branded her mind and emotions in one intense, unforgettable event. He needed to know about it, however painful it was going to be for her—and him. They had a lot to discuss before Jenna arrived, that was for damned sure.

Lily was hesitant about going into Jake's bedroom on the second floor of the gorgeous cabin. The door was open, the king-size bed unmade, dirty clothes dropped here and there on the highly waxed floor even though she could spot a clothes hamper from where she stood. She almost wanted to say, *typical bachelor pad.* He'd been in the military, and usually those men were organized and put their stuff away. They were taught that in boot camp.

Without thinking, she quickly gathered up all the dirty clothes and dropped them into the clothes hamper just inside the massive master bathroom. It was opulent, with some white tiles among the iridescent rainbow-colored tile floor, a handmade cedar stool, a chair at a vanity and two rainbow-colored glass bowls that doubled as sinks, on one side. The mirror had a cedar frame and looked as if it were growing out of the wooden wall. The tops of the double sink counter were composed of swirls of purple-, blue- and cream-colored granite that complemented the rainbow tiles on the floor. At one end was a shower that could easily hold two people, with at least eight shower heads placed here and there. The garden tub near the sinks was what drew her. And, surprisingly, there was a hot tub that could easily hold four people. That she checked out very closely because it could be a wonderful adjunct to Jenna's healing. Warm, pulsing water would create more circulation in the area of her surgery, which was always a good thing in speeding up the healing process.

The Jacuzzi hot tub at the other end was a swirl of white and blue, reminding her of the sky, with high wisps of cirrus clouds. She liked that the tub was positioned such that all a person had to do was hold on to the chrome metal railing and take three steps down into its heated depths. That was something Jenna could do after the first two weeks if her rehab went well, and with her doctor's permission. Dipping her fingers into the clear blue water, she saw the temperature was 102 Fahrenheit. It felt wonderful as the water sluiced through them. She wished there was a hot tub on the main floor, but there wasn't. Mentally, she put the hot tub on her list of things to talk to Jake about tonight.

Her heart skipped a beat as she rose and wiped her fingers on a lavender terry-cloth hand towel. A couple of times, she could have sworn Jake had wanted to say something to her that was personal. Maybe intimate? No, that couldn't be. Yet that flickering, heated look in his eyes for that one split second said so. *Impossible.* It was probably her misguided intuition, which wasn't always accurate because the PTSD had stolen that precious and necessary gift from her. That frustrated her. Walking out into the bedroom, which was literally the size of a huge living room, she quickly made his bed, fluffed the pillows and admired the white, purple and blue down comforter on top of it.

Atop an antique mahogany chest of drawers, she saw two photos in gold frames. Curious, she walked over and looked more closely at them. One was, she was sure, his mother and father. They were standing in front of a wooden swing on what was probably their home's front porch, his father's arm around Jenna's shoulder, both smiling like giddy teenagers. She wondered if Jake had snapped the photo. Knowing that his father had died of a heart attack at fifty-five, she grieved for Jake and Jenna because his parents looked happy with each other.

The second photo was of Jake in high school, in a football uniform, looking fit, proud and impossibly masculine, a football tucked tightly beneath his right arm, grinning broadly like a conquering hero. In the background, the stands were filled with people. His dark hair was a lot longer than it was now, giving him an almost swashbuckling pirate kind of look. Or maybe the ultimate risk-taker, unafraid, looking to do battle. Was that why he went into black ops to become a recon? To hide in enemy territory, discovering valuable information so that US and UN troops wouldn't be killed by them? She had met a number of recon Marines at the different firebases where she had been deployed. They were gruff, hardened, silent men, with a look in their eyes that said they were the ultimate hunters. Jake had that same piercing, eaglelike look, that same kind of Rock of Gibraltar confidence that dripped off all those men. So many questions to ask him! But would he open up and give her answers? That, Lily was unsure of.

Smiling a little, she was positive Jake was very popular with the ladies, no question. He oozed charisma even in that photo, as if completely unaware of his overwhelming male sexuality and its effect on women. So why was he alone here? He had so much going for him. Perhaps he did have a woman in his life and she just didn't know about it. That dampened some of her happiness, and she frowned. Her experience in love left her questioning whether anyone who fell in love ever had the relationship last. And then the PTSD hit, and she'd become immune to wanting any kind of relationship, pulled inward into her own pain and suffering.

Sighing, she turned and left, hurrying down the beautiful, graceful staircase. Her palm slid lightly across the warm, polished curved cedar balustrade with its gold and crimson coloring. She halted for a moment, simply absorbing the natural wood and beauty of this cabin that was a piece of architectural art.

Looking at the watch on her wrist, she sat down at the reddish mahogany table that probably dated from the early 1900s. The decor harkened back to that time. Steve might have made an ultramodern cabin with an open-concept kitchen-living room, but everything in it was an antique. And she loved antiques, feeling right at home in the cabin.

Maud had mentioned in passing that she had decorated the foreman's cabin when it was built. There were brightly colored, stained-glass lamps at either end of two couches that were placed in an L-shape in the living room. They looked like Tiffany lamps. Loving the colors, she skipped down the rest of the stairs. Now, it was time to rustle up some vittles. She only hoped Jake liked her cooking. Lily would find out shortly.

The odor of spaghetti laced with garlic filled the air as Jake stepped in at almost seven p.m. He'd called Lily at six, telling her that they were still unloading the last semi of cattle into the leased pasture. Taking off his Stetson, he dropped it on a hook near the door and shut it.

"I'll bet you're tired," Lily called from the kitchen.

Jake turned, seeing that she had found a green-and-white-checked apron and wrapped it around her waist. "Yeah. Sorry to be so late, but the next couple of weeks are going to be like this until we get all the leases filled. Smells good." He saw her cheeks suddenly go pink and he realized belatedly that Lily was blushing. She stood at the stove, two oven mittens on her hands.

"That's okay. I made spaghetti and meatballs. It was easy enough to put the oven on warm and cover the casserole with some foil."

"I'm going to wash up," he said, heading toward the stairs. "I'll be about ten minutes." He smelled of cow, for damned sure. Generally, he'd go upstairs when he arrived at the cabin, shuck out of his always dirty clothes, leaving them where they were and head for the hot tub to ease his many aching muscles, especially in his knees. Those joints had taken a beating when he was a recon. Right now, they ached like a perfectly matched set of banshees screaming for him to get off them and give them a rest. The hot tub would stop the tension and pain. He'd make it a five-minute soak.

Jake halted as he swung through the door of the master bedroom. His eyes widened. Everything was picked up. The bed was made. Hell, there was even a small blue vase with pasqueflowers, a pale lavender native to Wyoming, on the dresser. It was one of the first flowers to poke up its head after the brutal winter. Mouth quirking, he tried to pretend not to be pleased by a woman's touch in his sterile house. He moved to the bathroom. There, he saw a square glass vase with more of the same wildflowers between the double sinks. New, matching lavender-colored towels had been put out where his other towel had been before. He shook his head, rapidly disrobing. There was a fresh bar of soap, too, not the tiny sliver of one he'd used to wash his hands in one of those sinks.

A woman's touch.

It warmed his heart, though he tried to duck it and ignore it. Lily had made thoughtful touches here and there. Jake knew his mother would truly appreciate her attentions to detail. Now, for that lifesaving hot tub . . .

After five minutes, his knees stopped aching. He climbed out, went to the shower and washed away the cattle and manure odor, and the sweat and dirt from his body. He washed his short, dark hair, enjoying the lilac scent of the fresh bar of soap Lily had placed in the stall. Grabbing the large bath towel, he left the shower to stand on a sea-green-colored mat. The flowers made the place look . . . well . . . homey, he supposed. Maud was always prodding him to gussy up the cabin, but he'd resisted. He knew what his mother's home was like, and this cabin certainly looked sterile in comparison. Lily would fix that before Jenna arrived, he was sure.

Quickly drying off, he hurried to put on a pair of tan chinos, a dark green, long-sleeved polo shirt, which he pushed up to his elbows, a pair of moose leather moccasins and slid a brown leather belt into the loops of his pants. The smells emanating from the kitchen made his mouth water. He swore he smelled biscuits baking. What were the chances? He loved biscuits but wasn't a cook. The only time he got them was when he dropped over to Kassie's Café, where they made them every morning for their hungry breakfast patrons, who raved about them.

In no time, Jake was downstairs. He saw a pink vase with pasqueflowers in the center of the table, where they were going to eat. To his pleasure, there was a huge basket of biscuits straight out of the oven sitting there waiting for them. Lily had placed him at the head of the table, and she was to the right. There was a bowl of salad, slathered with thin, curled slices of mozzarella cheese and small red tomatoes and lightly covered with an Italian dressing.

"Need any help?" he asked, pulling out her chair for her.

"No," she said, easing the casserole out of the oven with mitten-covered hands. "What do you like to drink with your dinner?"

"Just water, but I can get that. Do you want some, too?"

She gave him a grateful look as she passed him and placed the ceramic dish on a dark blue metal trivet. "Yes, that would be fine. Thanks."

"Those biscuits are a nice surprise."

"Really? Kassie taught me how to make them. I was helping her in the kitchen at the café when I could. I wanted to somehow pay her back for her and Travis's generosity. I'm kind of regarded as a line cook." Straightening, she pulled off the mitts and placed a large spoon into the main course.

Bringing over the water, Jake placed a glass in front of each plate. He noticed she wasn't using the daily dinnerware he did: some cheap plastic plates he kept in one cupboard. Maud had bought some porcelain dinnerware for the cabin, with flowery red and pink roses painted on it, a long time ago. That was what was on the table now. Lily sat down, and he pushed the chair closer to the table for her. His mother had taught him to be a gentleman, but he saw how surprised and pleased she was by his gesture. Sitting down, he said, "Hand me your plate. How much spaghetti do you want?"

"Not much, Jake," she pleaded.

Mouth twisting, he grunted, "You're too damned skinny, Lily. Jenna will get on you about that, too, mark my words." He handed her the plate and picked up his own. He scooped four large spoonsful onto his plate, but he left room for a couple of those delicious-smelling biscuits.

"My parents said the same thing," she muttered, pulling the small salad in front of her and picking up a fork. "My friends from the Army who have PTSD aren't big eaters either."

"It's a standard symptom," he muttered, frowning. He offered her the basket of biscuits first. Lily shook her head. She was picking at the salad like a bird. Fuming inwardly, he placed two warm biscuits on the side of his plate. There were bright pink linen napkins on the table, which he supposed she'd discovered from another kitchen drawer. Jake hadn't looked through many of the cabinets, truth be told. Lily had probably gone through every one of them. He always grabbed a paper towel for a napkin. Well, it wouldn't be too hard to get used to a linen one, he guessed. And really, the table looked inviting, unlike when he ate there alone.

"Maud called me earlier," Lily said. "Your mom is due to arrive two days from now. We talked about getting a special medical bed and other supplies for her. They should be here before she arrives. There's a medical store in Jackson Hole."

He opened one of those huge, flaky biscuits and inhaled deeply, almost burning his fingers as he slathered butter across it. Lily had thoughtfully set a jar of honey and strawberry jam on the table. He picked up the honey. "Yes, she called me, too, keeping me in the loop with how fast things are happening. What room did you pick for her?"

"The room on the left, the one with the blue comforter on top."

"It's bigger than the other one."

"We'll have to get that special bed in there, where there's already a queen-size bed."

"Should I remove the queen?" He bit down on the biscuit, feeling as if he'd gone to heaven.

"No, we'll just push it up against the wall. Jenna will only need the special bed for three or four weeks, if her rehab goes as planned. Then she can graduate to the queen." She smiled a little. "Besides, that room has a nice flat-screen TV in it, plus a DVD player. The other one doesn't. Jenna will get bored, and I want to make sure she's occupied. I've got lots of plans for her. I'd rather have her tired at the end of every day but happy she could do things and keep engaged with life around her."

"Jenna is a world-class knitter," he told her. "Do you knit?"

"No. Do you?"

The line of Jake's mouth broke. "No." There was that spunkiness he liked about her so much. Her blue eyes glimmered with amusement and he damned near laughed out loud. How long had it been since he'd wanted to laugh? Jake couldn't remember. He hadn't earned the nickname Bear for nothing. He rarely, if ever, laughed. Or smiled.

"I think I'll call your mom tomorrow. I'll introduce myself, then ask her if she's bringing along her favorite things with her. What else does she like to do?"

"She's a camera buff. Loves photography. Has a real nice Canon camera."

"Lots to photograph around here. It's such beautiful country. What else?"

"She's a serious reader, fiction and nonfiction."

"I'll ask her what she likes to read, then. Make sure there's a stack of books nearby she can jump right in to."

He finished the biscuit in record time, now digging into the garlic-laced spaghetti. Jake almost groaned, it tasted so good.

"Is it all right?" Lily asked, trepidation in her tone.

He gave a brisk nod, his mouth full.

"Are you sure?"

He swallowed. "Yeah, it's good. I'm sure Jenna will demand really good food while she's here. She hates fast foods. Loves fresh anything. She loves to cook, too. And she has a ton of spice jars in her house in Casper."

"You don't cook?" She put her salad aside and drew over the other plate, swirling her fork into the steaming spaghetti.

"Not much. My parents tried to teach me, but I resisted."

She met his gaze. "I didn't think you cooked much."

"Oh? Because I'm a man?"

"No. There's just a lot of hotdog buns, weenies and other junk food in your refrigerator."

A chuckle arose in his throat. Lily missed nothing. "I usually get in late during the summer and fall, too tired to eat. I need something fast before I doze off in the chair." He saw sympathy come to her eyes. Jake tried to keep his focus there and not on her pretty lips. Lily had a fine, straight nose, high cheekbones and a full face that mirrored her every emotion. He liked that she didn't try to hide how she felt because he was bad at reading women accurately.

"Are you too tired tonight to give me a list of Jenna's favorite meals? Maud is going to take me to the grocery store in town tomorrow so we can stock up on things for her."

"Sure, I can. Want a list of foods I like, too?"

"Of course. I hope you're not going to order more hotdogs."

This time there was more than a slight rumble in his chest, a true, partial laugh.

Lily studied him openly, seemingly unafraid to make eye contact with him.

"You're funny," he muttered.

"Funny how? Funny odd? Funny humorous?"

He liked her jab back at him, holding him accountable for his comment. "Funny humorous. I think you'll probably see me smile at some point in the next two months."

"You don't smile?"

"Not often."

"But . . . why?"

"What's there to smile about? Our country is going to hell in a handbasket. There's people out there who don't think the democracy and freedom we enjoy is worth supporting."

Holding up her hands, she said, "I don't discuss politics or religion with anyone, Jake. It's a nonstarter for me."

"Smart lady." He hungrily ate the meal, savoring every bite. There were a number of spices in it. Jake couldn't tell what they were, but they sure tasted good together. He decided to change the topic. "Your biscuits are like eating heaven. They're really good, Lily." He liked the way her name rolled off his tongue. There was a natural sweetness and lightness to it. Almost lyrical-sounding to him. He noticed she had the old-fashioned 1900s radio on in the background, with soft classical music playing. Maud had bought it and had it rewired for him about six months ago, saying the cabin was too quiet. She was always adding new antiques to the place as she found them.

"Thanks. I love to cook. You have a wonderful spice rack, but nothing seems used. Now I know why. You don't have to spice up a hotdog, that's for sure."

Another rumble rolled through his chest. He took the second biscuit, opened it and used half of it to mop up what was left of that tasty, zesty marinara sauce. "Have you made coffee?"

"No. I didn't know if you wanted any."

"I'll make it. Do you want some?"

"Yes. I don't know of anyone in the military who isn't a coffee hound."

Yes, there was that very nice other side to Lily. She was a vet, no question, just like him. That made Jake happy for no particular reason, but it was an important part of her that had changed her forever, as it had him. "You're right about that. Usually, I'm up at five a.m. and out of here by six. I'll make a big pot of coffee and pour half of it into a quart thermos I carry on me, and when you get up, there will be enough left waiting for you."

"That's very nice." She looked around. "Do you mind if I do a little decorating?"

"Oh, you mean like those vases of flowers?" and he gestured to them.

"Well . . . sort of . . ." She chewed on her lower lip. "Would you mind if I could find some nice, leafy house-plants to put in Jenna's room and maybe out in the living room? Or in my bedroom?"

His brows raised. "Guess I never really thought of having plants in here. You have to water them."

"I'll water them," she promised.

"Sure. I'll leave you some money on the table tomorrow morning and when you go shopping in town, stop at Charlie Becker's Hay and Feed. His wife, Pixie, is one helluva baker. She brings fresh hot cookies, cinnamon rolls, brownies and all sorts of other baked goods into the store twice a day. She's the one who put in a small section of live plants at the store. That's the place to go to get what you want."

She smiled. "Thank you."

Jake felt his chest grow warm. Lily's smile was infectious. He wondered when or if the PTSD would rear its ugly head within her. Liking the easygoing connection that had sprung up between them, he said, "I like the flowers,

Lily. It makes this place look, well, nicer. I just don't have the kind of job that gives me the extra time I need to hunt them down."

"It brings life in here," she said. "I walked around the lake earlier today, and there are pasqueflowers by the hundreds blooming on the banks right now. I just couldn't pass them up. They probably won't last long in a vase, but at least they're alive and pretty."

And, Jake thought, *so are you . . .*

Chapter Four

June 3

Guilt ate at Jake as he entered the cabin the next evening, near eight o'clock. He spotted Lily coming out of Jenna's room. She looked weary. More guilt. He should have been here to oversee the medical items coming in, but he hadn't. Instantly, he saw Lily perk up when she saw him, her hello smile bright. It fed something deep within him.

"Hey, you're home!" she called, crossing the living room.

He closed the door and hooked the Stetson on the wall peg. "Long day," he admitted. "Did everything come in for Jenna today?"

She nodded and hurried into the kitchen, opening the oven. "Yes. Maud and I, plus two of her wranglers, came over to meet the truck this afternoon. We got everything in, including the medical supplies I'll need for her. We're ready."

"Good to hear. I'll be back in about fifteen minutes," he said, heading for the stairs. He smelled of mud and cow manure. It had rained last night, and the semi's bringing in the beef had buried themselves up to their axles on some of the parcels next to the dirt road between them. He'd spent more time getting a backhoe and chains on the bumpers of the trucks to free them so the cattle could be unloaded.

"Roast beef with all the trimmings tonight," she said.

Turning on the stairs, he saw she'd set the table for him. "Smells good," he grunted, turning, pushing himself on aching knees up that long, curved flight of stairs. He'd seen her face light up at his gruff words and wished he could be kinder, maybe less harsh toward her. If his dark demeanor bothered Lily, it didn't show. Still, the woman was a hard worker. She cared and was truly the right person to take care of his mother. She had that military responsibility toward others well in place. Jake was grateful. Worry about his mother's condition had weighed heavily upon him.

When he came down later, showered and in a set of clean clothes, he saw the pot roast, bowls of honey-glazed carrots, mashed potatoes, celery and apples set around his plate to choose from. There were several slices of whole wheat bread and butter as well. A glass of water was nearby. He heard noise down the hall and figured Lily was at work in Jenna's room. His stomach growled ominously; he'd missed lunch today, which probably contributed to his growly, low-blood-sugar mood.

Jake ate fast and he ate a lot. Best of all, Lily had made a dark, tasty gravy, which he poured over everything except the baked apple slices. Sometimes, he'd catch her moving from Jenna's room down the hall to her own, carrying items back and forth, but he didn't know what they were. Just as he finished, she came out to the kitchen.

"Phew, that was a busy day for both of us. Coffee?" and she held up a cup she'd placed on the counter earlier.

"Yes . . . please." Jake picked up his empty plate and flatware and brought it to the sink, where he rinsed them off. He wasn't about to take advantage of Lily being a woman and expect her to wait on him hand and foot. He wanted her focused on Jenna.

"I made dessert," she told him, taking two cups to the table. She added, "I hope you like bread pudding."

He straightened after putting the dishes into the dishwasher. "Seriously? Bread pudding?"

"Yes." She came back and put the creamer in front of him. "There's caramel sauce for it, if you want."

He stared at her. "I think I've died and gone to heaven."

"Why?" and she brought down two bowls from the cupboard.

"You're cooking things I like. Jenna loves bread pudding, by the way."

"Like mother, like son?" She moved around him to the fridge and brought out a can of whipped cream, handing it to him. "I'll bring over the dessert. Go sit down."

Jake nodded and did just that. He saw faint shadows beneath her eyes as she placed the bowl in front of him. "How'd you sleep last night?"

Grimacing, Lily said, "I had a nightmare." She wasn't proud of it but saw sympathy come to his expression. "I get them maybe once or twice a week."

"We're a pair," he said, drizzling the caramel across the warm bread pudding. "That's about the same rate I get mine, too."

"I wish they would stop." She sighed, taking the caramel from him. "I don't need sleep deprivation right now. I have to be alert and I will be, I promise."

He heard worry in her tone that she might not be able to care properly for Jenna. "I'm not concerned about that, Lily. You're a military vet. You'd cut off your right arm before you wouldn't be responsible for the other members in your team."

"Got that right." She shook her head as he offered her the whipped cream. The bread pudding in her bowl was a quarter of the amount in Jake's. Knowing he worked long, hard hours without relief, she knew he needed the extra food.

"Maybe you'll sleep the night through tonight," he said, lifting the spoon, pleasure thrumming through him at the vanilla and butterscotch tastiness of the pudding.

"I usually do," she reassured him. "When Maud and I went into town before the medical supplies were delivered, I got all the things your mom likes."

"She'll eat pretty much anything, Lily. Unlike me."

Chuckling, she said, "You're what I call a meat-and-potatoes kind of dude. I'm like Jenna: I'll try just about anything once. And I have a wide array of foods I enjoy."

"Guess that means my range is gonna expand, too. You can't cook two different meals for us."

"I could."

"No. I'll suffer in silence."

She tittered and gave him a wry look. "You're a foreman. I doubt you suffer in silence."

"You're probably right." He shifted gears. "How are you doing?"

"Adjusting, to be honest. I think I'll do better once Jenna arrives. She'll give me a sense of stability, a fixed routine, and I'm better when I have those guardrails. I used to be very adaptable, but not since Afghanistan."

"Well," he said, his voice low, "if you ever need a shoulder to cry on, look me up." He saw her glance away for a moment, her lips compressing. "Seriously."

Turning to him, she asked, "Do you ever cry?"

Caught off guard, he growled, "No."

"Why not? I find when I'm feeling overwhelmed, I

have to slink off to my quiet, dark cave and let it all go. I feel ashamed, crying in front of people. They don't understand . . ."

He pushed his emptied bowl aside, bringing over a cup of coffee. "That's one of the reasons, when I got out of the Marine Corps and went home to visit Jenna, that I didn't stay with her. It hurt her that I wouldn't take up residence in my old room in the house. I was afraid to let her know how much I'd changed. I tried to behave normally, but hell, only a knob on a dryer says Normal. I'm a different person now. I try to protect her from myself."

Her lips twisted, and she nodded. "I did stay with my parents after I got out of the Army. And it didn't work out. I think you were probably better off not staying with Jenna."

"Didn't like hurting her feelings, but it was too much to try to get her to understand what had changed me. I stayed at a nearby motel for five days and then came out here to try for the foreman's job. I got lucky and was chosen."

"I don't think luck had much to do with it," Lily said quietly. "Maud sings your praises to the heavens. Did you know that? She and Steve love you, I think, like one of their adopted sons."

He felt heat in his cheeks. "They have a bunch of adopted children who are now adults. I don't think Maud ever met a stray she didn't want to take home and help."

"She's a really good person. I haven't met Steve yet because he's in Australia on an architectural job."

"He and Maud are what Jenna would call *two peas in a pod*."

Smiling a little, Lily finished off the last of her dessert. She placed the bowl aside. "Well, if you ever need a shoulder to cry on, you come and see me. Military people never leave anyone behind. We take care of one another."

Her insight was remarkable, and Jake almost said those words to her. "I doubt I'll take you up on that. Crying isn't something I do."

"Men," she muttered distastefully, standing up. "You all have tear ducts just like we women do." She picked up the bowls and spoons. "If you just want to talk, I'll be there for you, Jake. Okay?"

He nodded. "Yeah. I hear you." He saw her roll her eyes and walk to the kitchen sink to rinse out the bowls. That spark of pluckiness was back in her eyes, her spine straighter, and he tried to keep his appreciation of her at bay. It was damned tough to do it, but he couldn't get entangled with her.

June 4

Lily was hoping Jake would be at the cabin when Jenna arrived, to welcome her. But he wasn't. She'd called him on his cell phone and it was dead. On this huge one-hundred-thousand-acre ranch, cell reception was spotty at best. He knew she was arriving at one today.

Maud was with Lily, who knew she was excited to see Jenna come to the ranch. Lily introduced herself once the gurney was out on the sidewalk. Jenna was in a hospital gown of light blue, blankets covering her to her waist and looking weary from the long drive across the state. Maud had given her a gentle, welcoming hug and urged the paramedics to get her inside because it was a cloudy day, the temperature only in the sixties. It was chilly for anyone who was ill.

Lily had gone ahead to show them where Jenna should be brought. She'd worked hard to ensure the room was bright, light and welcoming. This morning, after Jake had left, she'd gone out and picked more pasqueflowers from the lake edge for the vase she'd put on a dresser opposite the medical bed. It was the least she could do. Sure that Jenna missed her familiar surroundings, thrown out of her daily routines, the woman had given her a kind smile of sincere appreciation. Lily saw she had the same green eyes as Jake. And the same color hair, except for the many strands of silver mixed in.

Maud remained behind to keep Jenna company after she'd been transferred to the bed. The head paramedic gave Lily a file of medical transport papers, several prescription bottles of medication and the latest numbers on her blood pressure, pulse and temperature. She thanked him and the crew left, eager, she was sure, to get back to Casper before nightfall.

Quiet filtered into the large, warm room. Maud stood on one side of the bed, her hand in Jenna's. Lily came to the other side.

"How are you feeling, Mrs. Murdoch?"

Jenna wrinkled her nose. "Oh, call me Jenna. I hate formality, for the most part. I'm tired, but I feel fine. I'm excited to be here with Jake."

"Jake's got that trait of not being overly formal, too," Maud teased. "Did you notice, Lily?"

Grinning, Lily nodded. "Jake's eyes are the same color as yours," she said.

"My son takes after his father in other ways, though," she said. "Stoic. I'm sure you've noticed that little trait?"

"A little," Lily deadpanned. "I know Jake wanted to be here to see you."

"He's in the middle of grass leases," Jenna said. "For about a week, my son works from dawn past dusk. Doesn't he, Maud?"

"Yep, he sure does."

"He got in at eight last night," Lily told her.

"Probably be about that time tonight," Maud said. She released Jenna's hand. "Listen, I'm going to leave you two alone for now. You look tired, Jenna, and I know Lily needs to look at your surgery area. I'll drop by tomorrow afternoon. Maybe the three of us girls can have afternoon tea?"

"That's a good idea," Jenna said. "You know I love my tea."

Patting her hand gently, Maud said, "Indeed I do. I'll bring along a tin of lemon cookies Steve just sent me from Sydney. Cookies with tea are always delicious."

"Sounds good," Jenna said. "Thank you for all you're doing for me, Maud."

"Any time," she said, giving a wink to Lily before she left. "See you two later . . ."

Lily slid down the bars on one side of the bed. "I need to look at your scar area, Jenna. Make sure this trip didn't tear any stitches."

She groaned. "And here I thought it would be different."

Chuckling, Lily said, "No, I'm afraid all us nurses are the same. I want to make sure there's no redness or swelling."

"I know," she sighed, "it's a sign of infection. They've trained me well at the Casper hospital." Jenna pulled the blankets and sheet away from her left hip. Lily donned a pair of latex gloves and gently pulled her blue gown aside. The area had a long dressing on it, and she eased the tape away and pulled it up, observing the wound site. "Looks really good, Jenna." Lily laid the dressing back into place and pulled the gown down to cover her hip and butt. "Your primary physician's order is to get up once an hour to increase circulation in that area. I've got a walker over there. How do you feel about taking a spin around the cabin?" She had moved some of the furniture to make a circuit around the large living room easy for Jenna to navigate. Jake had helped her with the job last night.

"Ugh, I hate walking, but I know it's important. The nurses told me movement stops blood clots from forming and killing me. I really don't want to die."

Lily smiled and nodded. "They indoctrinated you well." Jenna was sitting up in what was known as Fowler's position, usually comfortable for many people with certain medical conditions. "Are you game?"

"Yes," she mumbled, frowning. Holding out her hand, Lily took it and helped maneuver Jenna's bare legs over the mattress, feet hanging down.

"I'm going to put socks on your feet," she told Jenna. "They have a nubby sole surface so you won't slip on the wood floors."

"Okay," she said, pushing her fingers through her short hair.

In no time, Lily had Jenna standing with the walker. She had placed a soft, wide belt around the woman's waist and walked to the side and slightly behind her, her hand firmly on that belt. If Jenna started to fall for whatever reason, Lily could stop it so she wouldn't cause more injury to herself. She guided Jenna through the opened doorway, to the right and down the shining cedar hall. "I've had patients in the past who refused to do this," she told Jenna, walking slowly beside her.

"I guess I could refuse, but the nurses told me that doing it speeded up the healing process. That," she said, giving Lily a deadly serious look, "is exactly what I want out of this, to get well sooner. I want to be free to walk again without any help. They said it would happen."

"We'll make it so," Lily promised. They made a slow circuit to the right, past the huge stone fireplace, then moving near the kitchen area, around the L-shaped couch and back to the hallway.

"This place needs a woman in it," Jenna muttered, giving the living room a frowning glance.

"I agree. I picked pasqueflowers from the edge of the small lake in front of the cabin."

"I suppose Jake didn't even notice?"

"He did notice. He liked them. I wasn't sure what he'd think." Lily guided Jenna back into the bedroom. Once there, she worked with her transfer. The medical bed could be raised or lowered, helping the person mount or dismount easily from the mattress. She guided Jenna to her bed. She looked very tired from her efforts. "How about you take a nap? Or are you hungry?" Lily lifted her legs onto the bed, then drew the covers up to her waist for her.

"I think I'd like a nap. Bet you'll wake me up in an hour for another walk?"

Lily pulled up the guardrail. "Not this time. You sleep as long as you want." She saw Jenna give her a grateful look. "I'll just come in quietly from time to time to see how you're doing." She pointed to an electronic buzzer on the side of the bed. "If you need me for anything, press this." She pulled a white plastic beeper out of her pocket. "I'll feel it vibrate and be right in."

"When I feel better, Lily, I want to know all about you. Maud called me and told me how sweet and unassuming you were. She was right. And I loved talking to you the other day. I knew we'd be a good match for each other."

"We're going to have two months together, Jenna. I'm sure we'll get to know each other really well. Now, go to sleep. I'll pull the drapes closed so it's dark in here. . . ."

Lily quietly left the room, leaving the door open a crack. She would start dinner with one ear keyed to Jenna's room.

* * *

When Jake arrived home at 8:30, the first thing he heard entering the cabin was laughter. He'd never heard Lily laugh before, and the sound of it made him feel warm inside. It reminded him of the burbling of a creek, which was soothing to the anxiety that lived within him. He shut the door, hung up his Stetson and made a beeline across the living room. Poking his head into the door of Jenna's room, he watched the two women talking. Both turned and saw him standing there.

"Jake!" his mother cried, opening her arms.

He nodded hello to Lily and walked to the other side of the bed. "Good to see you here with us, Jenna," and he leaned over to place a kiss on his mother's brow. She swept her arms around his broad shoulders, kissing his cheek time and again.

"It's so good to see you, Jake," she said, her voice wobbling. Releasing him, she gave him a watery smile. "It's been too long."

He took a chair and pulled it close to the bed. Lily had taken down the guardrail. He picked up Jenna's hand and held it between his. "I know it has. Been really busy. How are you doing? How was the trip over here?"

"Tiring." Jenna rolled her head to the left, giving Lily a warm look. "Lily is an angel, Jake. You did well in choosing her to be my nurse."

Giving Lily a glance, he said, "I had nothing to do with this. You can thank Maud for sleuthing around and finding Lily." He managed to give her a grateful look. Her cheeks pinked up. Such was the connection between them. "Lily came highly recommended."

"Well, I'm just glad to be home here with you, Jake. I

loved visiting you here once a year. It's a lovely cabin and that lake out front is just divine."

"You're stuck with us for a minimum of two months," he teased. Looking over at Lily, he asked, "Is her surgery doing okay?"

Nodding, she said, "It's fine. I'll be checking it several times a day and changing the dressings once a day."

"I'm also being forced to walk every hour," Jenna complained, her lips drawing into an amused smile as she gave Lily a warm look.

"I think Lily is going to help you get well faster," he said. Noticing the flush of Lily's cheeks, how she looked away when he praised her, Jake began to realize how much damage the PTSD had done to her. He could imagine her being a passionate nurse, filled with hope, dreams and aspirations. Understanding how PTSD took all that away, he was seeing her trying to reclaim her once idealistic way of looking at life. The symptoms stripped a person to their soul, and if there hadn't been a solid grounding in the first eighteen or so years of their life, they would have an even tougher climb out of those emotions, shame and humiliation. No one could understand it except another person who had similar symptoms. An ache formed in his heart for Lily. It was clear his mother, who had always been a good judge of character, doted on her.

Chapter Five

June 7

Lily screamed. She jackknifed into a sitting position on her bed. Breathing hard, her chest heaving, sweat trickling down her temples, she froze, fear paralyzing her. Bare, watery moonlight peeked around the heavy drapes at the only window in her bedroom. It gave her just enough light to swiftly absorb the entire silent room.

Shadows played tricks on her hyperalert mind. Enemies were here; her heart was pounding so hard, it was all she could hear. Whimpering, the sound stuck in her tight throat, and she scrambled off the bed, crouching down near the wall. Waiting. The screams of terrified children, the roars of terror and shocked cries of adults, the blasts of AK-47s ripping through the night, surrounded her. She could smell blood in the air. Hiding in a barn, the goats baaing, leaping around, eyes rolling, frantically pressing and pushing against one another, trying to escape the horror outside, only added to the cacophony deluging her distressed brain.

Scrunching her eyes shut, Lily pulled herself into a tight ball to remain hidden. She could smell the small room where she hid as the Taliban attacked the unarmed Afghan village in the middle of the night. It was dank, almost airless. Through a slit in the hundred-year-old wooden planks, she could see the goats leaping high into the air, coming down on their milling, frightened brethren in total panic, but they were imprisoned within a large wooden corral. There was no place for them to go.

A Special Forces sergeant had shoved her into the room earlier, when the attack had begun. He slammed the door shut and told her to stay put until it was over. He ran out, leaving her alone, horrified, paralyzed with fear as the enemy surged through the gates that had been blown open. Then the enemy soldiers flowed to the walled village like a tornado, wreaking revenge.

Lily didn't know what to do. The Army had not prepared her for a situation like this. How could they? Her life was hanging by a thread. The heavy footsteps of men running past, the galloping of horses careened around the barn. The blasts of thunderous AK-47 fire, triggered so near where she crouched, a thin wooden wall between her and the Taliban firing the weapon, made her scream. And then she slapped her hand over her mouth, realizing if the enemy heard her, they would know where she was hiding. She would die!

The acrid, metal smell of blood tainting the air hit her flared nostrils. Lily knew what blood smelled like. But not like this. It was warm and suffocative. It felt as if it was enclosing her, dripping down all around her, soaking her clothes. She was drowning in the blood of murder victims. The dank blackness of the small room closed in on her, her nostrils burning from the odor of gunfire, the bloodletting occurring around the barn. Hoarse shouts in foreign languages split the night, roars and orders thundering from American soldiers, all combined. She clapped her hands against her ears, her back against the wall, her knees drawn tightly up against her body. Lily couldn't catch her breath. She was sobbing. The cries of terrified children slammed through her, ripping her heart open. Children she'd known for years because she'd come back to this firebase, where the village sat in the nearby valley. She knew every child by name.

Her world was in utter turmoil. No one had expected this bloody attack. This was one of the safe villages in the valley, fully enclosed, with a five-foot-tall stucco and rock wall. Two ten-foot-high gates kept predators and the enemy out so the village slept safely each night. Those gates were only opened in the morning, during daylight hours. Too many predators on two legs moved in the night, so those gates were locked.

There was a sudden explosion, so sharp and deep, it slammed Lily into the gunnysacks scattered across the floor. Pain, jagged and sharp, raced through her ears. Pressure waves slapped through the barn, shaking it, shaking her. Goats were screaming in terror. What had just happened? She had no idea. Her life as a nurse and officer had been in a hospital setting, not a bloody, ongoing attack like this.

As she shakily sat up, Lily dazedly realized in alarm that she couldn't hear anything. The burning odor of the massive explosion filtered through the barn, the inner flesh of her nostrils smarting. Opening her mouth, she tried to breath in, but the odor made her start coughing and gagging. She fell down on the floor, clutching at her neck and chest, trying to draw in a clean breath of air. Impossible! Her throat felt as if it were on fire. It felt as if the tops of her lungs were burning. Was it a chemical explosion? Hazardous material? Something far worse? She lay there, gasping like a fish out of water, eyes bulging, hearing no sounds, trying to suck in fresh air. *Die . . . I'm going to die . . .*

Lily jerked, her arms around her knees, huddled against the wall, back against one of the brass legs of her bed. Suddenly, her mind canted and she blinked slowly, realizing she was no longer in the goat barn. Her ears popped, and she could hear herself sobbing for breath in the nearly dark bedroom. Air . . . she was inhaling clean, fresh, coolish air. She sucked deep drafts into her lungs, her entire body shaking with the vast surge of adrenaline. It felt so good to breath clean air! Eyes tightly closed, she concentrated on her breath, trying to slow down her hyperventilation, the edges of her mind telling her that she was in a flashback, replaying that deadly night.

A small whimper tore from her as she felt the claws of the memory, of that night, start to release her. It was such a relief! Still smelling the acrid odor, the funky smell of the goats, the dankness of her hiding place, she tried to control her breathing and slow it down. *Safe. I'm safe.* Her mind echoed that litany over and over again. She felt the coolness of the room, her knee-length cotton nightgown with its long sleeves.

Next, she realized where she was, the state and town, that this was Jake Murdoch's cabin. Reality began a drip, drip, drip into her fried, terrified mind, which was still partly back at the Afghan village and partly here and now. The memory was far more powerful than real life. It always was when a flashback hit her. Often, she felt as if she had two brains, one back there, the other here and now. Literally, she could feel the tug-of-war between them, and wondered which would win.

Hot tears squeezed from beneath her tightly shut eyes. They trailed down the edges of her cheeks, dripping off her jaw; she was helpless to stop them. Partly, the tears were a relief at knowing it *was* a flashback, that it wasn't real any longer. Partly, it was the loss of hundreds of innocent families that night when the Taliban came into the village to murder as many as they could because they were colluding with the Americans. She cried for all the women and men who were murdered in that attack, the loss of their innocent children. Lily had never forgotten any of them. Ever. They were branded into her memory and heart. She didn't want to forget them because they were good people caught in the terrible jaws of jihadists who took a peaceful religion and turned it into a war against those who wouldn't believe as they did. It was barbaric. Horrifying.

The chill in the room finally pulled her out of it. Lily had no idea how much time had passed; she never did when a flashback hit. Unlocking her stiffened arms from around her knees, she slowly allowed one leg and then the other to stretch outward from their cramped position. The clock on the dresser read four a.m. Shakily pushing her hair away from her eyes, she knew she had to get up. Slowly, more and more reality seeped into her traumatized, adrenaline-soaked brain. The horrifying memory was receding, like the ocean's tide. Lily knew the tide would come back in at some point.

Jerkily, she leaned forward until she was on the coolness of the cedar floor, on her hands and knees. Pulling the fabric away from her knees, she gripped the mattress, looking for purchase, looking for something to steady her unsteady world. The shadows in the room had changed; the moon had traveled for an hour or more from its position when she'd screamed herself awake. Then, the shadows had resembled the Taliban hunting her. Now, the shadows were more benign. But she didn't fool herself. That flashback would visit her again. She forced one foot outward, hauling herself up.

Falling onto the mattress, Lily crawled onto it, grabbing at the covers, chilled and shaking badly. As the adrenaline began to leave, it crashed her entire emotional and parasympathetic nervous systems. Collapsing, feeling weakness pervade her, she landed with her head on the pillow, pulling up her legs, curling into a fetal position for protection. Her breathing was steadier now; she was no longer hyperventilating. Closing her eyes, the warmth of the goose-down comforter made her feel safer, as if it were a wall between her and the flashback. A tremulous sigh escaped between her lips. Her gown was soaked with cold sweat. It smelled awful. Lily called it fear sweat because it stank. She didn't care; she was getting warm, the comforter like an island of safety around the emotion that still roiled within her.

All she wanted was to sleep, to escape her brain, which held these tragic memories and paralyzed her every time they replayed. Her thoughts canted to Jenna, and then to Jake. They were good people. In Jake, she saw someone else who was chased by demons. But he was a lot stronger than she was right now.

Every day, with incremental steps, Lily was trying to get a little stronger. It was in small ways, not large ones. Managing to live through a flashback more than showed her that she had the strength within her to keep moving forward. Earlier, the flashbacks had nearly destroyed her, leaving her helpless and unable to live normally for three or four days afterward. Now, she got through them in a few hours, sometimes in half a day. It wasn't pretty, but at least her real world now held together, no longer torn apart, drifting in and out of reality. That was progress. It was the last thought she had.

* * *

"Jake, did you hear Lily screaming last night?" Jenna looked up at her son, who had come in to see her before he left for work. She saw his black brows dip as he halted at the end of her bed. She had awakened because her door was partly open; if she needed help, someone would hear her.

"No, I didn't. Tell me more."

Jenna pushed her covers down around her waist. She had the bed in a slightly raised position because it was more comfortable on her healing surgery. "She was screaming. It jerked me awake. I've never heard that kind of cry from a human, Jake. It sent shivers down my spine. At first, I was disoriented because I thought I was in my home, not yours."

"You were jerked out of sleep," he rumbled.

"Yes, for sure." Jenna looked out the open door. "I wanted to go to her, but I knew I couldn't do it just yet. Maybe in another week, after my surgery heals up more, but not now. I had no way to get hold of you, to tell you what was happening."

Jake scratched his head. "I'll get Patrick to come over here today. I think we might need a buzzer you could press that would get hold of me. I know you have one for Lily."

"That's a good idea. But I'm concerned about her. She sounded like she was being murdered, Jake. I didn't know what to think."

He moved to the bed and reached out, taking his mother's hand. "Jenna, she's a military vet like me. I know she told you that she has PTSD."

"Is that what happened last night? She had a nightmare or something?"

"Probably." He released her hand and stood there, feeling his mother's darkening gaze on him.

"It was terrifying, Jake. My God, what has that poor woman gone through?"

"We all go through it if we're in combat, Jenna. She's not unique, believe me."

Tilting her head, she gave him an intense, sweeping look. "Is that why when you came home from the war, you didn't stay at our home?"

Moving uncomfortably, Jake looked away, his mouth thinning. The silence was telling. Finally, he tipped his head in her direction. "Yeah."

Sighing, Jenna reached out and gripped her son's hand, which had turned into a fist. "Oh, Jake, why didn't you tell me?"

He gently squeezed her hand, then released it. "I don't know. I just knew I'd startle you awake, like Lily woke you up last night. It's no way to live, Jenna."

She glanced out the door. "This is awful." She pressed her hand to her heart. "Oh, poor Lily! How can we help her, Jake? What can we do?"

Giving a painful shrug, Jake muttered, "Nothing. There's nothing that stops flashbacks and nightmares. We have absolutely no control over them. Sometimes," he hesitated, looking down at his worn cowboy boots, ". . . sometimes all we can do is take ourselves out of the equation. I didn't stay with you when I got home because I'm just like Lily. I'm sure she doesn't realize she woke you up last night. I'm sure she's ashamed and feeling pretty low after going through what she did last night."

"It's only six a.m. I'm hoping she's sleeping."

"Yeah, she probably is."

"Poor darling. She's so responsible and caring, Jake. This just breaks my heart. How can I help Lily?"

"Well, if you mention it to her, she'll probably feel lower than a snake's belly in a wheel rut."

"Does it affect her after having one?"

"Sure. When I left the corps, the first year was hard on

me. I would have a flashback at least once a week, sometimes twice. I was foreman here, and I was losing a lot of sleep." His mouth quirked. "That's how I got my nickname: Bear. I was growly, short and irritable. It's sleep deprivation, Jenna."

"You make a nightmare and flashback sound like separate things. Aren't they the same thing?"

"No. A flashback is a helluva lot more intense and can shake your world apart. You relive something you survived. Usually, it's about being in combat, feeling like you were going to die and not survive it. Flashbacks usually occur when there's a sound, a smell, a color or seeing something on TV or on the internet that triggers it. You're caught up in it. You're there, and you hear, smell, taste and see what that combat situation was when you were caught up in it. There's no way to get out of it. You're trapped. You aren't in control. You're swept up into what happened again."

"What if we woke Lily up? Wouldn't that stop it?"

Jake grimaced. "That's why a flashback is so devastating to people like us. And to the spouse or family who see it happen. If you were to touch Lily when she was caught up in the claws of that flashback? She wouldn't know it was you shaking her awake. She wouldn't hear you. She'd be locked in that experience. And she'd probably lash out and hit at you because she was back there, not here in the present."

"Oh," she whispered, shaking her head. "That's awful."

"I've seen marriages go on the rocks because of them," Jake growled. "The man or woman who's caught in the flashback, if touched, will strike out, thinking the other person is the enemy, attacking them. They're going to defend themselves."

"Then, how do I help Lily if it happens again?"

"Best to stand at the foot of her bed and quietly call her name. If you touch her in any way, you're just deepening her experience. She's a prisoner within it. It makes it worse for her. If you can just gently call her name, it might help release her a little sooner, but that's all you can do."

"My God, I didn't realize this, Jake. Why didn't you tell me?"

"I was ashamed, Jenna. I didn't want to admit I couldn't control myself. And I didn't want to keep waking you up at night, or maybe put you in danger if you tried to shake me awake. I've heard too many horror stories of a man coming home and not talking about his PTSD with his wife. And then, one night, he's hit with a flashback. The wife gets jerked awake, turns over and shakes her husband's shoulder. He turns and smashes his fist into her face or tries to choke her to death because he's trapped in the past and thinks he's going to die if he doesn't defend himself."

Rubbing her brow, Jenna gave him a long, sad look. "I feel so helpless."

"So do we."

"How long does a flashback last, Jake?"

"Could be minutes, sometimes fifteen or twenty minutes."

"How do you feel when you're coming out of it?"

"At first? You're there, not here," and he pointed down at the floor where he stood. "Slowly, your mind starts separating the past event from the present reality, and for a while, you're not sure where you are because you're emotionally overwhelmed and aren't free of the memories or feelings. It takes five or ten minutes, sometimes longer, depending upon the intensity of it, to realize you're here, not back there in the dangerous situation."

"A lot of confusion in your mind?"

"Exactly. And if you try to talk to me when I'm in that phase of coming out of it, strung between two different worlds, I may or may not hear you speaking to me. I may still be caught up in the sounds of battle or whatever is scaring me to death."

"And so I should just stand quietly and call your name, not touch you in any way?"

"Yes. The more I orient to the here and now, the more I'll start to hear you calling my name. Once I get a fix on your voice, I'll hone in on it, and it actually draws me out of the past faster than it would normally, back to the present."

"That's helpful to know," she murmured, her voice fraught with emotion.

"For both parties," Jake agreed. He looked at his watch. "I have to go. Are you going to discuss this with Lily?"

"I don't think so. At least, not right now. Maybe she'll talk to me about it."

"Doubtful," he said. "Remember, we're ashamed of ourselves. We feel bad we can't control our own body or mind." He settled the Stetson on his head. "Just give her latitude today. She's going to be wiped out."

"I'm sure," Jenna said, sympathy in her voice.

He leaned over, squeezing her hand. "Lily is lucky to be working with someone as understanding as you, Jenna."

"I'll see you tonight at dinner."

"Yes." He released her hand. "You're a Band-Aid on her wound. I know your kindness and care toward others. She's lucky to be here with you."

"And you," Jenna said gently. "Thank you for letting me know about the PTSD you carry. I wish . . . well, we'll talk more later." She could see the resistance in his eyes. Swept up on a wave of sadness, she realized just how many burdens from the war Jake and Lily continued to carry. "I love you, Son."

Jake nodded and leaned over, kissing her hair. "Back at you," he rumbled.

Lily tried to shake off the exhaustion that weighed her down as she hurried to Jenna's room. She'd overslept by half an hour. Peeking inside the room, she saw the woman was up, had dressed herself and was using the walker to get around.

"I'm so sorry I'm late," she said, coming into the room.

"Oh, no worries," Jenna assured her, giving her a warm smile as she eased out of the bathroom. "Look! I can finally get around by myself."

"Wow, that's progress. How is your leg feeling?"

"Tender, but no pain. Oh, I forgot to take my pain pill when I woke up."

Lily halted near her. "That's really good news. You're healing fast. Let me get the pill for you."

"Well, you've been giving me massages two or three times a day. I believe that's made a huge difference. Who doesn't love to get a massage?" and she smiled again into Lily's darkened eyes.

"Are you hungry?" She handed Jenna a glass of water and her medication. She dutifully took it and gave the glass back to her.

"I am. You know what I'd love to do, Lily? How about you follow along with me as I make it across the living room and sit at the kitchen table?"

"I'm with you," Lily assured her, resting her hand lightly on her shoulder. "Let's go for it." Jenna didn't say anything about her screaming, and Lily was relieved; she'd been afraid she might have awakened her in the night.

"I like strong, assertive women," Jenna remarked, moving her device on wheels to the hall. "We might be down, but we're not out!"

Lily remained at her side. "I don't like the other choice. Do you? Throw in the towel, wave a white flag of surrender?"

Snorting politely, Jenna said wryly, "Women are the stronger of the two genders, no question. And we're always the ones who carry so many more loads, seen and unseen, than any man ever does."

Smarting inwardly, Lily whispered, "You're so right about that." Right now, she felt like there were twenty-pound weights on each of her feet. She had finally fallen asleep after the flashback, but her rest was broken, restless and light. She knew she had to be alert and observant of Jenna to ensure her safety.

"Jake came in before he left for work," she said. "He made a huge omelet and said it was in the fridge. Maybe you don't have to make anything except some toast for me?"

"That was sweet of him," Lily said as they crossed the living room. There was one step to get up to the kitchen area. Resting her hand on Jenna's back, she watched her lift her walker with ease. Another sign she was gaining physical strength. "As soon as I get you to the table, I'll check it out. Want coffee, too?"

Jenna laughed and waited while Lily pulled out the chair at the end of the table for her. "A day without coffee is like a day without sunshine."

Grinning, and feeling a tad bit better because Jenna was such a sunbeam, Lily helped her sit down. Each chair had a comfy cushion on it, perfect for her. "We agree." Straightening, she placed the walker within arm's reach of Jenna and then headed to the refrigerator. Jake hadn't done this before and she warmed to his thoughtfulness. The way she felt right now, she wasn't sure she had the concentration necessary to make breakfast anyway. Had she awakened Jake with her screams last night? Did he know what had happened? That she'd had a merciless flashback? If anyone would know, it would be him. Lily needed to talk to him.

Chapter Six

June 7

Jake was disgruntled at his decision to come back to the cabin at noon. He never came back midday. But now he had. Pulling up in his truck, he put it in Park and turned off the engine. The day was sunny, the sky starting to show some clouds over the Wilson Range to the west of him. Dammit! He wanted to avoid the reason he was coming to the house. It wasn't to see how his mother was doing. No, what had been eating at his craw all morning long was their conversation about Lily. About her screaming, the sound carrying to Jenna's room and awakening her.

Mouth tight, he shut the door, his boots crunching across the gravel as he headed for the sidewalk that led to the gate and the cabin on the other side of it. Why the hell was he worried about Lily? She'd either had a flashback or a nightmare. But he knew the difference, and that was what ate at him. His own flashbacks the first year after leaving the military had nearly rendered him paralyzed in some ways, barely able to function like a normal human being. Thankfully, they were less frequent now, and if he got one only every three or four months, that was progress. There was nothing he could do to stop them or change them. And Lily couldn't either. He knew, as he pushed the gate open, that Lily was recently out of the military herself, so her issues were probably weekly, maybe more.

He wanted to talk with her, but he knew she was probably fixing Jenna lunch about now. It wasn't the right time. But something kept nudging him . . . hell, shoving him . . . to come home to check up on her. To see if she was okay. As he thunked up the stairs to the porch, he didn't know what to expect. He wasn't worried that Lily wouldn't do her job responsibly. She was a vet. She'd die before leaving her post. She wouldn't allow Jenna to get into medical trouble.

Drawing in a deep breath, he brushed his boots on the thick mat outside the door, gripped the knob and pushed it open. To his surprise, he saw Jenna sitting at the table, facing him.

Lily was in the kitchen, making sandwiches. She lifted her head at the sound of the door opening, and Jake got a good look at her pale features, the smudges beneath her eyes and the darkness clouding them. Her hair, which was usually in a ponytail, was free, somehow telling him she was at loose ends within herself. He'd always believed in his gut intuition and it had often saved his life in combat. In some ways, he was like a hound dog on a scent. He could sniff out a situation, a tenor of energy, and know if it was safe or a threat to him. As he took off his hat and settled it on a nearby peg, he closed the door.

"You got an extra sandwich, Lily?" He liked her name. Liked the musicality of it. There was shock in her eyes, her hands frozen over the cutting board for a moment.

"Er . . . yes . . . yes, of course."

"This is a nice surprise!" Jenna called from the table.

Frowning, Jake muttered, "I just happened to be in the area, was all." He tore his gaze from Lily, who had jump-started herself, finishing off three sandwiches at the kitchen counter. Forcing himself to move toward the table and not Lily, he said to his mother, "I didn't know you could get from your bedroom to out here."

"Lily's to blame," she said, giving the young woman a warm smile. Lily smiled back, but it was a tight, nervous one.

"That's good progress," Jake agreed. He halted at the chair, hands on the rail. "Lily? Would you like some help?"

"No . . . I'm fine. Would you like a turkey sandwich with lettuce and tomato on it?"

"Sounds good." He looked to the coffeepot and saw it was plugged in. "Jenna? You want some coffee?"

"Absolutely. I think it's done."

Nodding, Jake moved into the kitchen. Lily gave him a glance. There was worry on her face. She wasn't capable of hiding her feelings, and while that was good for him to see, it also meant she wasn't a game player. She wouldn't do well at a poker table, that's for sure. He pulled down three cups. "Want some, too?" he asked her, giving her a glance. She was placing a sandwich with a handful of Fritos on three plates.

"Yes, please."

Nodding, he filled the cups. She moved to the table, two of the plates in hand. On the way back, Jake got a better look at Lily. Her skin was stretched tight across her cheekbones. There was no color in her face at all. He sensed she'd had a flashback and he'd damn well like to be sure about it. They were handled differently from nightmares. As he slid a cup in Jenna's direction, he placed one next to him. Pulling out Lily's chair, he waited for her to arrive with her plate. He had a lot of questions for her, but none he could ask in front of his mother. Lily would be defensive in front of her, and Jake had no wish to make her feel humiliated or outed by him.

"This is very tasty, Lily." Jenna beamed across the table at her.

"Thanks."

"You put something zesty into it. What did you use?"

"A bit of horseradish with mayonnaise."

Jake pulled out the chair for her. She seemed flustered by his manners but sat down, quickly pulling her chair up to the table. He sat down at the head of the table, Jenna on his right and Lily on the left.

"Well, it's pitch perfect," Jenna praised. "I'll tell you, Jake, Lily is an incredible cook. I love everything she's made for us so far."

"Me too," Jake agreed, biting into the sandwich. It tasted good. Better than the protein bar he had stashed in the glove box of his truck.

"It's such a beautiful day today," Jenna said wistfully. "Are you going outside yet?"

"No. Lily says next week. But she's going to let me go out with my walker to the front porch, sit in the swing so I can watch the world go by, later today."

"Fresh air heals," Lily whispered, barely eating her sandwich. Her hand trembled as she picked up a Frito. "Sun, a breeze and just being out in nature is a prescription that always helps."

"You should go out," Jenna urged. "I have my eye on walking around that small lake in front of the house, Jake. But it's got long strands of grass and Lily is afraid I might get a foot tangled in it and fall."

"That can happen," he said. "Better to take it slow and easy."

"I wish I could ride a horse." Jenna sighed.

"That will come with time," Lily promised.

"Do you ride?" Jake asked her. He tried not to pry

into her life, but the question unexpectedly popped out of his mouth.

"No."

"I thought you were raised on a farm in Idaho."

"I was, but my dad kept a few milk cows, and we had a dog and lots of cats, but no horses. He was a potato farmer, not a rancher."

"You know," Jenna said, wiping her fingers on a paper napkin, "you haven't left this house since I arrived, Lily."

"I'm going to start going to the dog shelter next week, after I'm sure you can get around by yourself."

"Well," she sighed, looking out the window, "you're pale today and I think you need some sunshine." Tilting her head, she gave her son a fond look. "Jake? Could you take Lily around with you? She hasn't even seen Maud and Steve's ranch. It's huge. Maybe get her out for a bit of fresh air?"

Jake silently thanked his mother. He was sure she didn't realize he was looking for a way to get Lily alone. "Sure I can. Lily? I've got about two hours in this area of the ranch. You're welcome to ride along with me, and I can show you around. What do you think?" Never had he wanted anything more as he saw her lashes drop as she considered his request. Her hands were beneath the table and he was sure they were clasped. Maybe she was in the throes of an anxiety attack. She felt tentative.

Jenna reached across the table as Lily brought her hands up to it. "Go, Lily! There's no reason why we both have to be housebound."

Lily gave Jenna a half smile. "Two hours?"

"I'm going to hobble into the living room and work on my knitting. Go with Jake! You need to get out for a bit, I think."

Lily forced herself to look up at Jake. "Sure I won't be in the way?"

"No. I have stops to make, but you're welcome to climb out of the cab and come with me. More or less acquaint yourself with some of the ranch, if you want." Jake didn't want to press her unduly. Silently, though, he was urging Lily to say yes. Her expression was unsure. There was a scattering of fear in her large blue eyes, and he wondered if it was the remnants of the flashback she'd endured. His gut said yes, it was.

"Well . . . yes, I think I'd like that." Worriedly, Lily held Jenna's gaze. "Are you *sure* about this?"

Patting the pocket of her slacks, Jenna said, "My cell phone's on me. If I need you, I'll call."

"I'll take my cell phone for sure," Lily promised.

Jake watched her rise, her fingers having a subtle tremble as she gathered up the empty plates. He remembered all too well how damned shaky he was—inside and out—after a flashback hit him. He saw Lily chew on her lower lip as she hurried away to the kitchen, plates in hand. She was wearing a loose set of jeans that couldn't hide her nicely rounded hips or her long legs. Jake liked the way they swayed too much, unhappy with his body's clamoring needs. Rising, he said to Jenna, "I'll bring her back in two hours."

"Good," Jenna said. "If I get tired, I'll go lie down, but usually I like to watch some TV and knit after lunch."

Jake moved to his mother's chair and helped her pull it away from the table. He brought her walker to it to make the transfer easy on her. "Knit away," he teased, giving her a slight smile. Again, he wondered if Jenna had somehow sensed he wanted to talk to Lily in private. He never underestimated his mother's strong intuitiveness. After all, he'd gotten his own powerful gut check ability directly from her, and he was thankful for the times it had helped him save his life and the lives of the others with him.

He picked up everything else from the table, joining Lily in the kitchen. He felt a twinge as he saw her hands still trembling. What she needed—what he'd needed when it happened to him—was to crawl into the arms of a woman, in his case, and just be held. God, how many times had he wished for an embrace as he soaked the bedsheets with his sweat, sitting there shaking, his gut so damned tight it ached? Risking a glance in her direction, he saw her face was maybe even more pale than before. Did she not want to be with him? Not wanting to ask the question, his gut told him Lily would be better off if she got away from the house for a while. He knew he hated going into his bedroom after a flashback. Grabbing a blanket and pillow, he would make his way out to the living room and sleep on the couch. No, the bedroom always held the specter of the flashback. He never had one out on the couch.

Lily tried to quell her rolling stomach as she slid into the cab of Jake's huge three-quarter-ton pickup. The sun was bright, almost hurting her eyes.

"Here," Jake said, climbing in, "wear this." He handed her a black baseball cap with Wind River Ranch embroidered in red across the front.

Their fingers met briefly, and Lily was amazed at how much her stomach settled down after that. "Why . . . thank you. Is this your hat?"

"Sort of," he hedged, belting in and starting the engine. The truck purred to life. "I prefer a Stetson, but if I'm going to be on horseback or helping the wranglers in a corral, branding or vaccinating, I always throw that on my head instead." He managed a one-cornered smile. "Don't want to get my good Stetson dirty."

She laughed a little as she settled it on her head. Her thick brown hair wouldn't be tamed, so she took it off, stuffed her hand into the pocket of her jeans and drew out a rubber band. Quickly, she gathered her slightly wild hair into a ponytail. Then the cap went on easily. She glanced at Jake and saw him nod, pleased.

He drove over the graveled road and onto an asphalt one that would take them to the headquarters of the ranch. "I've got to stop at the medical dispensary and pick up a couple of boxes of syringes and vaccination bottles. I imagine you know a lot about those?"

She leaned back, feeling some of her tension melt, clasping her hands in her lap. "Just a little. I guess you have a group of your men vaccinating cattle today?"

"Yeah, but it's not cattle. It's buffalo."

"Oh. I didn't know Maud had any on her land. I thought they could give cattle brucellosis."

"Actually," Jake said, "brucellosis can attack cattle and bison or vice versa. I'm picking up the OCV, brucellosis vaccination. We're going to vaccinate some buffalo calves that are four months old today."

"I learn something new every day," she said, impressed by his knowledge.

"Maud's buffalo herd numbers a hundred. We had fifteen cows drop their calves the same day. At four months, we like to vaccinate. The wranglers already have the calves and mothers in specially built pens and a corral. They're waiting for me to bring the shots out to them."

"Do you have a vet give the shots?"

"Actually, our vet hopes like hell we'll do the vaccinating because bison are wild and don't like to be put in holding pens. They'll tear the hell out of a normal cattle pen, so we have to construct specially built corrals for this kind of thing so they don't wreck the place."

She laughed a little. "Even a little four-month-old buffalo calf is a handful?"

"Yeah, small but surprisingly strong. Plus, we have to watch the mothers, who we place in a pen next to the chute where we vaccinate. Some mothers get hyper and they have horns and go at the four-by-fours that make up the fence. Other mothers call to their calves but remain quiet. We never know what will happen."

"Sounds dangerous."

He glanced at her. "That's why I'd like you along. You're a nurse. If one of us gets nailed, you can be our medical help."

"So, there was a reason your mother suggested I go out with you this afternoon?"

"No. Jenna has always been a worrywart about me, so I never tell her I'm going to be tangling with a one-ton bull buffalo or cows with calves. She knows buffalo are twitchy at best and you can't guess what they'll do when wranglers ride up on horses to herd them from one pasture to another."

"I've seen bison in a zoo," she said, "but never out in the open like this." The Salt River Range, to the east, was still clothed in snow at the tops of the peaks. Below, a carpet of evergreens coated their slopes.

"I'll keep you out of harm's way," he promised. "Or you can stay in the truck and watch from there. Whatever makes you feel comfortable, Lily."

She felt her cheeks burning and lifted her left hand, fingers touching her cheek. The look Jake gave her stirred her as a woman. She was surprised at how her body reacted to that one warm glance. It had been over a year since she'd had relations with a man. There was a kindness in the tone of his voice, and she saw it in his green eyes. More tension bled out of her.

"Jenna worries about you, about the children she taught

through the years. I think she's one of those special human beings who truly cares about others. Nowadays," and she looked out the window for a moment, "it's become a rare thing."

"You care."

"Yes, yes, I do."

"A good trait to have in a human being," he agreed. Turning, he drove down a slight slope into the HQ area. There were barns, employee housing, a lot of corrals, twelve small cabins farther out for guests and the main buildings where the heart of the place beat. He parked in front of the medical facility, which sat next to the main offices. "Stay here. I'll be right back."

Nodding, she watched Jake move. He was lithe for his height and the breadth of his shoulders beneath the light-weight denim jacket. There was nothing about the man that didn't appeal to her. He wasn't pretty-boy attractive; rather, he had a face that had seen a lot, weathered a lot and was stoic-looking. She wished she could hear him laugh. What would it sound like? Jake always had a bright red kerchief around his neck and usually wore a long-sleeved chambray shirt. Jenna had grumped that her son must have eight chambray shirts in his closet, jeans to match and nothing else. They both got a giggle out of that comment. He didn't seem concerned about what he wore except that it was functional and as tough as he was. She noticed his boots were well scuffed, worn and had seen a lot of work as well. A pair of elkskin gloves sat between them on the seat. They, too, were worn. She enjoyed watching a pair of cow-boys on two bay horses clip-clop down the main road. Truly, this was the Old West she'd loved to read about as a teenager. *Lonesome Dove* was one of her favorite books.

Jake came back promptly, a red-and-white cooler in one

hand and a box of syringes in the other. He opened the door and handed her the small cooler.

"Tuck that between your feet?"

"Sure."

Next came the box of syringes and needles in a cardboard box. It fit on her lap easily and was lightweight.

"Thanks. I'm not used to having an assistant," he said, climbing in.

"I'm glad Jenna kicked me out of the house." She had rolled down the window. The truck was not one of those fancy electric car window types. It was fairly old, dents here and there, paint scuffs along with it just like the boots Jake wore.

"It's a nice day," he grunted, putting the vehicle into reverse, backing away from the buildings. "Enjoy this time of year around here because come September, the snow starts flying."

"Idaho doesn't have as long a winter as you do around here, thank goodness."

The breeze was fragrant with the scents of alfalfa hay, and of the horses she saw in one large oval corral down the road. They were all saddled, and she saw ranch guests going out for an afternoon ride. The place was alive with wranglers, men and women, horses, a chuck wagon and people coming to enjoy such a life. She saw Jake lift his hand from the steering wheel as three wranglers on horses were riding into the main area.

"How many people do you manage, Jake?"

"About a hundred and fifty in the busy season, from May through September. Then, a lot of them are seasonal workers. We're down to about fifty during the slow season, the winter."

"Where do all the other people go?"

"Some live around here and have a second livelihood.

Some live off their earnings and live in Wind River. Not many go to Jackson Hole because it's where the rich corporate people are, and rents are too high for them to afford." As he drove out of the area, he pointed to an area off to the right. "Maud and Steve started a program for wranglers and their families. If they worked a few years here, they would be given a free log house package and five acres to put it on. They had to build it, and Steve would bring in equipment to help get it erected. The land and home were then put in their name."

Her eyes widened with surprise. "That's so generous! I've never heard of anyone doing that."

"Well, Maud and Steve aren't your normal human beings either. They've made a point of hiring military people over others. They see how many of us are at loose ends when we come out of combat and need help of one sort or another. Unlike the VA, which has a spotty record of helping vets, they've been a bright spot for a lot of us."

"Having a home you own? That means something to anyone, whether they're a vet or not."

"Yeah," he said, glancing toward her, "that's true. But for vets with PTSD, there's no anchor to hang on to. You come home wounded in your heart and soul and all the VA wants to do is throw meds at you, numb you out and make you feel half dead. Here? Maud has a therapist from Jackson Hole, Ms. Hilbert, come down once a week, and we vets go to the auditorium where we talk and hash things out. And instead of meds, we get a horse assigned to us, we get a job that we want to do and we know if we stick with their program, a house and land of our own is the reward."

"I never knew about that," Lily whispered, suddenly emotional. "That's wonderful, Jake. Is that how you got your beautiful home?"

She saw one corner of his mouth drawn inward. "I don't

call it a home. It's just a house. And you know Steve built the foreman's house about twenty years ago."

"So, you don't have a cabin or land to call your own?"

"Well, the house is mine until I don't want the job as foreman anymore. It's a nice place but way too large for one man. Maud and Steve will give me a cabin package and land at that time."

"That's wonderful. That house is sure a lifesaver for your mom in her situation. And there's a room for me as well. Three people fit nicely in there. Heck, as large as it is, a family of six would love it."

"The last foreman was here at the ranch for twenty-five years, never married. He had to go back to Maine to care for his aging parents. That's how I got the job."

She watched the pastures, so lush with quick-growing grass beginning to spread out across the flat land. In each huge pasture, she saw Herefords eagerly chowing down on that nutritious grass. Each pasture seemed to stretch for as far as she could see toward the Salt River Range towering in the distance. "All these fence lines must take a beating in winter."

He snorted. "A helluva beating. We don't keep cattle here in the winter because temperatures are far too low; they'd die of exposure. The buffalo can tolerate it, but domestic cattle can't."

"But they have cattle ranches in southeast Wyoming."

"Yes, but the snowfall and temperatures there are a lot better than here." He pointed to a herd of brown-and-white Herefords off to her right. "These are all grass-leased pastures. A cattle ranch from Utah, Colorado, Arizona, New Mexico or Texas will truck their cattle up here from June through September, and the animals put on a lot of good weight due to the grass. Then they're trucked out of here by early October for the livestock yards. There's good money in grass leases, but you have to have the land to do it right, plus a lot of wranglers to keep those fence posts strong and the five strands of barbed wire tight. It's constant work."

Lily could see a pickup truck and four wranglers out doing just that: fence mending, along one side of the grass-lease pasture. "I know from my dad's potato farm about fences and rotting posts. We had it around the farm property along with some corrals and pastures for our milk cows."

"How old were you when you started driving fence line?"

She liked the glimmer of amusement in his eyes. "Twelve. My dad and I would drive up and down the road looking for rotted posts or sagging barbed wire. My mother, Sadie, gave me a twelfth birthday gift of a stout pair of elkskin gloves."

"Only kind to use," and he pointed to his, sitting between them. "You can handle the worst barbed wire with that thick leather. Deerskin will rip and tear, so we never use it here."

"My dad got me a straw cowboy hat and a blue neckerchief, saying that at twelve, it was time for me to learn about farm work."

"Did you like it?"

"I loved it. I loved going out with my dad. We had two black-and-white border collies that went with us. My mom would pack a big lunch for us, two thermoses of coffee for him and one of hot tea for me. I always looked forward to working with him. We had a lot of fun and laughs and got a lot of posts replaced and wire tightened up."

"But you've never been around horses?"

"No."

"Weren't you horse crazy as a kid?"

She smiled a little, hearing teasing in his tone. They were now driving on a dirt road, heading toward the Salt

Range. "I was, yes, but my dad didn't have time to take care of one."

"They're constant, daily work," Jake agreed.

"What about you? Did you grow up on a ranch?"

"No, my dad, who's gone now, owned a grocery store in Casper. From the time I was fourteen, I spent my summers on a nearby ranch, learning how to be a wrangler. It was good money and I liked being outdoors and around animals."

"I'm sorry you lost your dad. That had to have been awful."

He shrugged. "He died of a heart attack. I was already a recon Marine in Afghanistan and couldn't be reached or go home for the funeral. I was out on a top-secret assignment and radio silence couldn't be broken. When I got in off the op, two weeks later, they told me what had happened and I flew home."

She could hear the emotion carefully controlled in Jake's lowered tone. His fingers moved restively on the wheel when he spoke about his father. "I don't know what I'd do without my mom and dad. I just can't imagine them leaving me."

"Jenna took it hard. They really loved each other. And I grew up seeing what real love was about. At the time he passed, I was getting a lot of PTSD symptoms, although I didn't honestly recognize them until I went home after the funeral."

"Oh?"

"I'd been in the Marine Corps from age eighteen. My father died when I was twenty-five. My enlistment was up at twenty-seven and I got out. Let's just say I thought I'd return to Casper and run our family grocery store, but I couldn't hack it. My symptoms were such that I didn't even want to be around my mother and scare her half to death."

"What happened to the grocery store?"

"Jenna has a good manager and she still owns it, so my not taking over didn't scuttle the business." His black brows fell. "Let's just say I was a certified mess and didn't stay at home for long. I came west and got this job." He grimaced. "It saved my life."

She sat there digesting his heavy, forced words, as if he didn't really want to admit any of it to her. "I understand," she said softly. "I couldn't stay on the farm, even though I wanted to."

"Because of the PTSD?"

"Yes, very bad PTSD."

Jake slowed and turned down another, narrower dirt road. "I was wondering about that," he said, glancing at her momentarily.

"Oh?" Her stomach tightened and she grew fearful, her palms breaking out in sweat.

"Jenna told me this morning she'd heard you screaming last night."

"Oh God . . ."

Jake slowed the truck. "Jenna was worried about you."

Pulling her hand away from her eyes, she stared at him. "About my PTSD?"

"She knows about it on paper. But because I didn't go home and stay, like you did with your parents, she never understood that I'd get flashbacks and nightmares where I'd wake up screaming."

Her heart felt as if it were cringing in her chest and she placed her hand there. Jake was driving more slowly now. Up ahead, maybe half a mile away, she saw a truck, horses and wranglers waiting beside a high, stout corral. Inside it, she saw the buffalo and the calves. Swallowing hard, she managed to force out, "I had a flashback last night. I was so scared they'd happen here. Scared it would wake everyone."

"It didn't wake me upstairs. But Jenna heard it."

"I'm so sorry," she choked out, giving him a fearful glance.

"You looked tired when I came in at lunch. I figured you'd probably had one."

Wiping her upper lip, she managed, "Yes . . . I did. Was Jenna upset? Did it scare her?"

"She was concerned, was all," Jake soothed. "I told her you probably had a bad dream and explained about PTSD. She accepted my explanation."

Lily felt as if her whole life was hanging in the balance. What was she going to do? There was no way to control them.

"I–I can't do that again."

Shaking his head, he muttered, "It's not something you can control, Lily. What I'd suggest is to keep your door closed."

"But I'd told Jenna to keep our doors open so I could hear her if she needed help at night."

"I was thinking about that." Jake slowed the pickup and drove to just behind the group of wranglers. "I have an idea that might work. That way, when you have an episode, you won't wake Jenna and you'll be okay." He put the truck in Park and turned off the engine. "Wipe the worry off your face. Okay? You're not going to be fired. It's safe and so are you. Let's go."

Chapter Seven

June 7

It's safe and so are you.

Dizzied by his gruff, emotional words, Lily almost felt separated from her body for a moment. She got that way when a bubble of hope skimmed through her. It didn't happen often. In fact, hardly ever. Absorbing that sensation, the hope almost so palpable she could reach out and touch it, she climbed out of the truck, joining Jake, who waited for her at the front. There was too much going on right now for her to fully digest the enormity of his words, or the sense of overwhelming protection that seemed to fall around her when he held her gaze as he spoke to her. Lily had gotten used to feeling like an oyster without a shell since her breakdown. Her whole world revolved around not feeling safe anywhere, that there was nothing inside her to help her erect a protective shield so she could start to function somewhat normally once more. It was a help-less feeling, one she hated. She'd never been this way before.

Jake's unexpected response sent her into a euphoric state of hope. Right now, Lily knew she needed protection to cobble her shattered life back together again. But how to do it? How to make it happen? No therapist had the answer for her. Just now, however, Jake had made her feel safe for the first time since that night in the Afghan village. Lily had always felt sure of herself, felt capable, strong, and she had been living her life of service in a way she was passionate about. But not anymore.

One night had destroyed her world. Destroyed her. And she was careful to allow herself, even in this moment, to know she was making slow, torturous progress toward finding a new Lily to replace the old one that had been damaged. The worst part was not feeling safe out in the world at any time. And it involved every decision she made every day. How to fight to get a skin back on her raw body to protect herself from the hardness of this world. How to fight by the hour, sometimes by the minute, to find some small place she could relax. Never in her life had she ever thought about safety before that night. Her parents had raised her to stand up for her integrity, morals and values; they'd taught her that she had a voice and could speak up for herself and for others. *Not anymore.*

On some days, Lily wondered if she could make it through the next hour; the strength within her, which she thought was her core, was fragile, sometimes online, sometimes not. Every day was a struggle, a new mountain to try to climb.

Jake was a protector. It wasn't obvious. He was gruff and responded to others with a single word or as few words as he could. But she felt that sense of sanctuary he was offering her now. Just now, Lily felt that the tiny mustard seed of hope he'd shared with her would take root in her shattered soul.

Her maturity warned her not to project on Jake. To take it one day at a time with this enigmatic man she sensed hid behind hard, impenetrable walls of his own, who had to deal with his own struggles with PTSD. And yet, he had the strength to reach out to her, to tell her that not only was her job with Jenna was safe but *she* was safe. For a moment, Lily wondered if she'd made it all up. That it was something she wanted to hear so badly that her brain was screwing her up once more. Repeating words or concepts to make her feel better.

The truck slowed, and she lamented she didn't have the time to carefully sift through their conversation right now. Frustrated, she gently held this new awareness within her like an egg that might crack at any moment, putting it aside for now. Sensing a new world was opening up to her: ranch life, and Jake's nearness, for which she was grateful. Lily had just discovered he needed his own bulwark of quiet strength. That helped her to fight to become healthy and whole once more. He was a good role model.

To her surprise, as they drew up to the corral, she saw two of the four wranglers were women about her age. The other two were men in their late twenties, if she had to guess. Her window was open, and she heard one of the women call out to them. "Hey, Jake! You hired a new woman wrangler?" a redhead called out, tugging on her elkskin work gloves.

Lily climbed out and shut the door. Jake met her at the front of the truck. He brought his hand beneath Lily's elbow and gently steered her toward the group. He couldn't blame the men because Lily was sweetly attractive in an alluring, quiet way. It sure as hell called to him. "This is Lily Thompson. She's an RN and is taking care of my mother, who's staying with me while her broken hip heals up. She's an employee, not a wrangler." He guided her to the redhead, who had just called out. "This is Red Parker," he said. "She's one of our buffalo experts."

Red grinned and pushed her black baseball cap back on her hair, which was caught in a single braid between her shoulder blades. Taking off her glove, she thrust her hand forward. "Nice to meet you, Lily. I bet Jake brought you because we always have some kind of medical emergency when we have to vaccinate these wild, cantankerous buffalo."

Lily shook her hand, felt her palm roughened with calluses. "Nice to meet you, Red."

"And," Jake said, taking her next to the black-haired woman, "meet Elena Amell. Red is breaking her in to becoming a wrangler. She's been with the ranch for a year now."

"Welcome, Lily," and Elena smiled and shook her hand.

"Thanks. It's such a nice surprise to see women wranglers. I didn't even know they existed." She felt warmed by the grins the two women traded. It was good to be in the company of two very confident females and Lily silently lapped it up. She used to be just like them.

"You gotta be a vet," Red prodded. "Which branch? Elena and I are Army."

"Army, too."

Elena whooped.

Red's smile broadened. "Nice work, Jake."

"I had no part of hiring her. Maud did it all."

Red pulled her glove back on. "Next time I see her, I'll tell her she did good."

"What about us, Jake?"

The two hombres were giving her thorough looks. She knew that look, which made her feel unsafe once again. She was glad Jake was at her side, his hand comforting on her elbow, as if silently letting her know she wasn't alone. Since being kicked out of the Army, she hadn't thought much about herself as a woman. Just a broken human being trying to put herself back together, somehow. Someday.

"Lily, this is Steven Hogan. He was a paramedic in the Air Force before joining us."

"Hi, Steven," she said, shaking his hand. He was as tall as Jake, but leaner, with blond hair and blue eyes. He was sinfully handsome and he knew it, too. Stepping back, the second male wrangler took off his baseball cap and extended his work-worn hand to her. She felt safe with him.

"Casey Engel, ma'am. Nice to meet you. I was a Marine, like Jake, here."

"I never thought there was an ex-Marine," Lily teased, liking his gentle shake of her hand.

Casey's gray eyes danced with humor. "You're right, ma'am, once a Marine always a Marine. Right, Jake?"

"Yes," he answered, dropping his hand from Lily's elbow. He urged her over to the eight ten-foot-tall rail fences. "We have those calves to vaccinate," he told her, pointing to the other corral, where the four-month-old youngsters were huddled, pressed against the fence, bleating for their mothers, who stood on the opposite side.

"They don't look that hard to vaccinate," Lily said.

"Wait until you see them try to fight being driven into the chute," Red said, coming up on the other side of Lily. "Their kick can break your arm. They're small but mighty."

Elena came to stand just behind Lily's left shoulder, a few feet between them. "We had a wrangler last spring get kicked in the thigh by a six-month-old calf and it broke his bone."

Eyes widening, Lily gulped. "I have a lot to learn."

"You aren't putting her in there, are you, Jake?" Steven asked, sauntering up to the group.

"No. Lily is out of the cabin for some fresh air for another hour. I thought she might want to see the four of you hog-tie those calves."

Red caught Lily's glance. "You stay away from the fence a good two feet and just watch. Okay?"

"The only thing is that you'll get dust all over yourself," Elena warned her drily.

"I'm not afraid of a little dust," she said.

"You aren't a city person, are you?" Casey inquired.

Lily shook her head and told them about her family's potato farm in southern Idaho.

"And you're out here for how long?" Red wondered.

"Just until Jenna heals up. About two months, more or less, depending how long it takes."

"Well," Elena said, "maybe you'll fall in love with the Wind River Ranch. Who knows? Maybe we'll make a wrangler of you and you'll stay here with us."

"I did this kind of work on our potato farm," Lily said, gesturing to the fences.

"Good work-ethic background," Casey agreed.

"Let's get to vaccinating," Jake said, pulling on his gloves.

Lily stepped aside, allowing the wranglers to do just that. The sun felt warm upon her and she remained a few feet away from the heavily constructed corral. It was far more fortified than the kind used for cattle. Jake stood out in the crowd because of his size and height. She wasn't sure she wanted to watch because she feared someone might get injured. She hoped Red was wrong about a medical emergency. She didn't know what her reaction would be to the sight of a lot of blood since leaving the Army. Taking care of Jenna's stitches didn't bother her, but there was no blood.

Closing her eyes, she willed away what she'd seen the next morning in the Afghan village. Her stomach grew nauseated. No . . . she couldn't go there. Anxious at the possibility of another flashback stalking her, she forced herself to turn and go to the horses tied along the fence. The bleating and bawling of the calves rankled her nerves. They sounded similar to the cries of terror she'd heard from the Afghan children.

She didn't have much experience with horses, but there

was a flashy black-and-white pinto close to her. As she approached, the gelding turned his head, his blue gaze on hers. Halting, Lily thought the horse had the most beautiful eyes she'd ever seen. The animal nosed her arm, muzzle soft, his nudge slight but welcoming.

Smiling, she said, "Hi. What's your name?" She saw a pair of short leather chaps lying across the western saddle. On the leather waistband she saw "RED." They must belong to her. And this horse, too, must belong to her. Lily thought the showy pinto and the woman with the bright red hair suited each other.

"Can I come closer?" she asked the horse, uncertain. He was a big horse, with a broad chest, a long neck and thick, sturdy hindquarters. He looked like a tank to Lily, but his demeanor was easygoing, and she felt safe enough to take a step toward him, her hand tentatively outstretched.

His muzzle was velvety as she lightly stroked it. His ears were pointed toward her, and she felt as if he was just as inquisitive about her as she was about him. The pinto unexpectedly licked her hand with his long, pink tongue.

Laughing a little, Lily stepped back in surprise, her fingers and wrist wet.

The pinto nickered again, as if inviting her to come closer once more.

She absorbed the companionship the horse offered her. Eventually, all the other sounds—the wranglers talking with one another, the bleating of the buffalo calves—faded away. Thrilled when she combed her fingers through the pinto's black-and-white mane, feeling its strength, the shiny quality of the strands glinting in the sun, she once more felt a sense of safety. Oh, no question the horse was huge! She felt like an ant standing next to a big dog. The pinto never moved his large-hoofed feet, just casually switching his long tail back and forth from time to time. She could feel he liked being petted and enjoyed the attention. She became bolder, running her fingers through his short, shiny hair, down his long neck. A thrill raced through her, a vibration of happiness flooding her chest. It felt so good to become part of something bursting with life, with beauty and a sense of trust that had been so easily created between them.

Jake divided his attention between his knowledgeable and fully capable wranglers and covertly watching Lily in the distance. Something about this vaccination was disturbing her, and he thought it might be the sound, the noise or something else he couldn't put his finger on presently. When one of the buffalo calves started wailing for his mother while in the chute, he saw her wince, pull away and quickly walk toward the horses tied farther down. Her back was turned to him, so he couldn't read her expression. She was fragile. Hell, he had been, too, the first year out of the corps and thrown back into civilian life, grappling to appear normal when he knew he never would be again. He wished he knew her triggers: the sounds, smells, colors, faces, words, whatever. That he had no idea gnawed at him.

Twenty-five minutes later, all the calves were reunited with their worried buffalo mothers. Red had opened the end of the corral, and they all trotted out and into a larger pasture, where the rest of the herd was grazing about a mile away. After thanking his wranglers for a job well done, Jake headed across the corral, out the gate and toward Lily, who was standing and talking with a pinto gelding named Checkers. The horse was one of the string the wranglers could choose to ride on any given day. The horse raised his head in his direction as he deliberately approached from an angle so Lily could see him coming, trying not to scare the living daylights out of her. To this day, he never liked anyone approaching him from the rear. That was a deadly zone, and because all the wranglers were vets, they never approach anyone from that direction either.

He saw Lily lift her chin, turning her head slightly. Her tremulous smile made his heart thud with good feelings. Managing a poor semblance of a half-smile in return, he placed his hand on the gelding's rump. "I see you and Checkers have become best buds." Her eyes lit up, the darkness that had been there previously gone. There was even a slight pink tinge in her cheeks, no more marblelike flesh to be seen.

"Checkers? What a great name for him!" and she patted his neck fondly.

"Like black and white on a checkerboard," he agreed. "Steven named him when he came here as a one-year-old." He patted the horse's rump. "You look better."

"I guess it's the warmth of the sun on me, the breeze and Checkers' wonderful friendship. He's so gentle and yet so big."

Nodding, he said, "We use him as a trail horse for city kids who aren't used to being around horses. We call him the gentle giant."

"He's so sensitive. He gave me a horsey kiss on my hand. He licked it," and she held it up toward him so he could see.

Chuckling, feeling relief because Lily was no longer her introverted, serious self, Jake discovered this horse had done something good for her. "Well, if you like him, how about I give you some lessons on how to ride him in the coming days?" Her lips parted and his whole lower body blazed into a three-alarm fire. Lily wasn't teasing him or trying to subtly turn him on. No, it was such a childlike look of wonder in her response that it caught him off-guard. But then, he warned himself once more, she was fragile. She had no shell in which to hide, no way to protect her emotional responses. Checkers was a big, intimidating horse, but Jake would bet a month's pay that Lily saw him as a shield or a safety net.

"Really? I could do that? I mean, I would have to take care of Jenna's needs and taking her to physical therapy in Wind River first."

He wanted so badly to reach out and touch some of her runaway sable strands of hair but resisted, the sun glinting on the lighter, caramel-colored ones. Just then, she looked like a young woman who was fully and completely in love with life and all its promises. "Of course, but you'll have a spare hour or two every day. The house is only a mile from the headquarters and the barns where we keep these horses. I could let one of our wranglers know to keep Checkers in the barn for you on the day you'd like to ride."

"That sounds wonderful, but I know so little about horses."

"Don't worry, I'll teach you." He saw her becoming nervous. Did she not want him to teach her? He saw it as an excuse to spend some private time with Lily, his curiosity about her growing daily; he wanted to hear about her deployments, and to learn more about her experiences.

"Jenna said you're so busy right now with the grass leases."

"Oh that. No problem. I'm usually around HQ in the afternoons. My mornings are busy, but things ease up after one, unless there's an emergency."

She patted Checkers' neck. "I'd love to learn how to ride."

"I think Jenna would approve. Let's head back to the house. Our time is about up."

Nodding, she fell into step with him, buoyant.

"Did everything go okay with the babies being vaccinated?"

"Yes, like clockwork. Elena keeps the calves quiet while Red gives them their shot. Steven and Casey let the calves out and guide them to the other corral so they can rejoin their mothers. They've done this a time or two."

She looked over her shoulder, seeing all four wranglers mounting their horses. Turning, she looked up at Jake. "Your wranglers were very nice. I love that they're all vets like us. I guess it's easier, because they've probably been through hell on deployments, just like we have."

Jake opened the door to the truck for her. "Count on it." He placed his hand beneath her elbow, telling himself it was because his mother had taught him to be a gentleman. Now free of his gloves, he could feel the soft firmness of her skin as he helped her climb into the truck.

Compared to how Lily looked before the excursion and right now, there was a night-and-day difference, he noted, as he drove back to the house. The tension was gone from her body and face. Her hands were still in her lap, but her fingers no longer twisted in constant, fractious movement. She sat against the seat, relaxed, not ramrod straight. Best of all, natural color was back in her face. He sensed a quiet happiness around her. The outing had done her good, and so had meeting Checkers.

"I'll be home for dinner tonight at six," he told her, dropping her off at the front gate of the cabin. "Be sure to tell Jenna about your adventures."

"I will," Lily promised. "See you tonight," and she shut the door to the truck.

Jake hesitated, watching her walk up to the porch. Even her step was lighter. In his days as a recon Marine, it had been the little details that could make the difference between life and death out in the sandbox. Now, he utilized that skill in a different way. He really needed to get Lily to trust him more, to come clean with him. Maybe teaching her to ride would do it. He hoped like hell it would.

He didn't want to look too closely at why his crazy heart had taken a shine to Lily. He wasn't looking for a relationship. As Jake turned the truck, heading it out of the gravel driveway, his brows fell. He was worthless as a man thinking about a serious relationship with a woman. Since getting out of the corps, his love life, if it could be called that, had been sparse. Wind River Valley wasn't a place where he could pick up a woman, have a night with her and leave in the morning with no strings attached. Besides, his three-year struggle with PTSD had been his only focus. That and remaining a good manager for the ranch.

Lily, however, and for whatever reason, was making him yearn to have a genuine relationship again. But who wanted a PTSD-ridden man in their life? Waking her up with his screams? Afraid that if he had a flashback and she touched him out of concern, he might kill her with one movement of his hand. That scared the hell out of Jake. And Lily had demons of her own to contend with. Jake wasn't worried she'd kill him in the throes of a flashback. She hadn't been trained for hand-to-hand combat and wasn't as strong as he was.

There were so many hurdles staring at him that his desire seemed hopeless. And yet, her blue eyes shining with such life captured his heart. Never mind the soft shape of her full lips. For Jake, she was the whole package, and he felt damned to hell, cursed for life. He didn't deserve someone like her. What was he going to do? How could he tame his need for her?

* * *

Lily was cleaning up the kitchen at nine that night. Jenna had just gone to bed. Jake was in the living room, reading the Wind River Valley newspaper. She discovered he didn't like computers very much and used them grudgingly when he had to. Same with a cell phone. He was a throwback to another age, and her heart warmed to his old ways in today's world.

She put fresh coffee in the percolator and got it ready to plug in tomorrow morning, when Jake woke up at five a.m. There was a rhythm to the household now and she knew his schedule well enough to anticipate some little things that might make his day go easier. She had already made tuna fish sandwiches, which she found out he loved, and put them in a lunch sack in the fridge so he could grab and go in the morning.

When he'd dropped her off, Jenna had told her that Jake loved pineapple upside-down cake. They'd rummaged through the cabinets, finding all the ingredients. Jenna had given her the recipe from memory, and they'd spent the afternoon laughing. Jenna had told her more about Jake's childhood. By the time the cake was done, the fragrance of it filled the cabin. She'd then helped Jenna go through the daily physical therapy exercises. It would help her leg and hip heal. The older woman hated the rolling walker but used it grudgingly. Then they'd made one of Jake's favorite boyhood meals: tuna and noodles with crunched-up potato chips for a topping.

Her heart warmed even more as she saw the pleasure in his eyes as she'd placed the casserole on a trivet in the center of the table. Jenna laughed and patted his arm as he realized they'd made one of his favorite meals. He thanked them for it. Jake always gave Jenna, and then Lily, scoops of the steaming fare before piling the food on to his own plate. There wasn't much left, maybe lunch for the three of them, from that casserole. Jake had eaten a lot of it, and Lily secretly smiled because his expression was readable tonight as never before.

"Got a minute?" Jake asked.

She turned, seeing him come to the table. "Sure."

He pulled out a notepad from his pocket. "I thought we might sit down and figure out when I could teach you about horses and riding."

Wiping her hands on a towel, she said, "I'm starting back to work at the shelter in town tomorrow."

Jake pulled out a chair for her to sit down. "I heard you talking to Jenna about that earlier. That's all right. We'll work everyone's schedule into it and find times where you can learn to be a cowgirl instead of a spud farmer."

Laughing softly, Lily kept her voice low because she knew noise traveled down the hallway to Jenna's room. Scooting the chair forward, she said, "I'm always open to learning something new."

Jake sat down at the end of the table, Lily to his right. He opened the notepad. "Give me your shelter schedule."

"Three days a week, a half a day in the afternoon, from one to four p.m."

"So, you have four days you're at the cabin all day?"

"Yes." She watched him write everything down. Unconsciously, she inhaled his male scent. Jake always came home, climbed out of his dirty day clothes, took a quick shower and then put on clean duds. His beard darkened his face, but it only made him look stronger in her eyes. She liked his large, square hands, calluses across his palms, telling her how much physical work he did on a daily basis. "Do you have to work weekends, too, Jake?" The words popped out of her mouth before she could stop them.

"No, not usually, but sometimes things happen, and I

have to be there. What about you? Are there places or people you need to see on the weekends?"

Shaking her head, she said, "No. I haven't been in Wind River that long, so I only know the ladies at Kassie's Café." She saw a gleam come into his eyes, but he said nothing. She had no idea what that look might mean.

"It might be a good time to take you on your first couple of trail rides, then," he said, writing it down on his notebook. "I'm not so much in demand on weekends."

"Okay," she said, chewing on her lower lip for a moment, "but only if you have time."

"I'll take Jenna to the store this Saturday. She wants some of her favorite foods. Maybe you'd like to go along? I'll drive us into Jackson Hole. It's a nice place, and you might enjoy getting out of here for a while."

Jenna was at a point in her recovery where a fifty-mile drive each way wouldn't cause her issues. "Sure, I'd love to go along."

"Good. I thought we'd put Jenna in the rear cab seat and you could sit up front with me. Will that work?"

Lily liked that he was sensitive to his mother's needs. "Let's ask her. It might be nice that she could stretch out her leg in the removable cast."

Grunting, he noted it. "Do you have anything you need in Jackson Hole? It has anything you might want, unlike Wind River."

"Not really. My attention will be on Jenna, her comfort and if she's starting to tire at the grocery store."

"Right. I didn't think of that."

"You've never had a broken leg, so you wouldn't know."

A grin came to his mouth. "That's true."

She smiled and held his thoughtful gaze. There was an ease between them, a natural one, as if they'd always known each other. Liking that connection and trust, she added, "Have you ever had a broken bone, Jake?"

Holding up his left arm, he said, "My father gave me a palomino pony when I was seven. It was a birthday gift. My dad had him on a longe line. I was a pretty rough-and-tumble kid, hopped up on the pony and promptly slid off the other side, breaking my arm."

"Bad break?"

"Nah. Greenstick. It was a vertical crack in my upper arm bone."

"Your poor father must have been scared."

"He was. So was my mother, who was shooting me with her movie camera."

"What did you learn from that?"

She saw amusement gleam in his eyes. "Put a saddle on the pony and don't ride bareback."

Lily warmed beneath the intimate look he gave her. "I like finding out about you, Jake. About the normal things you did as a kid."

"What about you? Did you have any pets?"

"My parents always had a lot of cats who kept the rats and mice to a minimum on the farm. And we always had a dog around. I guess that's why I love volunteering over at the animal shelter."

"Because you miss having a dog in your life?"

"Yes. In Afghanistan, there were starving mutts in every village. I wrote to my mom and asked her to send me ten pounds of dried dog food so I could give them some food. I always carried a Ziploc of kibble in one of the pockets of my trousers."

"You're such a softy."

It was her turn to grin because she knew he was teasing her. Oh, how she longed for this kind of honest communication with Jake. She knew something had changed today at the corral but wasn't sure what it was until now. He seemed far more relaxed with her, almost wanting to find out more about her on a personal basis. "Softhearted." She opened her hands. "Before the village was overrun by Taliban, I always looked forward to helping the women, the children and the dogs."

"I'm surprised you don't have a dog right now."

"I want one, but when I couldn't stay at my parents' home to heal, I knew I didn't have room in my life for a dog." Her voice lowered. "Honestly, I felt like I couldn't even take care of myself properly. How was I going to take care of a dog that relied on me to feed and take care of her?"

Jake's mouth thinned for a moment, thinking over her words, which were laced with embarrassment. "Lily, you're in your first year of trying to deal with PTSD. Don't be ashamed you can't do everything you used to do."

"Did you?" she challenged.

"I was a hot mess when I left the corps. I wouldn't stay at Jenna's home because I had flashbacks and nightmares all the time. I visited a few days and then got a motel room. I was afraid she'd find me out, and I knew she wouldn't understand what I'd gone through or the demons I wrestle with to this day. I knew she'd try, but no one who hasn't been there, done that, is going to truly get it."

"I felt the same way with my parents. I love them dearly, and I tried to stay home and be normal . . ."

"Whatever the hell normal is," he growled, closing his notebook. Looking at the watch on his thick, hairy wrist, he said, "Let's hit the sack."

He was right. Normally, by nine p.m. the cabin quieted down, and by no later than ten, Lily was in bed. "You're right."

"Listen, one more thing. I had one of my wranglers come in earlier today and set up a buzzer system between your and Jenna's bedrooms. You'll find a small radio on your bed stand. Jenna has one, too. I already showed her how to press the top of it to send a signal to yours. Now I think both of you can sleep with your bedroom doors closed at night."

Shocked, she stared at him. She almost asked whether he'd heard her screaming. It was too shaming for her to blurt out. "That's nice, Jake. A good idea. Thank you."

Rising, he said, "I always sleep better if my door is closed. Good night . . ."

Chapter Eight

June 26

A few weeks later, Lily found herself standing off to one side in the concrete aisle of the barn. In the ties was beautiful, huge Checkers.

"He's so big, Jake," she whispered in awe, glad he was standing nearby. Lily could feel the heat of his body, the scent of sweet-smelling alfalfa swirling around her. She didn't try to hide her excitement. At last, they had found a window of time on Tuesday morning to begin to teach her how to take care of a horse properly, as well as learn how to ride one.

She glanced up at him, the shadows across his rugged-looking face as he cut a glance downward to her. This morning, at nine a.m., the sky was clear, the sun bright and it helped make this a special outing for her.

"Fifteen hands high," he agreed. "But horses are taller than Checkers. Thoroughbreds can be sixteen or even seventeen hands high," and he put his hand up. "Where my hand is? That would be the back of a sixteen-hand-high horse." He changed it, moving another four inches upward. "Here? That's the back of a seventeen-hand-high horse."

Gasping, she told him, "I can't imagine that! How do you climb on them to ride them?"

He chuckled. "With a long set of legs."

"I'm too short to do that."

"Naw." He cupped her elbow and led her closer to Checkers, whose eyelids were drooped half closed. He was a gentle gelding and perfect for Lily, who seemed like an excited nine-year-old. His heart bloomed with emotions he didn't want to feel. Around Lily, he just sort of started unraveling, and he had no way to stop it. This morning, her blue eyes shone with such life, it took his breath away. Maybe he was seeing her like she used to be.

"First," he told her, "Checkers comes from that box stall across the way," and he pointed toward the oak door that had been slid open. "You'll be responsible for putting a lead line on him, bringing him out here and hooking up the panic snaps to his halter so you can inspect him."

"Okay," she said, halting and studying the huge sliding door. All the other wranglers' horses were already gone for the day. The doors at either end had been slid open much earlier to allow light and fresh air through the huge building.

She took a deep breath of the sweet-smelling air. She was starting to want more physical contact with Jake. His gloved hand on her elbow was something she hungrily absorbed when it was there, which wasn't often. Lily sensed that if Jake felt she was in an uncertain situation, like now, he would remain close, hand on her elbow, keeping her reassured. She looked up at him.

"I have a confession to make to you." She saw his eyes tentatively narrowed on hers. "I'm not my old, risk-taking self anymore, still trying to gather together my parts and pieces after what happened in Afghanistan. I feel as if you understand how fragile I am right now. I don't like feeling that way, but I'm learning how to become stronger, and you seem to know that. Do you?" It was the first time she'd asked him such a personal question, unsure of how he would respond to her. This past week, Lily had felt an invisible bond forming between them. And it soothed her, and seemed to allow Jake to let down those walls he hid so well behind. That was speculation, however. She really didn't know. Searching his expression, she saw the corners of his mouth relax.

"I guess I'm like a sheepdog whose responsibility it is to keep his flock safe from wolves."

"You've always been that way with others?"

He grimaced. "Pretty much. Does it bother you, Lily?"

"No. You feed me your strength, whether you realize it or not. Right now, I know I'm not at my best."

"No one is when they have PTSD, and that's okay." He studied her. "Even though you feel vulnerable, your care of Jenna isn't in question. My mother loves you and I like hearing the two of you laugh and carry on with each other." He saw the worry leave her eyes. Jake didn't want her to think she was a burden to him or Jenna.

"Your mother is the best. I often find myself wishing she could meet my mom. They're so much alike!" and she grinned fondly, missing being home with her parents, wanting to see them once more.

"Can you go home to visit them?" he wondered.

"I will when I've grown myself a new shell or shield, so I don't feel like raw meat out here," and she gestured around the barn. "I told them that I had to get a handle on myself, that I was kind of on a journey of inner self-discovery."

"They understood that?"

"Mostly. You know yourself you can't lay your combat experiences on a civilian. There's just no way to bridge that divide. Or at least," she murmured, giving a sad shrug, "I haven't been able to."

"It's the same for all military who come home. It's an impossibility. I wish there was a way. It would help Jenna understand my . . . well . . . the eccentricities she'd never seen in me while I grew up."

"Jenna loves you dearly. I hope you know that. She talks about you all the time, telling me so many wonderful stories about your childhood in Casper." She saw him roll his eyes and she laughed. "Oh, they're great stories, Jake! She's so proud of you. Her whole life revolves around you."

"She does love me, despite my grouchy self," he admitted in a growl.

"You aren't unlovable," she pointed out archly, "despite what you might think about yourself. I see you doing good things for others all the time. Look what you're doing for me."

"You're a special case," he muttered, nudging her toward the tack room.

Lily felt special, but she didn't have the courage to tell Jake that. The fact that he'd opened up to her in such a personal way thrilled her.

He dropped his hand from her elbow at the door of the tack room, indicating for her to go on in. The wonderful, warm scent of clean leather, from the saddles hanging on the wall, the bridles and the martingales, surrounded her. She loved the combined scents of the alfalfa hay bales that were stacked up on the second floor of the barn above them and the leather. For the next few minutes, Jake showed her around. When finished, he picked up a small wooden toolbox, handing it to her.

"Checkers is next. This is your grooming box. Let's go out and get started."

Already, Lily could feel her anxiety dissolving. It was an amazing experience, as Jake showed her where to set down the toolbox, away from Checkers. He proceeded to show her how to walk and work around the big horse, who stood calmly, almost asleep standing in the ties. She learned to lift each of his massive hooves to clean out the frog on each with a hoof pick. She laughed a little nervously, but all Checkers did was switch his tail, eyes closed, trusting her with himself. Never had she felt such a rush of joy and hope since Afghanistan. And Jake was right there, her shadow. She could feel the warmth of his body close to hers, guiding her hand or supporting her wrist as she wrestled with the weight of that first hoof as she learned how to hold and clean Checkers' feet.

"Okay, you did good," Jake praised later, picking up the toolbox. "Excellent on brushing him, too. Now it's time to learn how to saddle this dude."

Lily followed Jake into the tack room. He showed her the nameplates above each set of saddles and bridles. Luckily for her, Checkers' huge, heavy saddle was at her height and she carried it, all thirty pounds of it, through the door and set it on its horn on the concrete floor. Jake brought along the horse's bright red, heavy wool blanket. In no time, she learned the proper way to place the blanket on his high withers and slide it back a bit with the grain of his fur. She struggled a lot to get the saddle up and over his back, but she was bound and determined to do it. She couldn't ride if she couldn't take care of the gelding properly, and Jake knew that as well as she did.

It took nearly an hour for her to do everything the first time.

"You'll get faster each time," Jake promised her, giving her a pleased look.

Dusting off her hands after putting the toolbox in the tack room, she patted Checkers' sleek neck. The gelding flicked his ears, liking her touch. "Do we have time to ride? I know you have a lot to do."

"We'll unclip him from the ties and you'll lead him out

to that corral down there," and he pointed out the opened barn doors. "Today, you'll learn to mount, dismount and then you can ride him at a walk for a bit within the corral."

Excitement thrummed through her. "That's great! Thank you! I can hardly wait to get in that saddle!"

Jake nodded and showed her the safe and proper way to lead a horse out of the barn. Lily's cheeks were a bright red because she'd been working hard. She probably didn't weigh over a hundred and thirty pounds, and hefting a large, bulky, thirty-pound saddle wasn't easy for her. But she did it. He liked seeing the grit in her expression, the determination to get Checkers ready for the ride. That said something good about Lily's heart and drive, even if she felt as if she were falling apart as she struggled to rebuild her strength and confidence. It made Jake admire her even more than he did already.

He had her lead Checkers to the center of the thick, sandy arena. Around them were wranglers coming and going. People who rented the many small log cabins wandered around or were in other arenas, getting ready for a trail ride. As the sun rose higher, it got warmer. Lily had been wearing a heavy denim jacket, but she took it off and hung it over the pipe rail of the fence. He tried to ignore her dark green, long-sleeved T-shirt because it outlined her body beautifully. Her hair was drawn up in a ponytail, swishing between her shoulder blades, the sun catching some of the caramel strands and highlighting them. It seemed the more she successfully managed horse protocols, the more confident she became. Jake tucked that observation away because he knew confidence was an antidote to feeling frail. Maybe working with a horse, being around one, was the kind of healing she needed. He wasn't sure, but it was an observation to remember.

After several failed attempts, Lily climbed into the

saddle. The first try, she hit Checkers in the rump with her foot, not lifting it high enough.

Checkers just flicked one ear back, patiently standing quietly.

The second time, she couldn't get the swing of hopping on one leg, the other foot in the stirrup. She ended up falling under Checkers' massive body.

Checkers didn't move. Jake helped get her to her feet. She brushed the sand off herself.

The third time, Lily puckered her lips, focused and got into the saddle. Thrilled, she threw up both her hands and gave a yip of joy.

Checkers snorted, as if to praise her gumption, but he didn't move.

Jake laughed for the first time in a long time. Lily beamed from the saddle, picking up the leather reins, smiling so big that all he wanted to do in that crazy moment was sweep her into his arms and kiss her breathless. Overpowering in his desire, he quickly reined himself in, realizing how effortlessly Lily had crawled in to claim his barricaded heart.

She couldn't know any of this, he decided. Jake understood, as few could, how long her healing was going to take. And many never made it to the point he had either. There was no relationship in her life, he was sure. Just as there wasn't in his. But now, he ached to have this laughing, giggling woman in his arms, warm, soft and willing. He already knew from their earlier conversations that she regarded him as more than just any old man in her life. No, a couple of times, Jake swore he saw yearning in her eyes, but then the look would disappear. His heart wanted to see that look again.

Jake walked over to her, gently nudging her fingers and the reins so she held them properly, with the correct amount of tension between the horse's mouth and her hands. He then affixed the toes of her tennis shoes, now caked with golden brown, sugarlike sand, so her toes pointed forward, toes up and heels down. That was the correct way to keep her calves against the horse's barrel. He pointed out that the position also forced her knees to push inward on the fenders, to help keep her in the saddle at different gaits. Lastly, he had her flatten her thighs against the horse, thereby allowing her legs to hold her for a proper riding carriage. Lily automatically sat straight in the saddle, shoulders back, a natural pose because of her military background.

She looked relaxed and confident. Stepping away, he told her about neck reining, a western tradition, laying one rein against the animal's neck and turning the horse in the opposite direction. The reins were her steering wheel. Lily burst out laughing over that analogy, but pretty soon, she found out the driver's wheel was really about those two reins.

For the next twenty minutes, Jake had her walk Checkers around the arena first one way, turning him around and then going in the other direction. The pinto was amenable, and Jake could tell he was paying close attention to Lily's hands. He did exactly as she wanted. The profound awe in her expression never ceased to tear at his heart. Never did she stop smiling or leaning over and enthusiastically patting Checkers' neck. The horse loved all the attention, snorting and tossing his head a bit, letting her know he enjoyed her touch. Jake would, too, and he tried to tamp down more sensual and sexual visions that wanted to crowd into his head. He wouldn't go there. Lily didn't deserve that from any man. Not even him. She was in the midst of a life-changing healing curve, and there was no way he was going to mess with it or hurt her progress in lieu of his own selfish desires and needs.

"That's enough," he called. "Bring Checkers into the center and stop him near me. Dismount." Jake nearly laughed again when he saw her lower lip push out in a genuine pout, making her look sultry, and oh so comely to him. Her cheeks were blazingly pink, her hair mussed by the riding, making her look wild and desirable. When she pulled Checkers to a stop, he watched with pride as she dismounted correctly the first time.

"Ugh!" Lily yelped, grabbing the saddle leather, looking down at her bowed legs. "I can hardly stand!"

Chuckling, he said, "Your legs have never wrapped around a barrel of something so large. That's what we call bowlegged."

Laughing, Lily worked to move her legs around, trying to get them to straighten. "I always wondered why some cowboys had legs that bowed out instead of standing up straight."

"Now you know their secret. Here, hand me the reins." He held out his hand as she took the looped reins over Checkers' head, stretching and leaning up to do it. Jake knew the movements would help her legs adjust to being on earth instead of floating in air around a horse's back. And sure enough, by the time she'd done that, her legs were no longer bowed out. He took the reins.

Lily patted Checkers, then threw her arms around his neck, pressing her face into his silky black-and-white mane. "Thank you, thank you, thank you, Checkers!" She kissed him, gave him a big hug and then released him.

Jake genuinely wished she'd done that to him, but he knew Checkers enjoyed the lavish hug because his ears drooped a bit, indicating in him, at least, that he truly enjoyed Lily's enthusiastic gratitude. He envied the horse.

"I still feel like my legs are bowed," Lily complained as they drove back to Jake's house. She rubbed the insides of her thighs because now they felt stretched and grouchy.

Chuckling, he said, "The more you ride, the quicker your legs will adjust, and that won't happen at all."

She sighed, placing her elbow on the doorframe, the window open, the wind heavy with the scent of sweet, lush grass growing in the pastures on either side of the dirt road that led to the cabin. "I'm not sure how often I can do it."

"It won't take you an hour next time to brush and saddle Checkers."

"Really?"

"Really. I've got some time day after tomorrow: ten a.m. Want to do it again?"

Did she ever. "I'd love to! Jenna and I are done with all her exercises by then."

"And I know she likes to sit on the couch and watch her favorite TV shows at that time of day."

"It's perfect." Lily rubbed her hands together. "This is so exciting. It's like opening up an entirely new window in my life. I loved brushing Checkers. He's so gentle and patient with me."

"Did you enjoy riding him?"

"Absolutely! I felt like I was on top of a twelve-foot ladder! What I loved the most was that swaying he did. I felt like a baby being rocked in the cradle."

"I call it horse meditation. Just lulls me into a nice, soft place where there's none of that anxiety eating away at me."

She gave him a pensive look, hands in her lap. "Yes, that's it. And the weirdest thing of all, Jake, is that I had no anxiety! I didn't from the time you started teaching me how to groom Checkers. It just," and she opened her hands, giving him a questioning look, ". . . went away. Even now, I feel like I used to, before the incident."

"Calm?"

"Very. It's such a nice break from that gut-eating anxiety that's always there in me." She peered intently at him. "Is it that way for you? For the other wranglers who have PTSD?"

Nodding, he added, "That's why Maud and Steve never went to ATVs instead of horses. They understood that horses work their quiet magic on humans, who respond in kind. If we rode around on ATVs all the time, the work would get done faster, but they don't dissolve the anxiety we get from riding or working around a horse. I don't know what it is, or what to call it, but it's like a horse is a sedative of some kind for all of us. And today, you experienced it, too."

"How long does it last? The calm, I mean?"

Shrugging, Jake said, "Probably a couple of hours. I know when I mount my horse, I can start to feel my anxiety instantly dialing back. Within fifteen minutes, I'm free of my symptoms. And because I've been doing this for three years, when I hang up my spurs at night, the anxiety usually stays away until the next morning."

Lily shook her head in disbelief. "I call that magic, Jake. How would scientists or even doctors explain this calming effect horses have on us?"

"I've been talking to Maud and Steve about creating a program for vets who have PTSD, bringing them out here, ten men and women at a time, teaching them to work around a horse, riding it and then helping us out as would-be wranglers. It would show them that there was something besides those awful medications, antianxiety drugs and sleeping pills, that can help calm the beast that resides within all of us."

"I would never have believed this," Lily whispered, suddenly emotional, "if you'd shared that with me earlier."

"I know." He slanted her a glance. "That's why I didn't tell you about it. I figured if it was going to work for you, you'd find out just like the rest of us did."

"Do you think that because we're animals, too, there's some kind of invisible connection between us and horses?"

"I think dogs have it with vets who are given a trained service dog to aid them in daily life. At least, that's what I've read in the articles I've come across. Having a service dog does the same thing as riding a horse."

"Maybe that's why I love working at the shelter."

"I thought about that when you told me you had a part-time job there. Does it help you?"

"Yes. Only my duties are many, and you can't ride a dog," and she grinned, sharing it with him.

"Point taken. But the dog is also a companion, someone who can sit at your feet, keep you company."

"Why don't you have a dog, Jake? It feels natural for you to have a buddy."

"I used to as a kid. When I got out of the corps, I was so messed up that it took every bit of my energy just to make it through the day. I had no energy left over to take care of anyone else at all, not even a dog. That's pretty sad, isn't it?"

Lily felt his loneliness for the first time. The searching look he gave her as he parked the truck in front of the cabin made her want to cry—for him. "My parents have a dog, a beautiful collie named Rachel. She's very old now, thirteen, but when I came home after getting out, she was always at my side. I can't tell you how many times I would bury my face in her long, thick ruff and cry my eyes out, cry until I had no tears left. She always sat there with me, not moving, just letting me hold her and bawl."

"And in your travels to find yourself, you ended up here in Wind River at a dog shelter. Something that gave you at least some comfort."

She studied him in the cloaking silence that built gently between them. Jake had his hands on the steering wheel, watching her, and it didn't make her feel stripped or raw. This was something new that she couldn't name, and it felt like a warm cloak was being tenderly placed around her shoulders. She loved these deep, searching talks with him. "It did. I guess I never saw that until you quantified it. I'm too mired in my anxiety to see much of anything."

He reached out, placing his roughened hand over hers, which were clasped in her lap. "In time, you will. You have to be patient with yourself, Lily. The first year is the hardest." Jake lifted his hand away. "You have me, the crew of the ranch, Maud and Steve. They all understand the issues. They want to help you. I want to help you because despite all you've survived, seen and heard, you haven't lost your ability to care for others. And so many with PTSD do lose that for some time afterward. Some never get it back, and that increases their level of suffering. Humans need one another whether we like it or not."

Her skin tingled wildly where his callused palm was draped across her clasped hands. Lily hadn't expected his tender gesture at all, and it shocked her in the best of ways. Human touch was something she yearned for more than anything else. What she'd give to have a caring hug. And yet, in reality, it was her choice because she didn't let anyone know what she'd been feeling.

"I don't ever want to lose my ability to care for others, whether animals or humans," she said in a tight-lipped whisper, battling back an urge to cry. Just one touch and she felt like someone had unzipped that vat of deeply hidden emotions. Somehow, Lily knew that if Jake ever placed his long, hard arms around her shoulders and drew her next to him, she would be all right. She would get through this. She would come out the other side of it healed, though not perfect.

That realization hit her so hard, it stunned her into silence as she tried to come to terms with it. She'd never looked to others as emotional support. But she needed that now. Wanting to burst into deep sobs, Lily fought against it. Jake wouldn't understand her reaction. She'd found that while recovering in the hospital. Tears were seen as a sign of weakness and nothing else, so she'd learned to button them up and swallow them. Only when she returned home to Idaho and Rachel came to sit with her had she allowed herself to hug the dog and bury her face in her fur and sob out all her terror and grief.

"I think," Jake said, opening the truck door, "you're a nurse for a reason. You're a service-oriented person, Lily. It gives you deep joy to help others, whether a two-legged human or a four-legged animal." He closed the door, came around the truck and opened her door for her.

"You all right?" and he gave her a brief, intense perusal.

"Uh . . . yes . . . yes, I'm okay. . . ."

Chapter Nine

June 26

Lily couldn't sleep that night. She was tossing and turning, replaying her conversation with Jake earlier in the day. Riding Checkers had brought a new level of awareness to her wounded world. The whole day had turned out to be a dream come true. Tonight, when Jake came home for dinner, he remained more open. Even Jenna noticed it, she thought, although she didn't say anything to her about it. There was a softening in him. He seemed to have enjoyed the outing with her.

Even now, her anxiety had not returned. Every couple of months she'd have an anxiety-free day, though she never knew why. Those days were like freedom, tasting the joy of feeling calm, centered and at peace within herself once more. And when those days happened, she dreaded the return of the anxiety, knowing it was going to come back. It always did.

This time was different, although she hadn't been able to define it until Jake had shared with her that horses and dogs seemed to tame and quiet the anxiety monster within the military vets. It made sense to her. She was raised with animals on their farm. They were a part of the family. The connection between animals and humans was well known. She sighed, opened her eyes, staring up at the dark ceiling above her bed. Jake's hand covering her own in that one spontaneous, completely unexpected moment, hovered strongly within her.

She had sensed from the beginning that the man behind the walls was far different from the gruff appearance he projected to everyone around him. Understanding walls meant protection, she accepted that about Jake. He, too, was wounded. He wasn't mean or nasty with people either. From what she could tell, he was a good leader and manager. She had never heard him yell at any of his wranglers, always praised them for what they did right and was patient when they made a mistake. That meant a lot to Lily. Being in the military, she'd met great officers and poor ones. And Jake struck her as a good, stable, sound leader.

He also had an element to him that she'd rarely seen in men. It was as if he sensed her real self, her rawness and inability to protect herself fully right now. She wished mightily he'd met her when she was well and whole. She wasn't the wilting flower he saw now. How she wished she could have her old, confidant self back! Jake seemed to believe she could retrieve it. He'd told her more than once that the first year was the toughest. He was three years into PTSD and seemed to have a handle on it. He looked normal to her and behaved that way out in the world. If only she could reach that point! Shortly after that, she fell into a deep, dreamless sleep.

Jake looked around the kitchen. He'd come in at noon in hopes of finding Lily. Jenna was knitting in the living room.

"Hi, Son," she greeted. "Nice to see you. I thought Lily said you were going to be gone all day in one of the pastures."

He took off his Stetson, stepped inside and shut the door. "I was, but I changed my mind. Where's Lily?"

Smiling, Jenna laid her knitting in her lap. "We got finished with my exercise routine and she walked over to the barns about an hour ago. She was dying to work with Checkers again, and I told her to go do it. She needs some space, and to get some fresh air, too."

"She walked to the barns? That's a mile away. Why didn't she drive her truck to the area?"

"Didn't seem to be a hurdle to her," Jenna said. "There was nothing else for her to do around here today and she wanted some good, physical exercise, deciding not to drive over there. You were going to be gone and she wanted to go see Checkers, groom him and be around him. I really think that horse has done something magical for her. She was telling me this morning that since that first ride three days ago, her anxiety is at an all-time low. She thinks if she works with Checkers more, it might help keep her anxiety down to a dull roar."

Scratching his head, he nodded. "I put my assistant in charge of the project. I was wanting to get her out to the barn today and thought I'd surprise her. I should have called her."

"So?" Jenna said archly, "drive down. I'm sure she'll be happy to see you. You two get along so well together."

"She's a good person" was all he'd admit. "I'll go hunt her down. Have you had lunch yet?"

"Yes. Go have fun."

"Did she take the cell phone with her?"

"Yes."

Jake nodded, threw his Stetson on his head and left.

Seeing Lily wasn't what he'd classify as fun. It went far deeper, an unknown emotion pushing him toward her. He was starving for more information about her. Since her first try at riding Checkers three days ago, he felt as if his heart and soul were being crushed through an invisible sieve in his chest.

Climbing into the truck, he took off for the head-quarters area.

Rubbing his chest, he saw the fluffy white clouds over the Wilson Range looking like they were a hat spread across the sharp peaks. Late June brought thunderstorms to the area, usually in the afternoon and early evening. He thought those clouds might be the beginnings of a storm. Needing to see Lily, just to hear her voice, listen to how she saw the world around her, made him relax. Jake didn't want to admit she was growing on him, becoming indispensable to his life, but she was. Jenna treated her like the daughter she'd always pined for but never had. What was happening to him?

He rolled his truck to a stop on a slight knoll where he could see the many activities going on in the main area of the ranch. In that one arena, he saw Lily on Checkers, riding slowly at a lazy clip-clop walk. Sometimes, she would use the reins to guide the gelding in another direction. Eyes narrowing, he saw she was constantly checking her posture, the position of her legs and feet, and he felt good about that. Lily was truly trying to ride properly, and he felt warmth, as well as pride, throughout him. She wasn't a quitter. She was a fighter.

After ten minutes, he drove down to the other side of the barn, where she wouldn't be aware of his presence. Lily walked Checkers out of the arena, dutifully shut the large gate and led him up the slight slope to the horse barn. There were a lot of trucks, wranglers and some riding horses in the vicinity. Headquarters was always a beehive of activity. As Lily entered the barn, Jake noticed she was walking slightly bowlegged, and he wondered how long she'd ridden Checkers. He'd find out, pushing his shoulder off the barn door and starting to walk down the clean aisle opposite where she'd just entered.

"Jake!" she called, waving to him, grinning. "What are you doing here?"

He couldn't help but give her a sour smile in return as he ambled toward her. "Thought I'd drop by to see how your ride went." He drowned in the shining life dancing in her blue eyes, her cheeks rosy with life. It was so rare to see her cheeks pink up; most of the time, she looked pale, her eyes dark as she wrestled with her inner demons. "Like some help?" he asked, standing off to one side as she turned Checkers around so he could be placed in the ties.

"No, I promised myself I was going to get this right." She laughed a little, catching his gaze. "I timed myself this morning. It only took me thirty-five minutes to take Checkers out of the stall, examine his feet and legs, brush and saddle him up."

He raised his brows, leaning against a huge beam that supported the roof, and rose from the first floor up to the third floor of the barn. "That's a big difference. What was Checkers doing as you ran around him timing yourself?"

She slipped the bridle off the pinto, hooking it over her arm and then picking up the first tie. "Very funny. He seemed more alert. He was probably wondering why I was rushing around like a madwoman." She clipped on the panic snap. Ducking beneath the horse's neck, she grabbed the second tie, clipping it to the other side of his halter. Straightening, she said, "Jenna told me this morning you would be gone all day."

Shrugging, he said, "After I got the big stuff out of the

way, I had my assistant handle the rest of it." Looking out the open doorway of the barn, he said, "I thought this might be a good day to slide in another riding lesson, but you beat me to it."

"That was so thoughtful," she said. "I enjoyed my long walk down the road to HQ. I left my truck at the cabin because it was such a beautiful afternoon."

Her hair was in a ponytail, tendrils mussed around her temples. She was so lively, almost bouncy. Best of all, confidence exuded from her. Had this ride done all of that? It must have, because he'd never seen Lily this animated, almost giddy as she worked the cinch loose on the saddle with her slender fingers. He was going to step in and help her, but right now, she needed to continue to build her confidence, not have someone short-circuit it because he felt she needed help. Lily hauled off the saddle, tucked her arms beneath it and carried it gingerly to the tack room.

She returned, wiping her hands on the thighs of her jeans, which had smudges of dirt here and there. More than likely, she propped each of Checkers' hooves on her thigh to clean them. He did the same thing with a big horse like that. "Something is happening," she told Jake as she reached into the grooming box and took out a rubber-toothed brush to gently dig up grit or grime from Checkers' back.

"What's that?" Today, Lily was far more confident in what she was doing. He wondered if she was the type of person who ran and reran a task in their mind until it became like breathing. Certainly, today it looked like she'd been doing this all her life.

She moved the rubber brush in small circles, gently loosening grease, sweat and dirt around Checkers' back where the saddle had been. "My anxiety, Jake. It's gone." Lily blew a strand of hair away from her eyes, giving him a glance across the horse's back. "Since the first ride."

"Yes?"

"My anxiety didn't come back for twenty-four hours. And then, when it started returning, it crept back."

"If a full-blown anxiety attack for you is a ten, what was the creeping-back number and did it stay at that level?"

"A five, which is amazing for me." Once done, she walked around Checkers and grabbed a curry comb out of the box. "It remained at that level. That just blew me away. I figured I'd try a test and decided to come here and work with Checkers to see if my anxiety would go away again." She grinned a little. "It did. It's gone. I'm hoping it will stay away another twenty-four hours."

He tipped the brim of his Stetson up a bit, watching her. The short-sleeved pink T-shirt showed off her pale limbs as she thoroughly curried the horse. "That's good," he praised.

"Is that why you love your job here, Jake? You said riding dials down the anxiety for you."

"It does for just about everyone. Some it doesn't, but for most of the wranglers, riding a horse dulls the anxiety a little to a lot, depending upon the person."

"And that's why you said Maud and Steve have horses here instead of trading them in on a bunch of ATVs," she reminded him.

"Right." He watched her get a dandy brush, one that was very soft and good for areas of the horse where there was no muscle, just skin against bones, like their legs. She worked hard, was thorough and Checkers hung his head, eyes half closed, enjoying the horsey spa time with Lily. Jake's skin riffled as he thought about those long fingers of hers caressing him. It was a dark secret he would keep. Ashamed of himself, he couldn't stop his need for Lily. What was it about her that drew him, drove him crazy, his dreams turning hot and sultry? He knew what it was like to want sex. But this went much deeper than just that. It bothered him because he had no way to turn it off or deflect the growing emotions he was feeling toward her.

"There!" Lily said proudly, releasing the ties after she placed the lead on the horse's halter. "Is it okay if I let him out back where he can get some grass and sunshine? He's earned it."

"Sure," Jake replied, walking with her, the echo of the horse's shod hooves hitting the concrete. They left the shade of the barn and she took the animal down a well-used trail to the pasture. Happiness bubbled within him, and this wasn't something he felt often. There was such peace in Lily's face as she led Checkers over to the gate that it made his heart soar. He wondered if, before the incident, there'd been a man in her life. She must have had one, he surmised, watching her slim, graceful form as she opened the gate and released Checkers into the pasture for the rest of the sunny day.

"How'd you like to drive into town with me? I need to pick up some items at Charlie Becker's Hay and Feed store." He saw her eyes gleam with excitement.

"Any chance I'll get to grab one of Pixie's cookies?"

Jake chuckled, the rumble moving through his chest. "Gal after my own heart. I'm sure we'll find something near the coffee station. Let's mosey on down and find out. . . ."

Lily tipped her head back against the seat, her arm hanging out the window of Jake's truck, the wind threading through her opened fingers. Life was suddenly, so sweetly, unexpectedly good that she felt as if she'd burst with joy. Jake hadn't erected that wall between them since the first time she'd rode Checkers. Something important had happened then, but she couldn't define what it meant. Maybe it was like the magic between her and Checkers that reduced her anxiety? Unsure, her lips parted, and she absorbed the wind flowing in the window from the speeding truck, plastering strands of her hair against her sweaty neck. How good it felt to be alive once again! Jake's nearness was a plus, although she tried to quell her need of him. In another month she would be leaving that beautiful house she silently called home. She knew Jake referred to it only as a house. But why? Everyone needed a home, not just a shell with a roof over their head. And he'd lived there three years and not made it his own in any way. Why? It was another personal question she wanted to ask him, but she knew the timing would have to be right to ask it, if she ever could.

"You look happy."

Rolling her head to the left, Lily barely opened her eyes, then met Jake's rugged profile as he devoted his attention to driving. "Do I?"

"Yes."

"How can you tell?"

"Your cheeks are flushed. When you first came to the ranch, you were always pale. I noticed when you and Jenna would get together, your cheeks got some color in them, as if you were enjoying your time together. Three days ago, when you and I worked with Checkers, your cheeks were flaming red by the end of your ride in the arena. I thought it meant you were happy. Were you at those times, Lily?"

Her lips curved slightly, and she watched his expression, which was readable now as he cast a quick glance in her direction, then went back to devoting his attention to his driving. How much she wanted to tell him that she liked this Jake far more than the man she'd first met. "I didn't realize that. Yes . . . very happy. Relief that I still feel no anxiety. Giddy that I can feel the wind through my fingers, smell the grass . . . little things that were taken away from me that have suddenly returned."

"You seem more alive, I guess. I'm not good with words sometimes."

He seemed awkward after admitting that, and Lily wanted to reach out and touch his thickly muscled forearm to reassure him, but that would have been too intimate a gesture. "You're a master of small details, Jake."

"You have to be to be a recon. It's the little things that can either save you from the enemy or get you killed."

"I never thought much about your skills, mainly because I rarely met a recon Marine in the medical clinic on our firebase."

"No, you probably wouldn't have. We worked in enemy territory for weeks or months at a time."

"That seems so stressful. Was that the cause of your PTSD?"

"Yes, it piled up on me over the years. I didn't realize it either. My focus was on surviving. When I was back at Bagram for an extended period, anxiety hit me hard. I went to the doctor at the base hospital, went through tests, and she said I had acquired PTSD." His mouth slashed for a moment. "Go figure. Out in enemy territory, cortisol, the hormone that works with adrenaline, kept me hyperalert because if I wasn't, I'd get killed. Out there, it was a plus that saved my hide. But back at base, or in the civilian world, cortisol is still there, pouring 24/7/365 into our blood, and it can't be shut off. So we go around in quiet agony in civilian life, feeling that same hyperalertness and anxiety."

"If only we could turn it off."

"Yeah," he muttered unhappily.

"Is riding a horse about the only thing that tamps it down, Jake?" She saw the emotion in his face for a moment and then he masked it.

"For me, it does the trick. I didn't want to use drugs or alcohol to anesthetize myself. I'd rather feel than become a zombie with no emotions."

"But not everyone is as strong as you are," she noted gently, watching his mouth soften at her quietly spoken words.

"I guess that's true. But you're strong, too, Lily."

She let loose an explosive laugh, then said with derision in her voice, "I don't see it that way. Right now, I'm a clam without a shell. I feel vulnerable because I can't protect myself or feel that I'm safe in the world. It's a horrible feeling that mixes with my nonstop anxiety. It takes everything I have within me to act or behave normally."

"I understand that," he murmured, giving her a sympathetic glance. "That's why I told you that you were safe here. I meant that. I know working with Jenna and being at the cabin has been good for you because I can see positive changes in you. You're more relaxed. And when I noticed your cheeks having color, I realized, or at least hoped, you were happy or close to it."

Gulping, Lily turned away, looking out the window, the breeze wonderful against her face and body. *Safe.* That word meant so much to her. Far more than she should allow it to. "I . . . uh . . . don't want to feel like this, believe me. It's not me, Jake. I wish you'd known me before. I was nothing like the woman you see now. I loved adventure, I took risks, I was brimming with confidence, with dreams of a wonderful future of service and helping to take pain away from those who had it. I was far more outgoing, not the hermit crab you see today." Her voice wobbled slightly. "I really miss who I was. I want her back. I fight so hard every day to try to get there, but I'm always failing, falling short. There are some days when I give up, and then that horrible depression hits me. I never had depression before in my life. It doesn't run in my family genetically either. But now I have it sometimes, and I hate it. It's like a wet, cold blanket covering me so I can barely breathe. All I want to do is escape the horrible feeling of helplessness. I see only darkness, never any light, and God knows I'm looking for a pinpoint of light when I get dragged down into those times."

He nodded, opening one hand on the steering wheel. "That's part of the PTSD symptoms. And right now, we have twenty-two good men and women who commit suicide every day to escape what you just described."

Sorrowfully, she gave him a glance. "I know. I keep telling myself I *won't* be one of them. But that utter darkness and loss of hope is so heavy and unbearable that I can hardly move. All I do is lie in bed, and that's just not me."

"Does it happen often?"

"It's been better the last couple of months. It used to hit me weekly for half a day or so." Shrugging, she said, "Since coming here, I've not experienced it. I feel lucky. I'm hoping it continues to stay away." Managing a wry look, she added, "Maybe this ranch is magic, you know?"

"I think it is, in some ways. I've given a lot of thought to why I'm feeling much better now than when I arrived here three years ago. Part of it is having a job where there's low stress, because that's what amps up the symptoms. There's a quiet rhythm and stability that ranching life gives you. You know daily what has to be done, and I think that fixed routine helps us vets. We know what's expected of us and we know we can handle the demands. And because of that, our stress levels don't spike, which cause the anxiety that tears the hell out of us on every level."

"Plus, riding a horse or working around animals helps?"

"Yes, that's all part of our low-stress recipe, I suppose." She considered their conversation as Jake pulled the truck into Charlie Becker's Hay and Feed store. It was a busy place, with a lot of flatbed trucks being loaded with grain sacks, straw or hay bales and other necessary ranch and farm materials at the two barn ramps. Most of the workers were male, but she saw several women wranglers coming and going from one of the many barns on the property. Would she ever be able to do what Red did at the ranch? It called to her and she liked the idea of being outdoors, out in nature, living a slower pace of life instead of the hectic one in the military.

"We're here," Jake said, giving her a brief, warm look. "Let's go into the store and see what Pixie made. See if anything's left after the locust swarm landed on it," and he chuckled.

She smiled and opened the door, getting out. "As I understand it, everyone in town knows the time Pixie arrives with her baked goodies."

Walking around the truck, he met her at the steps up to the porch. "She comes at eleven thirty, just in time for lunch." He lifted his nose. "I believe I smell cinnamon rolls," he said, opening the door to the store for her.

Sure enough, Lily was pleasantly surrounded with the hint of baked goods and cinnamon. Charlie Becker, in his midsixties, balding, a set of spectacles balanced precariously on his nose, lifted his hand in greeting.

"Hey, Lily! Long time no see!"

She smiled and walked with Jake, halting at the long wooden counter, behind which Charlie sat. He had an old-fashioned, ancient cash register, a small calculator in front of him beside his receipt book, where he wrote out bills. There was carbon paper beneath each page, so the buyer got a copy. "I've been busy."

"So Pixie tells me. You know how word gets around

like wildfire in Wind River?" and he waggled his gray, caterpillarlike eyebrows, grinning mischievously.

She laughed. "Yes. I'm taking care of Jake's mother, Jenna, for a couple of months while she recuperates from a broken femur."

"She's in the best of hands." He reached across the counter. "Look what the cat dragged in. Normally, one of your wranglers comes by instead of you, Jake. Long time no see."

"Every once in a while they let me out of my cell on the ranch," he deadpanned, shaking Charlie's long, parchment hand. "I brought Lily with me because she needs a few items; she's started to learn to ride."

Surprised, Lily turned, looking up at him. "What?"

"You need a few things," Jake repeated.

"But," she sputtered, "I don't have extra money to buy anything, Jake." And she didn't.

He held up his hand. "Charlie, put Lily's purchases on the ranch account for us?"

"Why sure."

Stunned, Lily muttered, "Wait a minute, Jake. Maud and Steve shouldn't pay for this!"

He gave her a calming smile. "It's okay, Lily. Maud saw you riding the other day and called me about it. They routinely provide what their wranglers need out of the ranch budget, and because you're working here for her, technically, she's extended it to you as well."

"Oh," she mumbled, giving him a wary glance. "I don't take handouts, Jake. I've always earned my own keep."

"You're earning your keep by taking such good care of Jenna and me."

She wasn't going to win this argument. Charlie gave her a merry look, then pointed his finger to the coffee service table at the rear of the large store.

"Hey, there are only two warm cinnamon rolls left. You oughta grab them before someone comes in here and steals them out from beneath your noses. Now, git! You can shop afterward."

The table held a huge coffee urn, Styrofoam cups, milk, sugar and spoons. And to the left of it was a huge platter Lily thought had probably contained more than two dozen thick, gooey and sinfully delicious-smelling cinnamon rolls. She heard Jake chuckle as he picked up a paper plate and handed it to her.

"They don't last long around here. Take your pick."

Their fingertips briefly touched, and she silently absorbed the contact. It always gave her pleasure to touch Jake, even if accidentally. "Thanks. I'll take the smaller of the two." She cut him a glance. "You're still a growing boy, Murdoch."

Snorting, he took the larger one, stabbing it with a white plastic fork. "I don't know about that. Want a cup of coffee to go with it?"

"Yes, thanks." Pixie Becker never made anything small in her life, Lily thought as she awkwardly guided the heavy, oblong cinnamon roll to the paper plate she had balanced in her other hand. It was obvious Jake had a lot of practice doing it in comparison to her. Pixie was Wind River's secret weapon of sorts. She loved baking and delighted in giving the townspeople something to make them smile. Life was hard, but Pixie no doubt made it easier.

"Come on over here," Jake invited, using his chin to point to a group of tables and chairs nearby.

The cinnamon roll was meltingly good as she savored the confection. Jake was making short work of his, too. The bell above the door jingled, and Lily recognized Shay and Reese Lockhart walking into the store. She knew them well. Setting her plate on the table, she murmured, "I'll be right back. I want to say hi to Shay and Reese."

"Lily!" Shay cried, spotting her coming up between the rows of cowboy clothes. "There you are!"

Laughing, Lily gently hugged a very pregnant Shay. "It's so good to see you! How have you been? How's your baby?" and she released her, stepping back.

Placing her hand on her seven-month bump, she said, "A day at a time. No one said pregnancy was fun."

Giving Shay an understanding look, she said, "Only two months to go, Shay. Then you can return to normal. Reese! How are you?" and she opened her arms, hugging the tall, lean cowboy.

"I'm better, I think, than Shay is." He laughed, giving her a light hug and releasing her. He turned to Jake as he wandered toward them. "Are you here doing ranch buying? Or out to get one of Pixie's world-famous cinnamon rolls?"

"Well," Lily hedged, ". . . sort of." She saw the joy in Shay's eyes, thinking how good she looked. Her father, Ray, had long been a cross for her to bear, and it hadn't changed. Lily had met her at the shelter when she first came to Wind River and they'd immediately become friends. "You look relaxed, Shay." And God knew with that father of hers, who was suing the ranch she owned to get it back, that was saying something.

Shay placed her purse on the counter, giving Charlie's hand a squeeze of hello. "I guess it's the pregnancy. Nothing's changed with my father. It's the same old stuff with him."

Sliding her arm around Shay, Lily gave her a tender hug. "It's going to come out fine in the end. Is there anything I can do for you in the meantime?"

Shay gave her a return hug. "No, not right now. Just

knowing you're close by, Lily, gives me a breather. If I suddenly go into labor, I'm calling you."

"But you have two great midwives here, Shay."

"I know, but it doesn't hurt to have a nurse in the mix. Right?"

Lily nodded. "I'll be there any time you need me."

"She will be," Jake intoned, coming over and giving Shay a quick hug of hello.

"Hi, Jake! Gosh, we don't get to see you very often! I told Reese the other day we needed to have a barbecue, invite everyone from the Wind River Ranch over so we could see you guys again. You've been missing in action."

Jake nodded. "A hundred grass leases, Shay. You know the work involved in that."

Groaning, Shay said, "Yes. We have twenty-five leases and poor Reese, Noah, Garret, Dair and Harper have been putting in dawn-to-dusk work. I don't know how you handle a hundred of them."

"Got a lot of wranglers who are busting their butts just like yours are. The rush is over soon enough. At least until mid-September."

Reese came over, shaking Jake's hand. "Good to see you. I told Shay that I was going to start calling you Ghost because we've not seen hide nor hair of you for so long."

Lily watched Jake's cheeks grow a dull red. Reese was an affable man, easygoing, highly intelligent and a good manager of people. So was Jake, but he wasn't as affable as Reese. When the men released each other's hands, she saw the friendship in their expressions. Everyone she knew respected them both mightily.

"Too late," Charlie called out, "Shay and Reese, you just missed the last two cinnamon rolls Pixie made."

Shay groaned. "Oh no! I *love* Pixie's cinnamon rolls! She doesn't make them often enough," and she pouted.

"I got half mine left," Lily said, grabbing her hand. "Come on, you can sit with me; we'll eat and talk."

Laughing, Shay said, "What a deal! Lead on, Lily!"

Jake watched the two women take off for the coffee area. "Reese? Tough luck. I already ate mine, so there's nothing left for you, pardner."

Reese smiled. "No worries. I think Shay will love getting even half of one."

"Yep, I know how much Shay loves 'em," Charlie said. "Right nice of Lily to share hers. Right nice."

Reese watched his wife, his expression tender. "Those two are good for each other. Shay's been having a time carrying the baby. She's been really uncomfortable. I know Lily can be a better support than I can in some cases."

"Oh," Charlie said, "there isn't a woman who doesn't suffer a fair amount while she's carryin' a young'un. With Lily comin' to town, bein' a nurse and all, that's made Shay feel a lot better, I'm sure."

"Hey," Jake said to Reese, "have Shay call Lily at my cabin any time she has a question or wants her to come and stay with her."

"How's your mother?" Reese asked.

"She's on the mend," Jake assured him. "Lily has been really good for her and Jenna is ahead of her healing schedule because of it. Lily has more time on her hands than she likes to admit, I think."

"Well," Reese murmured, taking off his Stetson momentarily and pushing his long fingers through his dark hair, "it might be nice if Lily could find a way to drop by once a week. I think Shay needs someone like her who has a medical background right now. I can feel her worrying, and she knows I don't have the answers she needs."

Jake nodded. "I'm fine with Lily taking one of the ranch trucks and driving over to her for a visit whenever she wants. I'll let her know she can talk with Shay and set something up."

Reese heaved a sigh. "Lily is becoming a guardian angel in Wind River," he murmured. "I'd welcome her over anytime so long as she's done with helping your mother first."

"I'm sure we can work something out," Jake said, clapping him on the shoulder. "Being a father is something to get used to, huh?"

Reese gave him a dry laugh. "In a lot of ways. I feel like I have two left hands with Shay pregnant. I wouldn't know what to do except for the classes we're both taking over at the community college. If I didn't have them, I'd feel lost and be of no help at all to Shay."

"Two more months, hombre," Charlie counseled wisely, shaking a finger toward the two men across the counter.

Chapter Ten

June 29

"Could you come over for a visit sometime soon?" Shay asked Lily.

Lily nodded, watching Shay slowly savor the last of the cinnamon roll. "Sure."

"I have your cell phone number. How about I call you tomorrow?"

"That would be fine. I'll be done helping Jenna with her exercises around nine."

Shay sighed, watching her husband, Charlie and Jake jawing at the counter. "I often wondered when Jake would get interested in living again," she murmured, giving Lily a keen look.

Frowning, Lily asked, "What do you mean?"

"It's no secret a very high percentage of the employees in this valley are ex-military. And they all have PTSD. Heck, I have it myself, although it seems to have lessened since I got pregnant." She swallowed the last of the roll. Wiping her lips with a paper napkin, she said, "When Jake came to Wind River Valley three years ago, he was in rough shape. Maud hired him, and I didn't see what she saw in him."

"Oh?"

Shay gave her a painful glance. "He was really jumpy. You sure didn't approach him from behind. He broke one guy's jaw who did that, when he was here to buy some stuff in Charlie's place. The wrangler didn't know what hit him. Charlie understood, of course, but the guy was a civilian and new to the area, so he didn't realize how many combat vets are in our valley. You don't come up behind them, pure and simple."

"Did Jake get thrown in jail?"

"No. But you know how fast word flies around here. After that, you could see men and women giving Jake a wide berth, no matter where he went."

"It must have been a really painful adjustment for him to make, too," Lily said, watching Jake laugh with the two men. He was all male. Hard muscle. Tall. Well-proportioned. She always enjoyed watching Jake's facial expressions since he rarely let that mask dissolve and she could read him better.

"I'm sure it was. I know you said you had PTSD also."

"Still do. But for some reason, it's been getting better since I came out to live with Jenna and Jake."

"Hmmm . . ."

Giving her a wry look, she saw a sparkle in Shay's blue eyes. "What?"

"I think Jake's sweet on you."

Her heart hammered once to underscore her surprise. She saw Shay's smile grow. "I don't think he is, Shay. Really."

"I saw him give you a very special look when you weren't aware just a few minutes ago."

"What look?" Lily demanded, confused.

"A man who's claimed his woman and is just checking to make sure she's okay. You know that look?"

"Of course I do."

Shrugging, Shay said, "It's the first time I've seen Jake interested in a woman. He's pretty much of a loner. He's had no love life since landing here in the valley. Did you know that?"

Squirming, Lily said, "I sort of guessed it because his home is pretty sterile-looking, no decorations and only two photos of loved ones or family. I never see him talking to anyone other than wranglers. He doesn't go out at night after he comes home, so I figured he didn't date."

Patting her thigh, Shay said, "He's a good guy, despite his gruff demeanor. He'd give the shirt off his back to anyone who asked. He's decent and honorable. You could do a lot worse, Lily."

Rolling her eyes, Lily whispered, "I'm not looking for a relationship, Shay. I'm nowhere near being whole enough to deal with someone else, much less myself. You know how our symptoms consume us."

"Ugh, tell me about it. When I first met Reese, he was looking for a job as a wrangler. I could tell he had PTSD. And later, when things calmed down a bit at the ranch, he owned up to knowing I had it, too. I didn't see how I could live with anyone, but it got to the point where I was really drawn to him. I was so scared. But he's so easygoing and patient, and he waited me out. He felt that despite our symptoms, we could have a wonderful life together. I didn't think we could. I'm glad I was wrong."

"Is the PTSD making your marriage more stressful?" Lily wondered.

Shay pushed back a curl from her cheek. "This may sound silly, but because we both have it, we know when to leave the other alone, or be a listener, or simply be support-ive in small yet important ways. It's nice to be able to share with Reese all the horror I experienced, and what it did to me in Afghanistan. He understood. He helped me make some serious breakthroughs that have really cleaned me out emotionally and made me feel better. And I've helped him in the same way." She blushed. "I guess you could say we've been the best therapists we've ever had because we love each other. Love heals, I've discovered."

Lily nodded. "I don't believe I could ever get close to anyone again, Shay."

"Maybe with the right person, huh?" Shay gestured toward the men. "Jake's a very patient man, like Reese. And I've been around him. The way he's reacting and acting around you is different. I truly think he likes you. Has he said anything to you?"

Lily grimaced. "Gosh, no. We have a professional relationship. I'm there to take care of his mother. In another month, my work will be finished."

"And then where will you go? Don't you have a position at the animal shelter?"

Giving a painful shrug, Lily whispered, "I honestly don't know. I have to get a job that pays my bills. I have to find a place to live. Kassie, bless her heart, has given me the small room at the back of her café rent free, but I can't keep living there. I've always earned my way, paid for everything. I won't go back and ask her for free help again. That wouldn't be right."

"Have you talked to Maud about a job at their ranch?"

"No . . . because I can see that what they need are wranglers." She opened her hands. "I'm not one. I came from a spud farm in Idaho."

Grinning, Shay patted her knee. "That's nothing to sneeze at. A farm or a ranch are the most demanding of all jobs as far as I'm concerned. Why not talk to Maud? She's always got plans, along with Steve, to expand into new and different areas. Maybe there's a job waiting for you that you don't even know about."

"It seems hopeless, Shay. I can't go back into the medical world because the sight of blood snaps me into a flashback. And when it happens, it can take me two or three days to come out of it."

"Don't sell Maud short, okay? Go see her. She might have a job in which you'll flourish."

"I'm not a cowgirl. That's the problem."

"But a ranch runs on more than just wranglers, trust me. Reese is our accountant, and that's a full-time job for him. Dair and Kira are always doing odd jobs other than wrangling for us at the Bar C. You could be a jack of all trades, perhaps, filling in here and there when needed. Sort of like them. I call Dair and Kira our troubleshooters. If there's a loose end, one of them or both go fix it."

"I'll bet they have a lot of mechanical skills, though."

"They do. But if they can't fix it, they come to me and we call in a specialist to do it."

Glumly, Lily wanted to believe Shay. "I know I need a skill where I'm seen as necessary. All I know is farming and nursing." And she couldn't go back to either one. Looking up, she saw Jake sauntering in her direction, his gaze on hers. Feeling a warm flush surround her heart, she saw a different look in his eyes. It startled her. It was tenderness. Lily had a tough time linking Jake with such an emotion. But there it was, in his eyes. She noticed the relaxed way his mouth had become as he held her gaze. Grief moved through her because she knew she wasn't ready for any kind of a relationship with a man. And yet, there it was in Jake's unshielded expression. It fed her hope. But it also fed her fear.

"Hey, can I steal Lily from you for a bit, Shay? We've got some shopping to do to get her ready for riding around the ranch."

"Go ahead!" She gently patted her swollen belly. "I stopped riding at five months. Poor Reese was terrified I'd fall off a horse or something, so I stopped." She smiled faintly. "I still miss riding, but that's something I can do after our baby is born."

Lily stood and reached out, squeezing Shay's shoulder. "Soon . . . just two more months."

Shay smiled. "I can hardly wait!"

"Hang in there," she murmured, walking away with Jake.

He slanted a glance in her direction. "You need several things." He picked up a wire basket and handed it to her. "First, a good set of leather work gloves."

Lily enjoyed being close to Jake. He was such a solid, grounded person that just being in his energy field calmed her. It was an important epiphany for her as she tried on several sizes of elkskin gloves.

"I like these," she said, holding up a pair for Jake to look at.

He took them, examining the stitching on the fingers, the thickness of the tanned hide. "These will work. Good choice. Okay, next is a cowboy hat."

"Oh," Lily groaned. "I'm not a cowboy, Jake!"

He gave her a patient look. "But you need to shield your eyes from the sunlight when you're riding."

Desperate, she looked down the long row. "There!" she said, turning on her heel and hurrying toward large stacks of colorful baseball caps. She liked red, so she picked one up, settling it on her head. Turning, she saw a slight tug at one corner of Jake's mouth. He halted.

"Baseball caps are worn by a lot of the wranglers. You'd rather have one of 'em?"

"Yes."

"Can't persuade you to buy a real hat?"

She ruffled over the word *real*. "I'm fine with this one," and she dropped it into the wire basket. Lily knew Stetsons cost a lot of money. This cap was $6.99. And it would work just fine.

"A straw hat is a lot less money than a Stetson, Lily. Why not try one on? The brim will not only protect your eyes and upper face, but if you get caught out in the rain, it will keep the water from running down your neck." He pointed to the baseball cap. "This one won't do that. Come on, just give it a try . . ."

She felt her resolve starting to erode. Jake could be very persuasive. His mellow voice washed right through her. "Well . . . okay . . . I'll try it, but no promises."

They walked down to the end of the aisle, where all the straw hats were stacked. Lily picked through them, feeling Jake's interest in her search for the perfect fit. Finally, she found one, liking its wide brim. Hesitantly, she went over to the long mirror and settled it on her head. She could feel Jake watching, but he didn't say anything. The hat reminded her of a straw hat her mother always wore when outside, not a real cowboy hat. Taking it off, she looked at the price: $12.98.

"Very nice, Lily."

Heat flooded her cheeks as she held it between her hands. "I kinda like it. My mom has a straw hat that looks like this one."

"Like mother, like daughter?" he teased.

All her worry left her. "I guess so. Okay, I'll take this one. Thanks for pushing me over here to look through them."

He chuckled. "No one can accuse you of being a pushover. You're a stubborn lady. Next, let's mosey on over to the women wranglers long-sleeved blouses."

Lily remembered Red wearing a blue-and-white-checkered cowboy shirt, the sleeves rolled up to below her elbows. She'd look strong, confident and deeply tanned. She knew she wasn't anything like Red and feeling counterfeit, she allowed Jake to lead her to a long row of women's blouses. It took her another twenty minutes before she'd chosen seven of them. Jake explained that one didn't wear a shirt or blouse more than one day around the ranch before it had to be washed. It was dirty, dusty and sometimes muddy work.

Lily had tried to dig in her heels on seven new blouses. That was a small fortune! "Jake, that's just too much money!"

"Maud knows you need a blouse a day when you're outside working."

Sputtering, Lily said, "But I'm not riding Checkers every day!"

"Okay," he rumbled, "how many days a week do you think you'll throw a leg over him?"

"Maybe three times a week?"

"Sounds about right. Okay, how about three blouses, then?"

"Yes," she muttered defiantly, "three is fine," and she picked a pink, an orange and a green one.

Glancing up, she saw a wry smile on Jake's mouth, his eyes filled with amusement.

"I'm not going to spend Maud's hard-earned money for nothing," she muttered, hanging up the other four.

"I get that."

"Are we done?"

"No. You need a pair of cowboy boots."

Lily considered it. "Won't my tennis shoes do?"

"No, and here's why." Jake led her over to the shoe department. He went to the women's wall and chose a pair of boots. Holding it down for her to look at, he nudged her over to the saddle department. Picking up one of the stirrups of the saddle, he placed the boot in it. "The reason this boot is narrower in the front is because if you have to fall off the horse or are thrown off, the tip of it will slide free, allowing you to fall completely off. If you wore a common shoe or work boot, the toe would most likely jam in the stirrup. Then," he said, arching a brow, "you'd get dragged. And that could break your foot, ankle or some other part of your leg, never mind dragging you over rocks and dirt. Getting dragged can kill you."

"I didn't know that," she admitted, digesting his argument, taking the boot, running her fingers across the narrow front of it.

"It's a safety reason."

She considered it. "Okay, let's go get me a pair of *cheap* boots. I saw the prices on them, Jake. I'm not paying two hundred dollars. No way," she fumed as she saw his grin reluctantly increase.

"Are you always like this, Lily?" he asked, walking with her to the shoe department.

"Like what?" she shot back, giving him a dark look.

"Maud is fine with whatever you want. It's not a question of money for her. She treats all her employees the same. She spends good money on gloves, for example, because we're always working with barbed wire. In her mind, it's better to buy a pair of thick elkskin gloves and pay a fair price for them than have one of her people slice open their hand or fingers and be unable to work for a couple of weeks while they heal. It's a business decision, Lily."

Lily didn't want to admit that Jake's reasonable answer made sense to her. She handed him the lone boot and went over to look at the women's assortment, checking out the prices as she went. There were boots made from ostrich and alligator hide, and they were expensive. Instead, she chose a plain pair made of cowhide, the cheapest ones there. "I'd like to try these on." She dared Jake to protest. To his credit, he just nodded, leaned down after she told him the size of her foot and handed her a box. However, there was an amused gleam in his eyes even if his smile had disappeared. She was glad he respected what she wanted instead of trying to argue her out of it or, worse, shame her into it. That wasn't the kind of man she wanted around, particularly if she was drawn to him whether she liked it or not. Jake gave her respect, and that was vital to Lily when it came to being in a close relationship. Sitting down, she pulled them on over her sock feet. Standing, she walked around. Coming back, she sat down again.

"These will do," she told him, pulling them off.

Jake took the pair and placed them in the wire basket. "Good choice."

She quickly tied her tennis shoes, giving him a questioning look. "I don't think Checkers will care one way or another."

Chuckling, Jake said, "We're done. Let's go."

Fine by her! She looked up to see Reese and Shay at the counter, talking with Charlie after picking up their purchases. They looked ready to leave. "I want to say goodbye to them," she said, hurrying ahead.

"Go. I'll take care of this," Jake said.

Grateful, she caught them just as Reese had opened the door. Lily called out to them, came up and hugged Shay and then Reese.

"Call me," Shay urged her.

Holding up her hand, Lily stepped back and said, "I promise. 'Bye . . ."

Jenna was thrilled to examine every package Lily brought home. Jake had left for the rest of the afternoon, so they were free to look through her new purchases.

"That's very nice of Maud to do this for you," Jenna said, moving her fingers across the deerskin gloves.

Lily sat in the chair next to the couch. She had made

fresh coffee and filled a thermos for Jake before he took off on his duties. "I'm not used to this, Jenna."

"What?"

"Someone paying for things I need."

Jenna gave her an understanding look as she opened the boot box on her lap. "You're used to working to earn what you buy. And it's hard to accept things like this from another person."

"I believe in charity, don't get me wrong. But all of these things cost money." Money she didn't have.

"I spent my life as a teacher, helping children who had so much less than I did growing up. There's also a charity in Casper I worked with closely that provides children with clothes, shoes and things they grow in and out of so fast."

"I never had to have charity," Lily grumbled, scowling at the goods next to Jenna. "I just don't feel right about it."

"Well, then, why don't you go see Maud about doing something about it? Maybe she has something you could do to work it off at the ranch while you're here."

Brightening, Lily said, "That's a great idea!"

Just then, the phone in the kitchen rang. Lily hopped up and ran to get it. "Hello?"

"It's me, Jake. I'm going to have a ranch truck brought over to the cabin for you to use. I know you have your vehicle, but here on the ranch, or on ranch business, I'd like you to drive it instead. Red and Jim are driving two trucks over there right now. Red will give you the keys to the ranch pickup. You're to use it as you see fit. Tomorrow morning, we'll take a ride in it. I'll show you where the gas pump is on the ranch so you can fill it with gasoline any time you need to."

"That's great," she said, thrilled. "I can take Jenna on trips around the ranch." She didn't want to admit that she had so little money that gas, which was high, wasn't something she could afford for her truck. Going to and from the animal shelter was a long trip for her and she didn't want to run out of gas.

"You could take her into town, drive to Jackson Hole or do whatever you want."

Lily felt hope fill her. "This is so thoughtful of you, Jake." Her voice grew hoarse for a moment. "Thank you." Had he somehow read her mind or known she was low on gas in her truck?

"You can thank me by making me that cherry pie you made a week ago. That was good."

Smiling, Lily felt herself going warm all over, her fingers tightening a bit around the phone. "That's an easy one. I'll make it for tomorrow night."

"Good enough. See you and Jenna tonight at six."

Lily hung up and told Jenna the good news. She saw Jenna's excited smile.

"You mean we can escape our prison?"

Giggling, Lily remained in the kitchen to start dinner. She had been using her own truck to take Jenna to appointments. "Yes. Isn't that nice of Jake to do that for us?" Jenna knew about her gas situation and accepted that they couldn't drive around too much, except going to and from her doctor's appointments in town. No extracurricular trips to Jackson Hole, for sure. Now, if Jenna wanted to go there to shop or have lunch, they could do it.

"That's my son," she said proudly. "Jake has always been a team player." She set the last package aside on the couch. "Need some help? Now that I can walk reasonably well, if slowly, I'm another set of hands."

Lily wanted Jenna as mobile as she could be at this stage in her healing process. "Yes, come on up. I thought I'd make us shepherd's pie tonight. Can you dice the carrots, onions and potatoes for me?"

Jenna got up gingerly, using her cane. "Sounds great."

Retrieving a cutting board and a good, sharp knife, she

set it down further along on the counter. In no time, they were putting the ingredients together. Lily absorbed the familylike atmosphere. She used to help her mother in the kitchen, making lunches and dinners. She loved it. There was a calming continuity to such work, and Jenna was so easy to be around. Lily could imagine after handling the chaos of thirty children in a classroom, she could easily deal with one other person in the kitchen.

"Did Jake get his patience from you?" Lily wondered, glancing over at Jenna, who was neatly chopping carrots into little squares.

"Oh, I think he got a dose of it from both me and his father."

"Jake reminds me a lot of my father," Lily admitted, retrieving frozen peas from the top of the fridge freezer.

"Will you visit them sometime in the near future, Lily?"

"I will, yes." She didn't want to get into her PTSD because she didn't know if Jake had ever sat down and had a good, long talk with his mother about his own issues.

"You know," Jenna said, grabbing a stalk of celery, "now that you're going to have wheels, you could drive over and drop in to see Maud."

"You were reading my mind," Lily said, beginning to make the dough for the bottom of the pie pan. "I really don't want to take charity. Tomorrow, after we get your exercises done, I'll go over to the main office and talk with her. I'd love to somehow pay her back for all the things we bought today."

"I wonder if Jake knows of some job you might fill. You could ask him at dinner tonight."

Lily wrinkled her nose, taking the rolling pin and smoothing out the pastry dough. "He didn't see using Maud's money as taking charity."

"Maud isn't the usual ranch owner," Jenna said wryly. "She and her husband are so generous, I sometimes wonder if they were aliens dropped down here to show us a better way to work with one another."

"What do you mean?" Lily gently laid the thin dough across the pie tin and then began to pinch the crust together with her fingers.

"Didn't Jake tell you? Any wrangler who stays on the ranch five years receives a log cabin. He or she has to build it, but a crane comes in and sets up the major bones of it. Then, they also give the wrangler five acres of land around it. The wrangler has a number of areas to choose from, too." She gestured around the house. "This cabin was built for the other foreman, who retired before Jake took over his job. Now he lives in Maine, taking care of his parents. Someday, he will have his own beautiful cabin here on the ranch when he wants to retire from being a foreman."

"Jake told me about that wonderful offer from the Whit-combs."

"And I just found out that they only hire military vets for the jobs around the ranch," Jenna said, nodding as she scooped up the celery, placing it in a nearby bowl. "They're the most generous people I've ever met. They also give our Casper charity a big donation every January, too. Maud once said they set up trust funds for their four adopted children, and they also plan to disperse a lot of what they have to charities around the country."

"That's just incredible," Lily said in awe. She took another bowl, getting ready to make the gravy that would hold the ingredients together. "When I came here, Kassie was telling me that they were the guardian angels of Wind River Valley. Now I know why."

"You'll see these five-acre log cabins all around the property. It's a hundred-thousand-acre ranch, and they have some beautiful areas where the wranglers can choose to put their homes."

"Why didn't the other foreman stay here and live in this

house? Or does the wrangler have to remain employed at the ranch to keep the home?"

"If a wrangler stays twenty years, they can own the cabin and live here forever after they retire. Jake said the other foreman has his parents in Maine. He's taking care of them there. His parents will be willing him a large 1930s Victorian, so he isn't out anything."

"I'll bet Jake loves this home." Lily looked around. "I'd love to live here the rest of my life. It's so gorgeous. So . . . alive."

"The first time Jake brought me here," Jenna said, "I told him this place was a home, not a house. It has three bedrooms; it's three thousand square feet. This cabin was built to have children in it. I can hear their laughter. I can see them playing on the stairs. I can see a dog for the family, too."

"I love what you see," Lily whispered, her heart swelling. "Maybe a cat, too?"

"Of course! I fantasize every time I come here, seeing each child with their own pet. Who knows? Maybe they have two dogs and two cats?" and she smiled dreamily.

"We always had a bunch of animals at our place." Lily sighed. "When I went to college, I missed my dog more than anything."

"This place absolutely needs a dog," Jenna agreed, frowning. She rinsed off the knife and set it in the dishwasher. Straightening, she added, "I know you work at the shelter. Why don't we go over there someday after you get that truck? I think Jake is very lonely here. He should have someone or something in his life."

Lily wanted to say that PTSD often made hermits out of those who suffered it. "I think you should bring that up to Jake first. After we leave, he's the one who'll be responsible for taking care of that dog. I don't know if he wants to do that or not. What do you think?" and she saw the older woman purse her lips for a moment.

"You're right. I'll talk to him tonight. Let's see if we can persuade him that he needs a buddy in his life."

"He seems lonely," Lily agreed.

"But you know what? Since you've been here, Jake actually looks better," Jenna noted. "I've visited him for a week every year and he was never like this."

Stirring the gravy over the gas stove, Lily said, "What do you mean?"

"He's more open than before. He used to hide all the time behind those walls he has around him. Mind you," and she shook her finger in Lily's direction, "Jake didn't used to be like that at all. He was far more extroverted when he was younger. Now, he's a dark man, and you never know what he's thinking or feeling unless he opens his mouth . . . which isn't often."

"I've found him really closed up, too," Lily said, sadness in her tone.

"With you here, he's blooming. Yes! Don't give me that look, Lily. Don't you see and feel his enjoyment in having you around? I certainly have seen and felt it. Haven't you?"

Chapter Eleven

June 29

Jake appreciated the tasty shepherd's pie the two women had made for dinner. The pie crust was light, buttery, flakey, and he savored it. He listened to them chatting about the day's activities, and how Jenna's exercises were, indeed, strengthening her hips and thighs as she continued to heal.

There was something good, something calming growing quietly within him. He wanted to say it was his mother, but inwardly, Jake knew it had to do with Lily also. Somehow, she had melted one of the walls he purposely kept in place because of his PTSD. And even more stunning was that he found his closeness to Lily blossoming almost daily. She wasn't a burr under his saddle. Instead, he'd found, over the weeks, that his anxiety had dialed way down when he came home after a hard day's work.

It wasn't anything special Lily did to make his anxiety level go down and sometimes go away completely. He enjoyed listening to the chats between her and his mother. They got along well, but then, both were the type who were what he'd term easy keepers. He knew he wasn't one. He was the rock and they were the water that flowed around him. Whatever the dynamics, it worked for the three of them. Even better was that his mother's health continued to improve, and he hadn't seen her that happy since his father's sudden death. His mother was far more positive now, and he felt that was due strictly to Lily entering Jenna's life.

He wanted to try to understand what, exactly, it was about Lily that made him, well . . . happy. Jake looked forward to coming home to this cabin after a long day, whereas before, it was just a box where he lived when not working. Even though he rarely contributed to their conversations, he found them interesting. His mother had a double degree, one in English and one in history. And Lily grooved on history as well. He liked history himself, so when Lily asked a question about ancient Babylon, Jenna was right there in lockstep with her, sharing her deep, broad base of knowledge of long-ago civilizations. He always learned something, too.

"Jake?"

Startled by his mother's voice, he snapped his head up. "What?" The word came out more growly than he'd intended. He'd been so focused on his thoughts that he hadn't heard her first call to get his attention. Clearing his throat, he said, "Did you ask me something?"

Jenna laughed and slid Lily a knowing glance. "Yes, I did. You were deep in thought."

"Shepherd's pie does that to me."

Lily laughed gaily, holding his gaze. "Seriously?"

Giving them a grudging grin, he felt his face was on fire. Blushing wasn't something he did at all. The merry expressions on the women's faces made him shrug. "I was thinking about some stuff," he admitted, giving Jenna an apologetic look. "What did I miss?"

"Oh," Jenna said, "not much. Lily and I were talking

earlier today about the possibility of you needing someone here after we leave. Like a dog."

His brows fell as he cut into the crust of the pie. "Oh."

"You had a dog growing up," Jenna reminded him archly. "You two were inseparable."

"Yeah, that's true," he admitted, chewing on the savory pie.

"Aren't you lonely here?" Lily asked tentatively.

"No."

Jenna gave him a frustrated look. "You seem happier with the two of us around, Jake. I've visited here before and this time is different."

"But it has nothing to do with a dog." He stared at his mother and saw consternation come to her expression. "By the time I get home at night, I'm whipped," he admitted. "I'm not lonely because I'm with wranglers all day long somewhere on this spread."

"Oh," Jenna murmured. "Well, I never thought of that."

Lily looked around the home. "This house is so big, Jake. And just one person lives in it. We thought you might get lonely."

"Not yet," he lied. Seeing the concern and sympathy in Lily's very readable features, he didn't want to get into why it was necessary for him to live alone. He knew she would understand, but his mother wouldn't. And he didn't want to go there with Jenna because even if she knew what his plethora of symptoms did to him, especially at night, after he'd fallen asleep, there was nothing to be done about them.

Crooking her lips, Jenna frowned. "I thought for sure you'd want a companion here, Jake."

"Maybe growing up," he said more gently. "But not now. A lot has changed, mostly me, and I don't need a dog to make myself feel like I have a buddy again." Because he had loved his dog from his days as a young kid. Jenna looked defeated. Glancing toward Lily, he saw concern in her eyes, but she said nothing.

"What about in the wintertime?" Jenna challenged. "There's nothing to do outside for eight months out of the year in this place, Jake."

He scraped his plate clean. "As foreman? I'm not sitting here doing nothing. There's horse riding gear, a lot of agricultural equipment that needs upkeep, and it keeps me busy. About three-quarters of our wranglers leave for other jobs in other less wintery states. So, I'm busy from dawn to dusk."

"I know my dad was always busy in the winter, Jenna, at our potato farm. He was always out in the barn, fixing equipment or repairing the barn itself. He didn't have anyone else working with him. Sometimes, I'd go out and help him, an extra set of hands." Lily cast Jake a look. "He worked six days a week in the winter. The demands were just different, but he was busy."

"Hmmm," Jenna said. "Okay, I learned something new tonight, too." She managed a warm smile. "I still think, Jake, that a dog would be a wonderful friend to have when you came to this huge, quiet place at night."

Nodding, Jake stood up and picked up all the plates. He did this every evening. If the women could do the cooking, he could do the cleaning afterward. "It's just one more thing I'd have to take care of," he said. "As foreman, I take care of the employees all the time."

"I see," Jenna murmured. "And it does make sense. You have a nice, big flat-screen TV you can watch," she said, gesturing to the wall where it hung in the living room.

He walked into the kitchen, rinsing the plates and flatware, transferring them to the dishwasher. "I like to catch the national news, but that's about all," he told his mother.

"And I'd rather knit than watch it," Jenna said.

Lily rose and went into the kitchen. She opened the fridge, pulling out a casserole. "Jake? I made some bread pudding for us for dessert."

He raised his brows, watching her bring it over to the counter. "Thanks. That was thoughtful." Jake finished his duties and then helped her take down small bowls from the cupboard. "You're spoiling me," he told Lily and Jenna.

"You'll miss us when we leave?" Jenna teased him.

Jake took the first two bowls of dessert, walking over to the table. "Yes, I will." Much more than either of them knew. Especially Lily. For a moment, a flash of his childhood came to him, strong and sweet, the happiness of their family, him as a lively ten-year-old. That same sense as a kid that all was right with the world shifted through him as he gave Jenna a bowl and set the other one where Lily would sit.

For a split second, he wondered if he could have that life again. The brutal reality of his symptoms instantly shattered that sliver of hope. No. It was impossible. As he walked into the kitchen, meeting Lily's wide, beautiful eyes, that soft smile on her lips, he wanted that feeling back so badly, his heart ached.

July 4

Lily crept quietly out of her bedroom. It was one a.m. and she'd had a nightmare. Dressed in her knee-length green cotton nightgown, a white chenille robe over it, she had pulled on her slippers and decided to get up. The house was quiet, and she absorbed that wonderful feeling it always gave her. Tiptoeing past Jenna's room, she headed down the passageway. There was always a night-light on in the kitchen, throwing just enough light that she wouldn't stumble over anything.

A movement caught her attention. Out of the shadows, she saw Jake. He was in a black T-shirt and black pajama bottoms, barefoot, at the stove.

He turned, as if sensing she was there. Lily hesitated. Should she go back to her room?

"Lily? What's wrong?"

Too late. She gulped, her heart speeding up as the deep shadows accentuated the powerful breadth of his chest and those broad shoulders of his. He looked endearingly like a little boy, his face sleepy-looking, dark strands of hair dipping down on his brow, uncombed. His masculinity was nearly overpowering to her interested body. Too often, she fantasized what it would be like to be held by this quiet, deep-thinking man. To feel the steel strength of his arms coming around her, holding her. "Nothing's wrong . . ."

He lifted a mug. "Couldn't sleep, so I'm making my mother's hot chocolate. Want some?"

Mildly shocked that his demeanor wasn't that of the gruff, walled Jake, she stood there uncertainly. He was even more appealing to her than ever before. Somewhere in Lily's canting senses, she managed a strangled, "Why yes . . . sure . . ." and she found herself being pushed forward by invisible hands on her back. More than anything, she'd craved quiet time, alone time with Jake. It had never happened—until now. Even though she warred within herself—Jake was her employer—as a woman, she was drawn helplessly to him as a man. It reminded Lily of when she'd had a crush on an eight-year-old boy in grade school. Just the way the shadows and grayness moved across his upper body, his now-exposed upper arms revealing thick biceps, made her eager to be in his company. Cautioning herself, she halted a good six feet away from him, seeing the pan on the stove and the carton of milk, box of chocolate, sugar, salt shaker and spice that said *cinnamon* on it.

"I couldn't sleep," she said, holding his shadowy gaze. Lily knew that look; she knew when a man was interested in her. Her arms were folded across her breasts as he gave her a swift, intense look. And then that hunger in his eyes was gone. Did her hunger for him show? She hoped not.

"Me either," he rumbled, opening the cabinet and pulling down a second mug. "Must be something in the air tonight. Probably the fireworks at Wind River the three of us watched reminded me too much of firefights in Afghanistan, dragged up a lot of other stuff I'd rather forget." He held up the bright blue mug.

"Is there anything I can do to help?" she asked.

"No . . . thanks," and he poured more milk into the pan, efficiently adding the other ingredients as well.

"Are you hungry?"

Looking around, she saw the toaster was out, the bread and butter nearby. "No. You?"

"Yeah. Pop in two slices of bread into that toaster for me?"

A warm, awakening feeling flowed into her lower body. "How much butter do you want on your toast?"

"A lot."

"The fireworks upset you?" she asked, moving outside her comfort zone. Always reminding herself she was an employee, not an intimate partner to him, she knew it was a very personal question. She saw him barely turn his head, his profile sharp.

"Yes. I went to bed and a nightmare hit me, if you want the raw truth. I figure you'd understand."

She managed a soft snort. "Jenna wanted to see the fireworks, so we both put ourselves out to be with her where she could see them. Because she doesn't know much about our PTSD, she had no idea it might upset us. I had a nightmare, too." She saw his profile relax, that strongly shaped mouth of his softening for a moment. "I used to get them three or four times a week when I first came home. It's been slowly diminishing." She pushed her hair away from her temple, watching the breadth of his back as he stirred the contents in the pan. "This is the longest I've gone without one."

"Have you had any since coming here?"

"Yes, the first night and now tonight." She blew out a breath of air. "But now, I can't believe they seem to have slowed down so much, almost stopped."

He chuckled a little.

It sounded like a drum to Lily. "What?"

"When you and Jenna arrived, I stopped having my flashbacks and nightmares. This is the first since your arrival." He turned, holding her gaze for a moment. "I was getting so I considered you and her my lucky rabbit's foot."

Her mouth quirking, she said, "I felt the same way, that by coming here, the chemistry of the house, you and Jenna all conspired to make me feel—I don't know . . . safe maybe. It's like the environment I grew up in as a kid."

"Something safe, warm and familiar. Right?"

She watched him turn off the stove and then carefully pour the steaming liquid into the mugs.

"Right."

But there was more, and Lily was afraid to voice her feelings to Jake because they were so damned intimate. Certainly not having an employer-employee discussion. She stepped forward, picking up the mugs and taking them to the table. The toast popped up.

"I'll get it."

She nodded and stood, watching him put water in the pan, then going to butter his toast. Deciding to sit down, she took a chair with her back to the living room, quietly absorbing every move he made. Jake was a big man, in top shape. The dark growth of beard shadowed part of his face, making him look dangerously appealing to her senses.

He brought the toast over on a plate and sat down, his elbow near hers. "Sure you don't want some?"

Shaking her head, she placed her hands around the warm mug. "No."

"This is the way I have mine," and he dipped part of the toast into the chocolate.

"I'm surprised you don't have some marshmallows around," she teased, cautiously sipping the steaming brew. The chocolate was rich, sweet and tasty.

"I'm not a marshmallow kind of guy."

"I didn't think you were."

He gave her an amused glance. "Well, now that I know you're a hot-chocolate-with-marshmallows woman, I'll make a point to pick up some the next time I'm in town."

Her lips flexed and she felt that warm, sensual connection building between them once again. Her hair was decidedly mussed, and she wore a frumpy chenille bathrobe that certainly wasn't sexy or alluring. And her simple, plain nightgown wasn't anything to write home about either. "What? You think this kind of unexpected meeting is going to take place again?"

"You have three and a half weeks to go here," he said, giving her a thoughtful look. "Anything can happen in that time."

Groaning, she whispered, "I've really gotten spoiled, being able to sleep deeply while I'm here. This nightmare jolted me, reminded me that I'm not free of them."

"Most vets would give their right arm to have only one a month."

"I know," she said, sad. Jake was hungry. He dipped his toast into his mug, and within ten minutes, it was gone. There was half a cup of chocolate left for him to drink, too. "How often do you get booted out of bed?"

"Well, it's been three years. I can usually count on a nightmare maybe every couple of weeks. I haven't had a flashback in nine months. I used to get them three or four times a month."

She sipped the chocolate she held near her lips. "It's nice to be able to share this with someone who understands." His face softened even more. The shock that he wasn't putting up his walls astounded Lily. She set the mug down, her fingers tightening around it a bit. "I know this is awfully personal, but you seem so different right now from the man who walks in that door at six every night."

Jake moved his jaw, looked away, then back at her. "I guess I could lie and say it's because I'm sleepy. The truth is, Lily, I've been wanting a backwater moment with you, just to talk to you and find out more of who you are."

Her heart beat rapidly for a moment. His voice was like gruff velvet being pulled lightly across her supersensitized flesh. Blinking, the silence settled between them, but it wasn't brittle or tense. "Funny," she offered with a slight, one-cornered lift of her lips, "I was looking for the same thing. I didn't think the man who walked out the door in the morning was the real Jake Murdoch. I know I'm really overstepping my bounds now, and maybe I should apologize. I know I'm here to take care of Jenna. I'm an employee."

"You are and you aren't," Jake rasped. "My mother dotes on you. I can see there's genuine affection between you."

"As I've said, your mother is a lot like mine," Lily said, fondness in her tone. "I enjoy her so much. This has been the best job I've had since getting out of the military. She makes it easy."

"I'm old enough now to appreciate my mother like never before."

"Me too."

The silence settled once more between them. Lily had a thousand questions for Jake, unsure what to ask and how to ask it. "I know military vets share something very special," she began haltingly, searching for words she hoped wouldn't screw up what she really wanted to say. "I guess . . . I've been looking for a home since I couldn't stay in my real one because of my symptoms." She gestured toward the high ceiling. "Being here? Being with the two of you? It's pulled me out of the hell I was slogging through since I got my honorable medical discharge. My parents wanted to help me, but I had no way to tell them how because I didn't know myself." She saw his mouth flatten, his gaze going to the mug held between his large, callused hands.

"I had the same problem when I didn't reenlist," he admitted gruffly. "I knew I couldn't stay with Jenna, even though she wanted that more than anything, wanted me to take over the grocery store." He gave her a dark look. "Can you imagine how those aisles made me feel? My anxiety amped up by a thousand when I would walk down one. I was expecting to be jumped by the Taliban. Closed in, narrow places get to me to this day."

Groaning, Lily whispered, "I've had a number of my A-team friends tell me the same thing."

"I couldn't shake it. I couldn't ignore it because every hair on my neck was standing up, my heart pounding so hard I thought it would rip out of my chest." He halted and scowled. "How do you tell a civilian about that? How can they put themselves in our shoes and see a simple grocery aisle in a completely different context, where it means life or death to us? My adrenaline automatically goes through the ceiling. It's not something I can control. I wished to hell I could."

She reached out, grazing the back of his hand, the dark hair across it. "I know. It's the same for me, but in a different way."

"What happened to you, Lily? What gave you the symptoms?" he asked quietly, holding her startled gaze. "It's a question I've wanted to ask you. I hope you can trust me enough to share it with me, but if you can't, I'll understand."

She felt paralyzed for a moment. "Jake . . . I can't do it here. Not with your mother here. I–I don't know what will happen if I start. I don't know if I'll lose it. I'm so afraid to give it voice. It will take me back to where I was when it happened." She tilted her head, holding his sympathetic gaze. "I want to tell you, but I'm so afraid of losing control. I've come so close to that abyss, so close to falling into the black hole I see in front of me when I have a really bad flashback. . . . I'm so scared if I step forward, I'll fall in and be swallowed up and gone forever. I can't do it right now."

He reached out, gripping her hand, squeezing it gently and then releasing it.

"You don't have to go there, Lily. I understand. But you were an RN, so I couldn't piece together how it might have happened . . . your symptoms, that is."

Swallowing hard, she felt the coldness beginning to creep into her toes and feet. It was a warning sign of a flashback beginning to stalk her. "I can't . . . it's already starting to hit me, Jake. Let's talk about anything else. When I can, if I can, I'll tell you, but not right now. I'm still too raw from it."

"Then let's talk about Checkers."

Instantly, through her closed eyes, she saw her friend, the paint gelding. And she began to feel the tendrils of iciness that were starting up her ankles, numbing her, making her feel freezing cold recede. "Y-yes, Checkers." She opened her eyes, sliding her other hand around the mug, seeking the warmth of the ceramic.

"I'd like to take you riding tomorrow. Our first trail ride. I think you're ready for it. You've done a lot of good ground work with him in the arena. And you look comfortable in the saddle."

She absorbed his low, mellow tone, which felt like the warm, rich hot chocolate being poured into her lower legs, ankles, feet and toes. The care vibrated in his voice, filled with an invisible caress, a support she hungrily embraced. "I—I'd like that."

"You can wear your gloves, your straw hat and your cowboy boots and break them in."

Lily realized what he was doing. She was like a raging bull, moving toward the red flag he was waving at her, trying to minimize the flashback. Intuitively, she knew Jake was purposely guiding her imagery, focusing her, getting her as far away from the brink of the black hole that still haunted and terrorized her. If only it would go away! Disappear! Forcing her mind, which was tumbling, trying to focus because that was the only way to get away from the stalking flashback, she said, "I'll wear all my new gear."

"I was thinking of an easy trail. There's a straight two miles that parallels our asphalt road. It ends up at two hills that have pine trees all over them. When you ride around the farthest hill, there's a beautiful flower meadow about a quarter of a mile down the slope. I think you'd really like to see that."

"Will Checkers want to eat the flowers?"

He chuckled a little. "Only if you let him. You're the boss; you keep his head up with the reins. How about I drop by tomorrow at around eleven? You can make us a lunch and I'll pack it in the saddlebags on my horse. I think you could use a couple of hours of sun."

"Sounds good," she said.

"We can have a picnic in a nice little spot off the slope of one of the hills. It will give you a view of the ranch."

The silence settled over them, and Lily didn't feel the need to break it. Neither did Jake. He finished his coca and set the mug on the table. She was almost finished.

"When will we be back?"

"Probably by around one. Why?"

"I have my volunteer time at the shelter from two to about five tomorrow."

"You should make it. Do you do any vet work there, considering you're an RN?"

"Sometimes I'll take a dog or cat over to the vet for examination, but I'm just there to hold and calm the animal."

"We have a new small animal vet who just moved into town," Jake said. "Have you met her yet? Dr. Ann Sharp?"

"Yes, and she's the best. I really like her."

"How do you handle the suffering you see there?" Jake wondered. "You were through a lot already in Afghanistan."

"I don't know. Animals have always calmed me, and I feel love from them. I like giving my time over there because now they need my love in return. They've been thrown away, dropped off in the middle of nowhere to try to survive, and I want to be there to make a small difference in their lives."

"You're still serving," he said quietly, giving her a look of praise.

"How do you mean?" She straightened up and pushed the empty mug away from her. Lily didn't want this time with Jake to end. He was open with her for the first time.

"Nursing is a service career. Right?"

"Yes, it is. Just never thought of it in that way."

"Did you get that from your father or mother?"

She smiled a little, remembering what he'd said about wanting to know her on a more personal level. "Let's put it this way: When I was four, my parents gave me a Winnie-the-Pooh bear. I promptly bandaged it up with some of my mother's head scarves. I don't honestly remember it, but she has video of me blathering away about how Pooh broke his arm and I had to fix it."

A grudging smile pulled at his mouth. "So, any stuffed animal got the ER treatment after that?"

Laughing a little, Lily said, "Yes, they all did. Mom got it, and when I was seven, Santa Claus left me a doctor's bag with a stethoscope and bandages in it. I was in heaven." She saw his eyes light up with laughter. "I guess, looking back at that time, I was already in my chosen field. When I went to junior high, I started taking courses that would get me into college someday. I really loved being a nurse. When I graduated, I went into ortho because I loved working with the bones and joints of the body."

"Do you think someday you might go back into ortho?"

Giving a painful shrug, Lily whispered, "I don't know. Not yet . . . It brings back too many fresh memories for me. I wanted to do something different, like helping Jenna. There's no blood involved either. I could never be an ortho surgery nurse again because of it."

"PTSD changes us," he agreed in a low tone fraught with emotion. "I was going to spend twenty in the service. I had my whole life laid out in front of me."

"Yes, well," she said drily, "so did I. When we're in our early twenties, Jake, we're so young, so hopeful . . ."

"That idealism we're all born with takes it on the nose after we enter the military."

"It didn't for me until . . . well, the one incident that destroyed my hope." She could see turmoil in his dark green eyes, feel a sense of protectiveness gently encasing her. Was it possible Jake had invisible arms he was wrapping around her shoulders? It sure felt like it to Lily. Releasing a long sigh, she said, "I guess I still hope. When I'm with the dogs at the shelter, I feel hope for them. Maybe I haven't completely lost my way."

"Animals have a way of luring our better human emotions to the surface," Jake said. "Checkers is good for you, too. I'm glad you're making time for him to become part of your life."

"Only for the next month." She frowned. "I need to get

a steady job. I can't rely on part-time work. And I don't want to stay in the room Kassie give me for free."

"Maud's always looking for office staff," he said. "Matter of fact, her assistant, Helen, is retiring next month. Do you type?"

"On a computer keyboard, yes."

"Have you thought of something like becoming an office assistant? Won't involve any blood, that's for sure. And Maud is easy to work for, so you won't be buried under stress and demands. Might be a possible job for you, Lily."

She brightened a little. "Thanks, Jake. I meant to drive over to see her, but I haven't yet. I'll get over there in a day or two to ask her."

"You're looking tired, Lily. Your eyelids are drooping. Why don't we hit the sack?"

She stood and pushed away the chair. "Sounds good."

"I'll put the mugs in the dishwasher," he said. "You go ahead."

There was something vulnerable and almost boyish about Jake as she stared up at him as he rose from his chair. "I really like this, Jake," she said. "Usually, you have walls around you. But you don't now. Why?"

He collected the mugs. "I don't have an answer, Lily. I don't know. Maybe it's you."

Chapter Twelve

July 6

"*I don't have an answer, Lily. I don't know. Maybe it's you.*"

Lily couldn't get Jake's response out of her head. Or her heart. The man was like fog: silent, nearly invisible, impossible to grasp where he was coming from. Did she want to think about getting into a relationship with him? It hadn't occurred to her until recently. Jake was opening up to her. She wasn't some young innocent in the world of men and women. There was something good growing between them, and she didn't try to stop those feelings because her symptoms were better as a result. She knew part of it was because of Jenna, who reminded her of her mother, who she loved fiercely. Lily missed her family acutely.

Frowning, she drove her pickup down the highway toward the ranch after finishing up at the shelter. In another twenty minutes, she'd be home, in time for dinner at six. Jenna was getting to the point where she was walking without help. She loved working in the kitchen and had promised to make Jake and her dinner tonight, which Lily appreciated. Outside, the sun was setting in the west, not yet touching the Wilson Range peaks, though it would shortly.

Her thoughts moved to her first trail ride yesterday with Jake. Her inner thighs were still stiff and sore from that two-hour jaunt. And she walked funny, too, feeling as if her legs were bowed, for about an hour after returning to the barn. Jake had ridden one of the string horses at the ranch, a bright red sorrel gelding with four flashy white socks with a wide blaze down his face. She loved the quiet plodding of Checkers, who followed the more active gelding Jake rode.

Jake never talked about what he'd said to her that late night. She wanted to broach it but was fearful for a lot of good reasons. First, she was an employee, not a friend, not a possible lover. She was a temporary, understanding she would be gone in weeks. Jenna would be going back across the state to Casper, where she lived, and her job would be over. And Lily was tentative because her focus was on trying to heal, not accidentally meeting a man who might be an equal in her life. Yet there it was, staring back at her, teasing and making her ache inwardly for something outside herself. The loneliness pierced through her at times as she fought silently to try to be normal. During yesterday's ride, when they stopped for a picnic on the slope of one of the hills, Jake had continued to unveil a little more of himself. Like her, he'd had a good set of parents, but she could see that when his father died, it had left a wound in him that still hadn't completely healed.

Slats of sunlight shot like golden lasers across the wide valley, the fingers highlighting the many shades of green across it. Lily was finding summer was indeed a beautiful time here on the western side of Wyoming. The scent of lush grass permeated the air and she loved it, inhaling it deeply. The two-lane highway was pretty much deserted at this time. Most people who worked during the day were already arriving home to join their families.

She missed her own family, leaving an ache in her heart. Guilt warred within Lily, even though she faithfully called her parents every weekend to fill them in on how she was doing, avoiding the PTSD stuff, of course. They were relieved she had a job, even if it was only two months long. If only there was some way to bridge the gap between civilians and military people. Their worlds were literally so far apart, their unique realities so different from one another. Jake, however, had given her an outlet, and for that she was more than grateful. Every time they tentatively walked around their symptoms, she felt a little bit more of her was healed.

A dark shape appeared about half a mile ahead of her, walking along the shoulder on her side of the road. What was it? She slowed, worried it might be a coyote that might cross in front of her. Or maybe a wolf from one of the packs who lived in the nearby mountain ranges. She didn't want to hit an animal, so she slowed down even more.

There was a barbed-wire ranch fence off the gravel shoulder, grass on the other side and about twenty head of Hereford cows munching away, ignoring the animal passing nearby. As she coasted closer, she saw it was a black-and-white dog. Her belly was protruding; she was obviously very pregnant. She was limping on one of her legs. Making a mewing sound of sympathy for how bedraggled the dog looked, Lily checked traffic one last time. There was none. She pulled over in front of the dog, her pink tongue lolling out the side of her mouth, head down, ears down, not at all alert. It looked like a Border collie. The dog's fur was matted, uncombed, ratty-looking. Lily would bet anything someone had dumped the pregnant collie and left her to fend for herself weeks, if not a month earlier.

Sliding out, she walked to the rear of the truck and watched the dog for a reaction. Her head was hanging down, and she was obviously tired and weary. Kneeling, Lily called, "Hey girl, come here," and she patted her knee.

Instantly, the dog lifted her ears, picking up her pace a little toward her.

Lily saw she had the most beautiful crystalline blue eyes and remembered that some Border collies had that color. The dog was limping on her right front paw. As she drew closer, she could see the animal was starved. Her heart turned with even more distress for her. There was no collar on her. For sure, someone had dropped her off, wanting to get rid of her, And she was so pregnant, Lily wondered if she wasn't already in labor.

"Hey," she cooed as the dog slowed cautiously, wariness in her eyes as she looked Lily up and down, deciding whether she was friend or enemy. Then she lurched forward.

With a quick intake of breath, Lily opened her arms.

The pregnant dog collapsed into her arms, nearly knocking her backward. Regaining her balance, she felt the dog trembling and whining pitifully.

"It's all right, all right, sweetie . . ." she whispered, moving her hand lightly over her black head, which had a white blaze down the center of it, her muzzle the same color. "You're all right now. Everything's going to be all right from here on out. . . ." Her voice strained as she slid her hand knowingly down the thick, dull-looking fur of her body. Tears filled Lily's eyes. The dog was horribly thin. Lily wanted to cry over her condition, but bit down on her lower lip to stop the reaction. The memory of Afghan children, their ribs prominent in their too-thin bodies, slammed into her as well.

"I have to give you a name," she said, the dog studying her intently, as if begging her silently for help. Lily swore she could see desperate pleading in her beautiful blue eyes. "How about Sage?" Because there was a lot of this plant in dry areas of Wyoming. She felt the dog trembling more and she whispered, "Okay, hold on. . . . I'm going to carry you to the truck and take you home with me." She was a medium-size dog and should weigh around fifty pounds. Lily grew scared as she pushed to her feet, the dog in her arms. Sage was probably no more than forty pounds at present. Pregnant, starving and alone. As she came to the passenger side, she knelt and allowed the dog to lie on the gravel at her feet for a moment, so she could open the door. Sage was too exhausted to stand any longer. She lay unmoving, panting heavily.

Urgency thrummed through Lily. Lifting the dog into the seat, she made sure she was as comfortable as she could be under the circumstances. Sage lay down, eyes closed, breathing heavily. Shutting the door as quietly as possible, Lily hurried around the front of the vehicle and climbed in. Knowing Jake wouldn't be home until six, her mind raced as she put the truck in gear, checked for traffic, which was nonexistent, and drove back onto the empty road. Patting her gently on the shoulder, she said in a choked tone, "I'm taking you home, Sage. Just hang on. . . ."

July 6

"Jenna," Lily called urgently, breathless as she opened the door to the cabin, "I have a very sick, very pregnant dog with me."

Jenna, who was setting the kitchen table, raised her brows. Because of her own medical condition, she still couldn't move fast. But she could keep the door open for Lily, who had turned around, hurrying toward the porch steps. She came back carrying the black-and-white dog in her arms just as Jenna reached the entrance.

"She's starved and very weak," Lily explained, taking her into the living room, gently placing her on the leather couch.

"What can I do?" Jenna asked, shutting the door.

"Can you stay with her? I'm calling her Sage. She's very close to having puppies. I think she might be in labor." Turning, she saw Jenna coming toward her, worry on her face.

"Go," she said, waving. "I'll stay with Sage."

"I'll get her some water first," Lily said, more to herself than Jenna, hurrying past her. "I think she just needs some loving company right now."

Jenna went over, leaning down, gently petting Sage's head. The dog's brushy tail beat once with thanks for her kindness. "I'll give her all the loving she wants."

Lily grabbed a bowl and put some fresh water in it, balancing it and trying not to spill it as she hurried into the living room. She handed it to Jenna, who had brought over a chair and was sitting next to Sage, talking soothingly to her. "Here. Hold the bowl down and see if she wants to drink. I'm going to find an old blanket or something to place under her. She's so dirty. She needs a bath."

"Yes, go ahead." The moment Jenna placed the bowl of water near Sage, she lifted her head and plunged her muzzle into it, gulping the liquid, droplets flying all over. "Oh, you poor dog," she whispered.

Lily discovered an old blanket in the closet of her bedroom. The dark green polyester had seen much better days but was perfect for her purposes. Gripping it, she hurried back to the living room. Sage had drunk all the water in the bowl. Her muzzle was dripping. She was probably weak from thirst, for starters. With Jenna's help, they carefully placed the blanket beneath Sage's body. Lily may have been imagining it, but she thought the dog's eyes didn't seem as dull as before. In no time, she was back with a second bowl of water and handed it to Jenna. Again, Sage eagerly gulped down the liquid until the container was empty.

"She's so thirsty," Jenna said worriedly, moving her hand across her back. "I can feel her entire backbone. She was slowly starving to death, Lily."

"I know. And she's bursting with puppies."

"Look, her nipples are leaking," Jenna said. "Sage is close to birthing."

Lily moved to the kitchen. "I think the only thing that could give her some energy is maybe chicken broth. She's too thin to eat a lot of food. She'll just throw it right back up."

"Agreed," Jenna called over her shoulder. "Where did you find her?"

Lily told her the story, opening a can of soup, separating the noodles from the broth. She warmed up the liquid just a little in the microwave, then placed it in another bowl. Kneeling near the dog's head, she said, "Let's see if she'll drink this broth . . ." and held her breath.

Just the scent made Sage lift her head, now a bit stronger because the water was infusing her body. With a grateful look up at Lily, she began lapping up the chicken broth. In no time, it was gone, and she was looking for more.

"How many more cans of soup do you have?" Jenna asked, her hand comforting on Sage's shoulder.

"I don't know," Lily admitted, worried. "Stay with her.

I'll go look in the pantry. That's where most of the canned goods are stored."

"Great idea!" Jenna laughed a little. "Look, Sage is more alert. She's watching that bowl in your hands as if she hopes there's more where that came from."

Thrilled, Lily stood up and hurried through the kitchen to the pantry. To her relief, she found four more cans of chicken soup. There seemed to be four of everything, and she silently thanked Jake for stocking up. Carrying the cans in her arms, she moved to the can opener on the counter. "Found four, Jenna!" she called, excited.

"Oh, wonderful! Sage's eyes are looking better, Lily. She's able to keep her head up."

"All good news," Lily said, smiling. Losing track of time, with Jenna's help, she fed Sage all four cans of chicken broth.

"I think that's enough for now. Her digestive system is probably pretty overwhelmed at this point. It's going to take it a bit of time to come back online."

"You learned this broth trick at the shelter?" Jenna asked.

"Yes." She chewed on her lip. "I really need to get the vet, Dr. Sharp, out here."

"Give her a call," Jenna urged. "Or should you drive into Wind River with Sage? Take her to her office?"

Glancing at her watch, she said, "Dr. Sharp closes her clinic at five, but I have her home phone number. I'm going to call her. I'm almost positive Sage is in labor and I don't want to move her around anymore than necessary. I need the doctor's help and guidance in this."

Jenna nodded. "Call her. I'll keep Sage company."

Hurrying to the kitchen phone, Lily made the call. As she stood waiting, she looked at the clock on the wall. It was nearly six. What was Jake going to think of her bringing this poor dog into his home? Would he be upset? Lily wasn't sure, but she hoped he wouldn't be.

Jake was mystified as the town's vet, Ann Sharp, drove up to the parking area just as he got out of his truck. He was fifteen minutes late.

"Hey Ann, good to see you," he called. She was in her early thirties, a widow; her husband, Jack, died of a heart attack two years earlier. He saw her smile and she waved in his direction.

"Jake, I could use your help."

Frowning, he nodded and walked over to her vet rig, a truck and cab designed for animal house calls. "Sure. What are you doing here?"

"Lily found a starving stray dog on the highway coming home tonight," the redhead explained, opening the back doors. She pulled out a very large willow basket and two sterile plastic liners. "The dog is close to labor."

"Oh," Jake said, stunned.

"Lily called and told me everything," Ann said, grabbing her vet bag, then shutting the doors. "Come on, follow me in."

He met her friendly smile, his arms filled with the large wicker basket. "Lead the way, Doc."

Laughing, Ann mounted the steps quickly and knocked on the door.

Lily answered it. "Thanks for coming," she said, stepping aside. She saw Jake and the quizzical look on his face. "Jake . . ."

"I hear you're helping a stray pregnant dog," he teased drily, walking into the cabin. He saw his mother sitting next to where the dog lay on the couch and he lifted his hand in greeting to her.

Lily shut the door and took the white liners off his arms, following Ann down the stairs. "I hope you're not upset I picked her up."

Shrugging, he placed the basket near where Jenna was sitting with Sage, who was now panting heavily. "No, it's okay."

Ann smiled at Jenna and introduced herself. Jenna slowly rose, and Lily placed her hand beneath her elbow, guiding her to a nearby overstuffed chair. Jake stood there, assessing the dog, who was now lying on her side. She was a prettily marked dog, black and white, her brows above her eyes a golden-brown color. There was a lot going on. When Lily returned, he remained out of the way to allow the women to work together. Ann had her stethoscope on and was listening to Sage's heart, and then checked her milk-swollen nipples. In the meantime, she directed Lily to place a piece of plastic in the wicker basket to make a nest. They would transfer Sage there.

Ann straightened. "Jake? Can you put the basket in that corner?" and she pointed to a dimly lit area off to one side of the room. "She'll feel better, safer, if she's in a quiet, out-of-the-way area. She's going to start birthing a puppy about every half hour."

Jake nodded. "Sure can."

"How many puppies do you think she'll have?" Lily asked as she watched Jake carry the basket to the corner. He had dried mud splatters on the jeans that hugged his long, hard thighs and lower legs. He had a quiet, controlled power about him, and she felt he was just as excited as they were about Sage bringing her puppies into the world.

"I palpated six of them, but there could be more," Ann said.

"Six," Lily whispered. "And they're going to need every bit of nutrition Sage has."

"She's been on her own for a long time and running on dry," Ann cautioned, looping the stethoscope around her neck. "Have you fed her anything yet?"

"Chicken broth," Lily explained, pointing to the five open cans sitting on the kitchen counter.

"Good call," Ann praised. "Sage is in very poor shape. I want you to keep offering water to her every half hour. I don't think we can give her bits of chicken right now, but maybe later. I'll have to monitor her as she births her pups."

"We have some leftover baked chicken," Jenna said, pointing toward the fridge. "I'll pull it out and shred it so she can eat some later."

"Great," Ann said. She smiled and nodded her thanks to Jake, who had set the basket on the floor. "I think she'll feel less exposed there."

In the next five minutes, Lily picked up Sage and transferred her to the long, oval basket after Jake scooped up the green blanket and placed it inside. She settled the mother dog into it. She had plenty of room and appeared to be comfortable. Jake then retrieved two wooden stools so no one had to kneel on the floor to give the dog water or keep her company. Jenna went to serve everyone dinner. Lily wanted to remain with Sage, who licked her hand, her blue eyes filled with adoration. She felt such a strong kinship with the dog.

Jake excused himself, then, and went up to his bedroom to take a shower and get a change of clothes. When he came back down, the mouthwatering scent of turkey sausage and broccoli pasta filled the air. Even Sage lifted her nose, sniffing the yummy scent. Lily continued to pet the dog and murmur soothing sounds to her. Ann was filling her plate from the steaming casserole and so was Jake.

The vet had said it could be any time for the first puppy to arrive. She was so excited.

"Hey," Jake called softly, offering her a plate, "you need to eat, too. Take this. You can eat here if you want." He handed her flatware and a napkin.

Surprised, she took the white plate and smiled up at him. "Thank you." She saw something in his green eyes but couldn't decipher it, except that it made her feel warm and cared for. "Are you upset I brought her home?" she asked.

"No." He straightened and moved aside as Ann came over and made herself comfortable on the other stool, near Sage's tail. "I'd expect you to do this. You have a soft heart."

Nodding, she choked out, "This reminds me so much of the Afghan villages I tended, the kids, the mothers . . ."

"Did you care for animals, too?" Jake asked, holding her watery gaze.

"Yes . . . sometimes. There were always dogs around, and they were just as thin and scrawny as Sage here."

"Seeing her brought it all back?"

She pushed her fork around in the pasta, the bright red peppers a contrast to the broccoli. "A lot . . ." and that was all she could say.

Leaning down, he rested his hand on her shoulder for a moment. "It's all right. I'm here if you need me or want to talk about it at any time."

Lily gave a jerky nod, unable to meet his gaze. She lamented him removing his large, warm hand from her shoulder. Jake's compassion was surprising now because he usually was so brusque and unavailable. But not now. He must have a soft heart for dogs, just like all the women did, and that pleased her.

"I'm going to join Jenna at the table and keep her company. If you need anything else, let me know."

Swallowing hard at his gentleness and understanding, Lily fought back tears. "Y–yes . . ."

Jake forced himself to move away. He knew animals of any kind liked to be left alone when birthing. As he walked across the shining wood floor, he knew Sage was comforted by Lily and Ann's presence beside her. He knew a lot about animal birthing and Sage was in good hands with those two ladies.

He didn't want to be moved emotionally by how hopeful and happy Lily looked right now. Animals made her happy, that was for sure. All three women were excited about the coming of the puppies. Hell, so was he. Sage was a pretty-looking dog, and it bothered him greatly that someone had dumped her to die. Wyoming wasn't a kind place to animals anyway. With snow eight or nine months out of the year, many didn't survive.

"This is so exciting!" Jenna said as he filled his plate.

He smiled a little. "We go from no dogs to seven?" His mother glowed.

"No one can ignore a puppy, Jake. They're just so darned cute. You'll love them, too!"

He chewed his food, his eye on Lily and Ann for a moment, and then he devoted his full attention to Jenna. "We don't even have a dog kennel built."

"Well, Son, when you were barely three years old we had a beautiful black Lab, Susie. I don't think you remember her, do you?"

"Vaguely," Jake admitted, taking a piece of garlic toast that had been slathered with butter.

"Susie had ten pups! And at six weeks old, we sold every one of them because she'd been bred to a champion black Labrador. But in the six weeks the pups were opening their eyes, getting to know their world and getting acquainted with humans"—she tapped his lower arm smartly, a gleam in her eyes—"we used to set you in with Susie in the laundry room and those puppies would just love you to death! You loved them, too, and you were so happy to be with them."

"I don't remember."

Jenna chuckled and squeezed his hand. "Well, you're going to get your chance to remember that time again."

Chapter Thirteen

July 6

Jake stayed out of the way, but he was just as emotionally invested as the women who sat around the wicker basket, tending to the dog. Ann Sharp had been right about the weakened Border collie needing human help to birth her pups. Ann had brought everything she needed, and he'd helped her bring in those items from her van. By nine p.m., Sage had birthed six puppies.

He hung around the edges, listening to the soft but excited voices of the women, the whispers showering Sage with love and praise. Ann took each puppy as it was born and cleaned it off because the mother was simply too weak to do it herself. Then, she passed the puppy to Jenna to dry it off, and she gave it to Lily, who placed it in front of the mother's nose. Sage would sniff, lick and nuzzle her offspring. Then Jenna would pick up the baby and place her at one of the dog's milk-swollen nipples. Even though Sage was exhausted, the puppies were in a relatively healthy state, according to Ann. None of the puppies were fat. Indeed, Ann noted they were all about a third less in weight than was normal for their breed, but that was due to the starvation of the mother.

Jenna turned and looked over at Jake where he sat in a nearby chair. "Jake? Come take my place. My leg is aching, and I need to get out of this position."

Rising, he went over and helped his mother stand. She was growing stiff from being in one position on that short wooden stool for hours. Jenna looked down at her watch.

"Hey, ladies, I need to get myself ready for bed. I'm tuckered out."

Lily nodded. "Do you want some help?"

"No, I'm fine. I'll ask Jake to be my crutch and take me to my room. Then, he can come back and take my place."

Jake saw Lily beam at that suggestion. It made him feel good. "If you want me," he told the vet.

"Of course we do!" Ann said. "There isn't a human being alive who doesn't want to be around just-born, wriggly, happy puppies."

He couldn't deny that. Jenna said good night to everyone and nudged him toward the hall. He cut his stride a lot because she was slow, and he could see she had stiffened up. "Maybe a hot shower?" he asked her as they walked.

"I think so. I was getting good at climbing into and out of the tub for a bath, but my leg is too stiff to do anything like that tonight."

"Do you want Lily to help you when you shower?" he wondered. Usually, he had nothing to do with their nightly routine. More often than not, he was in the living room reading the news on his iPad before going to bed at around ten.

"No, I'm fine, Jake. Just getting tired," and she gave him a kind glance. "Age."

"Glad I'm not there yet," he teased, opening the bedroom door for her.

"It happens to all of us," she promised. "Thanks. Good

night," and she squeezed his hand. "Go keep Lily company. She's enthralled with the puppies. And I know you are, too."

Jake nodded and left, wondering how his mother knew that. He certainly hadn't broadcasted it, though he'd learned a long time ago that women had this all-terrain radar, picking up stuff he never thought about. Smiling slightly, he headed to the living room. He liked that Ann had taught Lily how to help a dog give birth and take care of the puppies afterward. His gaze fastened on Lily's profile as she gently used her index finger, touching each wriggly puppy, worrying the nipple they had chosen to drink from.

"Come," Lily called, "sit with us. Ann will give you latex gloves to wear."

Ann handed him a pair. After he struggled into them, she gave him a dry white towel. "Your job is to dry the next puppy. When you're done, pass it on to Lily so Sage can smell her new baby, welcome it into the world and lick it hello. That's the bonding moment."

He sat on the small stool and got comfortable. Lily was about six inches away from him. Unable to get enough of absorbing the joy radiating from her face, her cheeks pink, her blue eyes sparkling, he wished for a deeper connection with her. Tonight certainly wasn't it, but he wanted quiet, personal time with her.

"Oh, here comes number seven!" Ann said, pleased, her gloved hand catching the next baby.

Lily made happy sounds. "This one is butterscotch and white," she said. "That makes three of that color, one mixed and the rest black and white like Sage."

"I'm positive she was bred to another Border collie," Ann said, working quickly to remove the sac and examining the squirming pup. "This makes four females and three males. And I'll bet the daddy was this same color. Here you go, Jake," and she placed the puppy in his waiting cupped hands, the towel across them.

"Thanks," he rumbled. His hands were so large and the puppy so tiny in comparison. This wriggling little tyke, gleaming wet, was making grunting sounds and moving around, its eyes closed. It made Jake smile. He carefully and gently wiped the puppy off. Handing it to Lily, he asked, "Have you named all of them yet?"

Lily giggled and took the baby. "Oh, heavens no! I want to watch them for a few days, maybe a week, before we start giving them names." She placed the baby in front of Sage's nose. They had continued to give her water and Jenna had hand-fed her some chicken earlier, which she'd gobbled down. Ann wanted the dog to have only a little bit of food. Her digestive system wasn't ready for a large meal after being starved for so long. An hour ago, Lily had given her more chicken broth because Jake had located two more cans for her in the pantry. Sage was able to give her puppies milk and she would lie exhausted between each birth, spread out on her side, relaxed and no longer panting heavily. She was so glad Ann was here to tell them how Sage was doing.

"You're a good mom," Jake told her, holding her gaze.

Feeling heat rush to her cheeks, Lily avoided his gaze, feeling how vulnerable he was becoming. Birth had a funny way of stripping everyone's mask away and allowing their hearts to shine instead. "I guess it just comes naturally," she said, watching Sage lift her head and lick her baby from stem to stern. "Isn't this a wonderful moment? I loved helping the women in labor in Afghanistan. They had midwives who knew so much about pregnancy and labor. I always marveled when a baby would take that first breath of air into her or his lungs. It was such a rush."

"Do you get a rush with each puppy being born?"

"I do." She took the newly welcomed puppy and placed

it down on the soft green blanket and guided its small mouth to an awaiting nipple. She straightened, watching the baby latch on and suck mightily. Sage lay there, her eyes closed, dozing. "Does this affect you, Jake?"

"Sure. It's a special time." He tried not to allow his gaze to linger on her softly curved lips. Lately, his last thoughts as he fell into sleep were about kissing Lily. Imagining how her mouth would feel beneath his, if she fit his mouth as perfectly as he thought she might. And other sultrier thoughts he'd never share with anyone. Lily was quietly sexy. Jake had tried to quantify the womanly charisma that called to him. She was never a flirt. And her clothes always covered her body, never revealing much skin at all. He wondered if that was because of her experience in Afghanistan, or if she was just an introvert who didn't fit into the overloaded world of extroverts, some who bared their bodies proudly, without apology. Maybe he was a prude, but there was something sensual and exciting about a woman fully clothed, allowing him to undress her one piece at a time.

Ann stood up and gently examined Sage's abdomen, which was now flabby, no longer looking like an overfilled balloon. "I think she's done. I don't feel any more babies inside her."

Lily saw it was midnight. "Why don't you go home, then, Ann? You've had an awfully long day and night."

Snapping off the gloves, Ann dropped them in a plastic bag for refuse. "I think I'll do that."

"Is there anything I need to do for Sage?"

"She'll probably want to get up soon and go outside to pee. Maybe poop. You should go with her."

"Do you think she has the strength to walk out there or should I carry her?"

Ann laughed softly. "She just birthed seven healthy pups. She's stronger than you think. I'd put a leash on her and let her pick the pace. This place is strange for her and she knows you, so she'll probably feel secure in your presence. I think if you stay with her and let her wander around as she wants to do her thing, things will turn out just fine."

"What about later?"

"After she comes in? Give her about half a cup of chicken. That will continue to strengthen her and keep nudging her dormant digestion back to life. I'd put a big bowl of water next to her bed so she can drink throughout the night."

"Will you be around tomorrow in case I have a question or something?"

Ann grabbed her jacket off the arm of the chair. "Sure. Call me anytime, at the clinic or at home. What's important is that Sage begin to lick and potty them. If she doesn't do that, let me know early, because you might have to do it for her if she's too weak."

Wrinkling her nose, Lily said, "I sure hope she's up to doing it."

Snickering, Ann closed her vet bag and stood up. "Sage is probably about three years old by my guesstimate. She's young and strong, despite being starved. She has heart. My bet is that a good night's sleep, drinking water and getting some food in her belly will make her a lot stronger tomorrow morning and she'll take care of her pups."

"I'll walk you to your van," Jake said, rising.

"Sounds good." Ann came over and patted Lily's shoulder. "You were terrific and so was Jenna. We did good! It's a happy ending for Sage."

Jake came in and saw Lily down on her knees, gently sliding her hand along Sage's back. The dog's fur was in terrible shape, scruffy, dirty and stiff with lack of care. He came over to the basket, remembering to always come at an angle where Lily could see him coming. She lifted her chin and smiled up at him.

"Do you want to trade places? It's so nice to be able to lay my hands across all the puppies. They're dry, their fur so silky smooth. They're so adorable."

He knelt, keeping some room between them. He might want many things from her, but he wasn't going to let her know that. At least not yet. "They're so tiny."

"Yes, but so alive, wriggling, pushing and eating." She straightened, her hands coming to rest on her thighs. "What a day. What a night. Did you get enough for dinner? Did Jenna?"

"Yes," he said. "Did you?" and he searched her eyes, which were filled with happiness, yet he sensed how tired she was becoming.

"Absolutely." She gently rubbed Sage's inner ear. The dog groaned with pleasure, her eyes barely opening. "It's past midnight. Everything has happened so fast."

"How are you doing?" he asked, trailing an index finger down the multicolored puppy's back.

"Tired but happy."

"Did this whole thing become a flashback for you?" and he held her gaze.

Pursing her lips for a moment, she sighed. "At first I was afraid the blood and other fluids would trigger me. But for whatever reason, they didn't. I was so glad," and she pushed some strands of her hair behind her ear.

"Me too. I was watching you for reaction."

She studied him. "I think you're slowly becoming my big, bad guard dog. Or am I wrong?"

It was his turn to feel uncomfortable, and he pushed his hands down the thighs of his chinos. "I guess one good thing about having the same symptoms is that we know what to look for in the other person. I don't know what I'd do, but I think both of us would try to be a support to the other if it happened."

She nodded and stroked the youngest puppy. "I'm so glad I found Sage. Somehow," and she shrugged a little, "tonight has been a miracle for me."

"How so?" he asked, hungry to have this alone time with her.

Leaning over, she gently touched each puppy's fur, watching each wriggle in reaction. "I feel so at peace. I can't explain it. My anxiety is gone. It hasn't happened at all since I saw Sage on the highway. Sometimes I'll get a half a day with no anxiety. I don't know what makes it go away, but it always comes back. I had low-level anxiety driving home, but after I saw Sage, it disappeared." She made a worried expression. "I'm sure it will be back."

"Maybe less so," he murmured, watching her eyes grow shadowed. Lily was always in contact with either Sage or her puppies. Her gesture was always graceful, her long fingers reminding him of a dancer's. "Being home for three years, my anxiety has gotten a lot better. Maybe fifty percent."

"What do you think dialed it back?"

Shrugging, he gently touched the black-and-white pup on the end. "It seems getting back to nature, working around the animals, especially the horses, helped me a lot."

"The way Checkers calms me," she said, nodding.

"I can see the tension in your face dissolve when you're working around him or riding him," Jake said. He saw surprise flare in her eyes. "I used to be a recon Marine," he reminded her. "We have a knack of seeing very small details, so I'm more observant than most people."

She touched her cheek. "Looks like I can't hide anything from you." She said it part in jest, but also with a bit of chagrin.

He held up a hand. "I promise never to use it against you."

"You don't strike me as the type to do that to anyone, Jake. You're not a mean person."

His heart swelled over her quietly offered comment. He wanted to have Lily admire him in small, important ways, and this was one of them. "You've been around Jenna long enough to know my parents raised me right. My dad was my role model. He was kind, thoughtful and sensitive. I could go to him and ask about anything and not be embarrassed."

"And Jenna was a schoolteacher. You were lucky like me, Jake. We both have great parents. I'm really sorry your dad died so early in your life. Jenna has told me so much about him. I think she's still just as much in love with him as she was when he was alive."

Grunting, Jake said, "I never realized how much they loved each other until I got older. They had something very special. And yes, when my dad died, it took Jenna a full year to get back to teaching. It broke her in a lot of ways. And in some ways, she's never recovered."

"That's what she said," Lily offered quietly, seeing the pain in his eyes, missing his father even now. "I've never experienced that kind of love, I guess."

"Me neither." He gave her a wry look. "We're a pair, aren't we? Stoved in with PTSD, alone and kind of bad at social stuff."

She rubbed her brow. "Yes, I'm a hot mess. I admit it."

"Hey," he growled, reaching out, sliding his hand across her shoulders, "don't say that. Considering what you went through, and you've just moved back to civilian life, I'm amazed at your strength, Lily." He forced himself to pull his hand away. How badly he wanted to explore her, but he knew it wouldn't be right. Not now. More importantly, Lily needed to be held. How many nights had he wished for the warmth and softness of a woman in his bed, beside him? It wasn't about sex. It was about being held and comforted because of the war that was continually churning through his body and soul. Just to be held. How many times had he ached for human companionship? To have a woman's arms come around his body and simply hold him? Jake had lost count. He switched his focus to Lily, who'd seemed to perk up a bit when he'd gently slid his hand across her shoulders.

"I look at you, Jake, and I know you're three years into being a civilian with those symptoms. You give me hope because you don't seem to be as destabilized as I am."

He grunted. "Don't be fooled. I have my days; it's just that as time wears on, I have less and less of them. You're in your first year, and not only do you have to grapple with the adjustment to being a civilian, you have these symptoms on your heels every day, without rest. It's really tough the first year, and I think you're doing fine. You're a strong person, whether you realize it or not."

It was her turn to grimace. "I don't feel strong at all. There are so many things that stop me from finding work."

"Well," he soothed, "go talk to Maud about becoming her assistant. I'm sure she would like to know you're interested." And part of his reason was purely personal. He'd become used to having Lily in his life, in his cabin. She made it come to life with her little touches here and there.

Jake knew how anxious Lily was to find a job after Jenna recovered and went home to Casper. He wanted it just as badly for her. But he didn't like the idea of her leaving the cabin. How could he share that with her? What would she think of him for suggesting it? Lily would probably give him a fish-eyed look of wariness, and Jake didn't want her to think of him in that light. She looked up to him, admired and respected him. There was no way he wanted to diminish the way she saw him.

"I'll go to Maud's tomorrow," Lily promised, softly sliding her finger down the back of one of the puppies. She switched subjects. "Are you okay with Sage and her babies being here in the house for now? I think if we could stabilize her and get some meat on her bones, they'll be better off before I take them to the shelter in Wind River."

"Is that what you want to do?" He'd seen sadness in her eyes and heard it in her voice as she asked him.

"Well," she whispered unsteadily, "not really, but this isn't my house. I work here. I need to have a plan for Sage. It's up to you, Jake."

He could feel her wanting the mother and puppies here. Maybe that was his ace in the hole. "What would you think of being a sort of babysitter for them? You could keep them here. I could have some of the wranglers create a nice pen outside for when they get older, make some doghouses for them to sleep in, and you could raise them. They're going to need human handling and I'm out in the field all day. You could stay here and train them, get them used to being around people. Would you like to do that?"

She stared at him. "Are you serious?"

"Sure. I like dogs. I don't want to see them suffer any more than you do. I have the space inside and outside. It wouldn't take much to create safe areas for them as they grow. What do you think?"

Never had Jake wanted anyone to say yes more than right then. He tried to appear nonchalant, as if it didn't matter one way or another if Lily decided to leave and take the dogs with her. "I would pay you to do it. I'm sure Maud would hire you as her assistant, too. I wouldn't expect you to take care of them after you quit work for the day."

"You mean, live here? Stay here and raise the puppies until they were of an age to be given to good homes?"

"Yeah," he said, "something like that. They need human help and guidance. I can't give them anything except a roof over their heads, food and vet care. You have a nice way with animals, Lily. I know you love Sage and her puppies."

He refused to feel guilty about corralling her into this new job that would keep her at the cabin. Keep her close to him, even though he didn't really know why. Jake knew he was a hard bastard. Not a mean one. Just unavailable in a warm, human sense. She didn't know it was due to his symptoms, but he knew she was right. Would this extra time help him become available to Lily? To show her the sides of himself that he hid? And what would she think? Puppies were whelped and usually ready to be given away at six to eight weeks. That would give him another two months with Lily under his roof. He saw her thinking about his offer. Inwardly, he was holding his breath. What would she say? Would she stay or go?

Chapter Fourteen

July 7

Lily's heart was pounding in her chest, and she wondered if Jake could hear it. Barely believing her ears, she studied his hard, unreadable features. "You wouldn't mind? I mean, if Maud will hire me as her assistant, you'd let me rent a bedroom here and take care of Sage?"

She tried to ignore her growing feelings for Jake. Being around him this long, despite his hard outer shell, she was discovering more and more about him every day. He was a kind man who cared deeply. She could see the pleasure come to his eyes as he watched the puppies nursing.

Swallowing hard, she said, "I could pay you rent for the room."

"No," he growled, shaking his head, "the room, the food and everything you have here now is part of the deal. I'll pay you to take care of Sage and raise her puppies. That's probably two more months here."

She stroked Sage's head. She lay with her eyes closed, but Lily knew she needed affection and attention right now. "I'd love to do that, Jake, but you don't need to pay me to help Sage. I'd do it for free."

"I know that," he rumbled, "but you need to start saving money to build a nest egg for your future. This would be a way to do it. I'm fine with you not paying rent. If I could trade for you making me dinner at night, that would be fair. Maud has her housekeepers come over here once a week, as you know, to clean the place. So it isn't something I'd expect you to do."

"What if Maud doesn't think I'm right for the position, Jake?"

"I'd still want you to stay here and take care of Sage."

Drawing in a ragged breath, she said, "I'd like to, Jake." She laid her hand on several of the puppies, who were now curling up, tummies full and sleeping. "I'll take you up on your offer. Thank you . . ."

Hope bolted through Jake as he saw a sheen of tears come to her eyes. And then she swallowed and looked away, fighting them back. "Sounds good," he murmured. "We can make this work. It will be good for everyone." In some ways, he felt like a thief, stealing the time to be with Lily but not letting on why he wanted her to stay with him. Jake knew she wasn't looking for a relationship. Lily was trying to survive, to adjust back into civilian life.

She reached out, touching his lower arm. "Thank you for being there for all of us. It means a lot to me. . . ."

Lily tried to tamp down her anxiety as she took the steps up to Maud's office on the crisp, clear morning. It was nearly ten, and she'd called earlier to make the appointment. She had finished helping Jenna with her morning exercises at nine. She was almost well enough to go home. Lily would miss Jenna when that day came.

"Hey," Maud called from inside the office, "come on in, Lily."

"Hi," she said tentatively, shutting the door behind

her. In the summer, it was cool and in the forties in the morning. There was heat on in the office and it felt good. "I'm here for the interview."

Maud stood and gestured toward her inner office at the end of the hall. "Come on in. Want some coffee?"

"No, thank you. I just finished breakfast with Jenna." Besides, her stomach was so tight with fear that Maud wouldn't think she would measure up for the job that Lily was battling nausea. She got that way whenever something important to her hung in the balance. It was as if her old self, who had the capacity to put such moments into context, had been lost. Now she had this awful reaction in moments of severe stress. She had trained herself to appear calm outwardly, but she was far from feeling that way inside. Maud pulled up a chair beside her desk as they walked into the small office at the far end of the building. She quietly closed the door once Lily had entered. "Have a seat," she invited, sitting down at her desk. "And relax, will you? This isn't going to be the Inquisition," she teased, giving her a concerned look.

Sitting, her purse on her lap, her hands tight around it, Lily said, "I'm a little nervous."

"It's okay, don't worry about it," Maud said, gathering up some papers. "Here, I'd like you to look at these. My assistant, Helen, handles these sorts of things all the time and so would you. She has free rein to make them her own, and I'd like you to do that, too. Jake said you're the most responsible person he's ever met. Jenna sings your praises. I think you'd be perfect for this job, but you have to know what's involved. Okay?"

Heartened, Lily took the sheaf of papers, feeling marginally better. Her stomach stopped roiling. "Yes, okay."

"Take a moment to look through them. Your job here would involve typing, keeping my files in alphabetical order, answering the phone, faxing stuff, and making

reservations for the tourists who stay with us." She gestured
to her right, where there were five-foot-tall dark green
metal file drawers against one wall of the office. "Steve
wants me to move into the twenty-first century and put all
those files and their information on a computer, but I don't
trust the internet. They get hacked, and I don't like the idea
of our employees or tourists having their private information for sale on the Dark Web. So I do everything the
old-fashioned way, like before computers and the internet
came into being."

"I don't blame you," Lily said, slowly perusing each
paper. "This looks pretty straightforward to me, Maud."

"You'd also be the first person tourists meet when they
come to get the keys to their cabins. Are you comfortable
with that, Lily? With working with small groups of
people?"

"Sure. There's nothing here I can't handle."

Sitting back in her black leather chair, Maud studied her
for a moment. "Good. As my assistant, you'll do a little of
everything."

"I get bored easily, so this would be a great job for me.
I like variety."

Smiling, Maud said, "I spoke to Jake earlier this morning. He told me how you rescued a starving dog along the
highway, that she had seven puppies last night."

Coloring, Lily felt heat stealing up her neck and into her
face. "Oh . . . that. Well, I love my volunteer work at the
shelter. I couldn't let a poor, starving dog just keep walking
on the shoulder of the highway. I was so relieved when
Jake said it was okay to let them grow up at his place until
they're old enough to be given away to good homes."

"Yes, he was telling me that he's going to pay you to
care for them. I was going to offer you one of our employee houses, but he told me you were willing to remain
at his cabin and care for them until then."

"It's the best of many worlds," Lily said. "I love babies of any kind and I grew up with a dog, like Jake did. I was shocked at his offer, but I was so relieved he wanted me to help him with Sage. I wasn't sure how he'd feel about me bringing home a pregnant, stray dog."

"Well, as foreman, he's people-centric" Maud said drily. "I know he appears hard and unreadable, but he's got a big heart, compassionate, which is why he's been a superior manager for our ranch hands. They love him because he's fair-minded, he doesn't expect perfection from anyone and he's got everyone's back. Which is typical of anyone who has been in the military. The downside is that he's not at home very much. He puts in fourteen-hour days during the summer, always out working with his wranglers."

"I know."

"He's a good man."

Nodding, Lily wanted to say more, but she resisted because what she wanted to say was personal.

"Do you want the job, Lily? You're a known quality here on the ranch and Jake has vouched for you. You'll work five days a week from nine a.m. to four p.m. Weekends off. I pay my people well because I want them to know we value them and their contribution. I'll start you out at sixty thousand dollars a year. You'll be the hub of the ranch here, so your responsibilities will be important, many and we can't function without someone like you as the rudder to our ship. What do you say?"

Stunned, she stared at Maud. "Sixty thousand dollars?" she whispered.

"Yes. With yearly raises. You'll have a comprehensive health insurance plan, too. The best in Wyoming. And if you remain in the job for five years, we'll offer you a cabin package and five acres of your choice on the ranch. What do you say?"

For a moment, Lily felt as if her broken, fragile reality

had fallen over a cliff and, instead, she'd found herself in the middle of a fabulous dream. She put down the sheaf of papers on Maud's large, rectangular bird's-eye maple desk. "I'd love to take the job."

Nodding, Maud said, "Good. Helen is at the dentist in Wind River right now, but she'll be here at one this afternoon and will start training you for the next two weeks, before she retires. You'll know how everything operates so we have a seamless transition. And as you know, we all dress down around here. We're a working ranch. You wear what you want, but it doesn't have to be fancy. No heels. Those things are horrible for women's feet. Wear simple, comfortable shoes, Lily. I don't care if you wear cowboy duds or not. Okay?"

"Okay," she said, disbelief in her voice. "I'll be here at one to start training."

Maud sat up in her chair. "Good. Maybe Jake should take you out to Kassie's for dinner to celebrate your new job."

It was nearly six when Lily returned home. The first thing she did was feed Sage, then take her outside. The dog remained at her side as they stepped out on the porch. Her babies had been fed and were sleeping in small piles here and there in the wicker basket. Lily made a gesture with her hand and Sage bounded off the porch, loping toward the pond to do her business. She saw Jake's truck in the distance, a rooster tail of dust rising in its wake as he drove down the dirt road, coming toward the cabin.

Standing there, Lily watched with joy as Sage, who was much stronger now, sniffed here and there, squatted to pee and then followed a few more scents into the lush grass around the edge of the pond before trotting back toward the cabin and her.

Jake slowed as he came through the entrance, spotting

Sage, who was moving to where Lily was standing. He parked and shut off the truck engine, enjoying watching Lily smiling and leaning down to pet the scruffy, terribly thin dog. It struck him that this scene was something he'd dreamed about so many times when he was in the military. He'd ached for a life like his parents had: a house, happiness and laughter. He'd lost that dream as his symptoms overwhelmed him. Now, it seemed that dream might be possible because Lily had unexpectedly walked into his solitary and drab life. Still, Jake didn't dare put too much hope into the situation. But he wanted to. He slid out of the truck, taking a notebook with him, and shut the door. Turning, he raised his hand to Lily, who was waiting there, watching him.

She smiled and waved to him. His heart swelled with a quiet euphoria. When she smiled, it went straight to his soul. She had the sweetest smile, her lips perfectly shaped, as far as he was concerned. And that contagious smile of hers was always reflected in her sparkling blue eyes. She was a woman who wore her heart on her sleeve, like his mother did, and that called to him strongly. Lily was open, vulnerable and trusting. She wasn't the kind of person to put on airs or manipulate others. Jenna was the same way. What you saw was what you got. He liked the entire package, hoping against all hope that Lily might like him, might look at him as a long-term relationship possibility.

Sage wagged her tail at him in a friendly hello of her own as he ascended the stairs. Jake leaned down and patted her head.

"She's looking a lot better," he told Lily as he straightened.

"Ann said she'd bounce back and she was right. I gave her solid food this morning, and then more when I returned from seeing Maud. She's to get fed three times a day from now on."

He slid his hand to the small of Lily's back, guiding her toward the door. "How'd it go with Maud? Were you hired?"

Lily hungrily absorbed the momentary heat of his hand barely making contact with her back. It felt good. He dropped his hand almost as quickly as he'd rested it there as he came around her and opened the door for them.

Sage bounded in first, heading straight to her wicker basket to check on her brood, who were still sleeping soundly.

"She hired me. I worked with her assistant, Helen, from one to four p.m. I'll work with her every afternoon for the next two weeks to learn the routine of the office."

Jake hung his hat on a peg and shut the door. "Is it a job you think you'll enjoy?"

"Absolutely. Just getting to work around Maud, who's so easygoing, will reduce my stress level," Lily said, with emotion behind her words. "Jenna is taking a nap right now." She looked up at the clock on the kitchen wall. "We're going to eat in forty minutes. I'll wake her up while you're cleaning up."

"Good," he said, watching Sage as she nosed and licked her pups. Finished, she turned and came into the kitchen, claws clacking on the wooden floor as she made her way to a small niche near the pantry that Lily had set up as her eating station. He could hear Sage happily crunching dried kibble with relish. There was a large bowl of water nearby as well.

"I'll see you in a little bit."

"Okay."

Sage trotted up to her, licking Lily's hand, her eyes adoring and happy. Lily laughed softly, leaned over and ruffled her fur. "I'm going to give you another few days, then it's bath time for you!"

* * *

"Jake, I'm about ready to go home." Jenna sat at the kitchen table after dessert, a cup of coffee in her hands, giving her son a smile.

"Are you sure?" he asked, frowning. "It's only been five weeks."

Jenna shrugged. "With Lily's help, I've zoomed past all the standard medical expectations for healing even though I'm in my midsixties. I couldn't have asked for a better coach and caregiver."

"You miss your home, don't you?" Lily asked gently.

"Yes, very much. I love it here, I love to visit, but my life, my friends, everything I've done and do, are in Casper."

Giving her a nod, Jake said, "I understand. Has the doctor given you permission to go home?"

"Yes. A few days ago." Jenna smiled again. "And then Sage came into our lives and I just couldn't stand not being here to make sure she and her puppies would make it. And she will survive. Now, it's time for me to go home."

Lily saw different emotions flit across Jake's face. Having his mother here had been good for him. Over the weeks he'd softened, the mask he wore dissolved. Jenna had confided to her that now he was more like the old Jake she knew, from before he'd gone off to war. That had made Jenna happy, and Lily had seen the fears she had for her son ease greatly as a result. Jenna had confided that she knew something bad had happened to Jake in the military, but she could never get him to talk about it. Her worry had ebbed, however, the longer she'd remained with them. Yes, this had been a positive and healing time for all of them, herself included. Lily felt incredibly happy having these two people in her life.

Jake sipped his coffee. "We'll miss you, but I know you have a huge network of friends and charities you work with in Casper."

Jenna nodded. "Thanks for understanding. I hope I'm

still allowed to visit you once a year?" and she smiled over at him, giving him a teasing look.

Jake nodded. "You're always welcome here."

"Lily, would you help me pack later? I'd like to fly back to Casper tomorrow morning, if possible. One of my friends will pick me up at the airport and drive me home." The corners of her eyes crinkled. "Then you two can get on with your lives. And I'm so happy to hear you're staying here for Sage, Lily."

"I'm excited about helping her and her puppies," Lily said.

"I noticed," Jake said to his mother, "that you seemed to be drawn to one pup in particular. Do you want a dog back in your life?"

"You don't miss anything, do you?" Jenna baited her son. "I've fallen in love with that little yellow-and-white female. I've even given her a name: Butterscotch. She loves cuddling with me and whines when I put her down in the brood. When I pick her back up, she makes happy little sounds and doesn't want to be separated from me. I feel the same way about her."

"I know the one you mean," Lily said, smiling with her. "Maybe Jake and I could drive her over to you after she's weaned. Would you like that, Jenna?"

"Oh, I'd love that! Just being around these puppies brings so many good memories of Jake growing up with his dog. When Chet died so suddenly, I felt horribly alone. Thinking about that time, I realized if I'd had a dog to blunt some of that loneliness, I wouldn't have felt so depressed. I'd like to remedy that now. I believe in synchronicity, that things happen for a reason. Sage picked you to help her survive, Lily. And with your beautiful heart, you brought her here, to Jake's cabin. And he opened his heart to Sage as well." Her voice lowered with feeling. "Lily, you've been such a blessing to all of us, you truly have. I'm going to miss you as much as I'll miss Jake."

Hot tears welled up in Lily's eyes and she lowered her lashes as Jenna gripped her hand and gently squeezed it. Swallowing hard, she forced her reaction down, as she always did because if she didn't, she was afraid she'd never stop crying. And no one in the military wanted to see a woman sobbing, grief-stricken by her trauma. No, everyone jammed emotions down to do their job. She understood that, but now, as a civilian, especially the last weeks living with Jenna and Jake, her emotions were always rising, and she wasn't sure how to go about handling them. It had been so long since she'd cried. The only time she had was on that horrific night in the Afghan village.

"I'll miss you terribly, Jenna," she said, her voice a little wobbly.

"I'll be as close as your phone, Skype or an email, dear. Just because I'm leaving doesn't mean I'm losing touch with you. All right?"

"I've loved every moment here with you, Jenna. You're such a positive force in the world. I admire you so much. It sort of blunts my missing my mom and dad."

"Then it's a mutual admiration society, because I admire you equally. What we have in common is Jake," and she gave her son an affectionate pat on his arm.

Jake gave Lily a glance. "I like your idea of bringing Butterscotch to Jenna. We'll drive across Wyoming on a Friday, deliver that little puppy to you, Jenna, stay overnight and come home on Sunday. It will be something we'll all look forward to, if you're okay with that plan?"

Jenna sighed and smiled a little more. "That would be wonderful! I'll love seeing both of you and Butterscotch. Who would ever have thought my breaking my hip would turn out so well?"

Lily looked at how her own life had turned in a direction she'd never anticipated, much less thought would happen. She'd had her life mapped out, to be an RN in civilian life after twenty years in the military. It had all looked so smooth and doable. But life, as she well knew, had abrupt twists and turns no one could anticipate. And now she was surviving, barely holding on, trying to reclaim what she'd lost in Afghanistan. She didn't see any happily ever after for herself, still too mired in just surviving each day that faced her. "I wish I had some of your hopefulness, Jenna."

"You have it. I know you do. Sage and the puppies are starting to make nice changes in you, Lily. They'll continue. Trust me on that."

Giving Jake a quick glance, Lily knew it was both the mother and son who were infusing her, slowly but surely, with hope. And it felt good, even though it might come and go. Life was tenuous, but just feeling hope instead of that awful blackness was like sunlight on her barren soul. Jake fed her in one way, Jenna in another. "Well," she told Jenna, choking up, "you and Jake are blessings in my life I never thought possible."

Chapter Fifteen

July 16

Lily drew in her breath as she sat cross-legged in front of Sage's wicker basket. All the puppy's eyes were opening at ten days old! Everyone but her favorite, Athena. She was the runt, but Lily hoped they might open tomorrow.

Everything was ready for dinner, the cabin fragrant with the smell of a well-seasoned, garlic-laced marinara sauce. Jake would be here any minute now, and she was excited to share the news with him. Glad that Jenna was doing well at her home in Casper, she looked forward to keeping in touch with her via Skype and emails. It was nice to have her, plus her parents, to communicate with on a weekly basis. She'd missed doing that so much after being separated from the service.

The door opened. Looking up, she saw Jake give her a look of hello. More than anything, she loved the tender look that was there for her alone. They'd come so far on a quiet level with each other, neither of them talking about their growing closeness.

"Hey! Six of the puppy's eyes are opening! Come see!"

Jake crouched down beside her, leaving just a few inches

separating them. "Look at that," he murmured, awe in his voice. He picked up Athena. "Hers are still closed."

"I think it's because she's the runt. Maybe tomorrow, I hope." She thrilled to his gentleness with the puppies.

He put the squirming puppy into her awaiting hands. "Look at their eyes. Amazing," and he reached out, petting Sage, who responded by eagerly licking his hand. She lay with her puppies, her once-gaunt sides filling out more and more every day with good food and loving care.

"I know." Lily stroked Athena, who nestled happily between her breasts. "I can hardly wait to see what color hers are."

He glanced at her. "What do you wish for?"

"Blue eyes. That's just the most beautiful color." She sighed. Setting Athena back into the basket, she said, "Spaghetti and meatballs for dinner tonight. Toasted garlic bread. Sound good?"

Rising, Jake held out his hand to her. "Does it ever. You're spoiling me rotten."

Any reason to touch Jake was a good one for her. She slid her fingers into his and unwound from her sitting position. "Thanks," she said, not wanting to leave his warm, callused hand. She felt such a powerful pull toward him, she had to fight herself daily. "I need to get the garlic toast into the oven."

"I'll go grab a quick shower and be back down in a few."

Absorbing the quiet intimacy that always sprang between them, Lily had never felt happier. She missed Jenna terribly, but since she'd left, they'd had a chance to explore what they had together. Oh, it was never discussed, but it was there. Going to the counter, she took the cookie pan, where the bread was brushed with butter and garlic, and slid it into the heated oven. Everything seemed so perfect. She needed to talk to Jake about all of it. Lily was no longer willing to remain silent about what was happening between them.

"Something on your mind?" Jake coaxed as they finished their meal and had coffee afterward. "You look thoughtful." She sat at his right elbow, at the head of the table. He wanted Lily to know she deserved that place of honor.

"Yes. A lot, in fact. I'm not sure how you're going to take what I'm about to say, Jake, but there's been an undercurrent between us ever since I came to live in your home. I know men have a tough time speaking up, but we need to share how we really feel about each other. I can't make any serious decisions about my life until I know."

Leaning back in his chair, he studied her. Lily was allowing her hair to grow longer, and it was now beneath her ears, giving her a girlish look. "You're right," he acknowledged. "Let's talk, then. It's past time." There was fear and anxiety in the glance she gave him, but one of the many things he'd learned about her was that she'd challenge the fear, not let it stop her from moving forward. That was real courage, possessing an inner strength to plow through the gauntlet called life, in his opinion.

"Good," she whispered, clearly relieved. "I came here to do a job, not to become attracted to a man. I was mired in myself, swallowed up by my symptoms, on the edge of starvation, unable to keep a job because of them. On top of that, I was having a hard time adjusting to civilian life." Holding his gaze, she pressed on. "This could all be one-sided, and if it is, that's okay. I'll deal with it." Pushing her emptied coffee cup to one side, she clasped her hands on the table. "Jake, I'm drawn to you. At first, I wasn't even conscious of it. All I knew was that I felt safe and protected when you were around me and Jenna. After all I'd been through, that sensation felt so good. It anchored me, grounded me and allowed me the room to start to heal. It never occurred to me that you were interested in me at all. I accepted what was happening within me. Too much was going on for me to sit down and feel my way through it. But then, as the weeks passed, I slowly began to realize we had something going on between us." She shook her head, appearing stymied by it all. "I thought I was making it up at first. It couldn't be true, so I began to look for clues from you to prove it was just me being messed up inside my head, and I couldn't sort it out at that stage."

"To see if what you felt was mutual?"

She licked her lower lip, his gaze holding her. "Yes."

"It is, Lily."

She blinked. "Really? It's not just me?"

He managed a half shrug and gave her a wry look. "I wasn't looking for a relationship either. My focus was on my mother's health when you walked into our lives. I was drawn to you, but I brushed it off as me being lonely and not realizing it. I focused on my job and my mother. Later, it became pretty obvious to me that I was seriously attracted to you."

"Oh," she whispered, frowning. Opening her hands, she pushed some strands of hair from her cheek, her gaze darting away from his. "Then you weren't looking for someone in your life either?"

"No. The first two years here at the ranch were a special hell for me, and I wasn't about to get entangled in any serious relationship because of it. This third year, I started to feel as if I was coming out of a long, dark tunnel, feeling more stable and confident than ever before." He shared a look with her. "And then you walked into our lives."

"I guess it's mutual, then?" and she searched his dark

green eyes, her heart beating heavily in her chest, shock rolling through her.

"I think it is. How do you feel right now about us?"

"I'm in shock. I thought it was all one-sided."

A rumble went through his chest. "You're a brave woman, Lily. I've been trying to find a time and place to sit down and tell you how I feel about you, but it just didn't seem to happen." He gazed over at the wicker basket, where Sage was feeding her plump little puppies. "Like tonight? I had planned to do just that, but when I came in and the puppy's eyes were opening, I knew it wasn't the right time."

"Something is always cropping up in the evenings because of Sage and her babies," Lily agreed quietly. "I was trying to find a window of opportunity to discuss what was going on inside me. But I never could find an opening either. I guess . . . if I'm honest, I was afraid to bring it up. I thought you might get angry. Or worse, fire me. My mind goes crazy, shifts into hyperreaction, and I still haven't figured out a way to see through it to know the truth or reality. I hate the overemotional reactions I have to everything. I never used to be like this."

"I would never fire you, Lily. As for your hyper reactions, in time, you'll be able to tell the difference. You're less than six months out of the service, so don't be hard on yourself. And besides that, our focus was on Jenna," he murmured. "As it should have been."

Dipping her head, she said, "Thank you for letting me know that." Inhaling deeply, she continued in a soft voice, "So? Where does that put us with each other right now?"

"I guess we'll find out." Amused, Jake added, "Things were kind of growing between us even when we weren't really aware of it at first. Later, I guess we were both afraid to speak about it to each other. Fear of rejection has a big seat at our table."

"I don't want to go back into silence about this, Jake. I'm the kind of person who needs to share, to talk, to know what's going on within you, your thoughts, as well as sharing mine with you. I guess that's why I wanted to speak to you tonight. Fear of the unknown pushed me to open up."

"Fear?" He frowned.

Flattening her hands against the table, she nodded. "Look, as you said, I'm less than six months out of the service. I've got raging PTSD symptoms. I'm a hot mess, Jake. I know you've agreed with me on where I'm at in this cycle because of other conversations we've had. You've told me how your first year out of the Marines was hell on you, too." Her jaw tightened, eyes flashing with frustration. "I'm afraid of every day because I'm so broken. I'm afraid I won't be able to cobble myself back together. I try, and sometimes I feel a part of me starting to settle back into a familiar routine and I feel hope once more. But then, the next day or two, something happens, and I feel like I've taken two steps backward. I'm terrified I'll never get well. I'll never be normal again."

"That's the way healing goes, from what I can see," he offered quietly, holding her teary gaze. "What we've seen and suffered through makes for such a lonely inner journey. I know what you're saying. You're not alone, Lily. You have parents who love you. Jenna treats you like the daughter she always wished for and never had." A corner of his mouth tipped upward. "Until now." Reaching out, he took her hand, which was curved on her thigh, giving it a comforting squeeze and then releasing it. "And you have me. I can help you measure your progress because I've already been where you are. I want to give you hope because that's what I needed when I crawled through that first year alone."

Sniffing, she quickly wiped the tears from her eyes, afraid they would become a flood, and she didn't want that to happen. Not now. This conversation was too important. Too necessary. "And you have been an important part of my progress. I don't think I'd be where I am today without your experience and support. I loved having your mother here. I felt it an honor to care for her. Whether she knew it or not, she stabilized me in some ways, and that helped me. She gave me a more solid footing within myself."

"I felt lucky growing up with her and my father," he agreed. "Almost daily, I could see you were changing, becoming more confident about yourself. I know Jenna saw you were blooming right before our eyes." He managed a softened smile. "You've done a lot of healing since you've been here, Lily. And that's all good."

She clasped her hands, forcing herself to hold his patient gaze. "And then there was you, Jake. You fed me in another way. I wasn't afraid of your gruff exterior. I knew you were a good person inside because Jenna was good. And I was proved right on that over time. You didn't treat me as being broken or lost. I was, but you didn't emphasize it. Instead, you allowed me to be on a long tether to range around until I could find another way home within myself. I felt you sensed where I was at any given time, gave me the space to flounder and were always nearby in case I needed to grab out and hold on to your hand. You pulled me out or up from the inner quagmire I was always getting trapped in."

He sighed and shook his head. "I recognized it because I'd already been where you are, Lily. I know the anguish and pain. I didn't want to see you go through it. I wanted to help short-circuit it by being a support."

She reached over, touching the back of his hand briefly. "I owe you so much."

"I hope whatever is between us isn't about what we might owe each other."

She managed a quirk of her mouth. "I don't think anyone's generosity, for whatever reason, is ever given back to the giver. I realized what you were doing with me on bad days or nights. I realized you saw my struggles. You gave me hope to hang on, to keep fighting to get well or," she grimaced, "find my 'new normal.'"

"I wanted to help you end some of your pain, was all. I don't like to see anyone, human or animal, suffering."

"You're a softy inside, Jake Murdoch."

He grinned unevenly. "Don't tell anyone else, okay? I've got just about everyone else on the ranch buffaloed."

She laughed a little, then sobered. "Yes, and I go around trying to fool everyone by being 'normal,' when we know there's no such thing for us anymore."

"I didn't want to fool you that I was normal either," he began awkwardly. "There was something vulnerable about you that grabbed at me. There's a lot of goodness in you. I don't know if it's because you were a nurse and love helping people or something more. Whatever it is, it's a beautiful part of you." He sat up and pushed the chair back. "Come on. Let's go sit on the couch and continue our talk there."

"Sure." She pushed back and stood uncertainly, feeling as if they'd just made a vital connection with one another. Maybe her gumption had helped to create it. She wasn't sure, but she followed him into the living room. She took the end of the couch and Jake sat about three feet away from her, elbows on his knees, hands clasped, looking serious. "I don't know about you, but it feels good for me to get this off my chest."

"Same here." He went silent.

Lily waited, sensing he was struggling for words.

Jake's voice was low, off-key. "You're magic to me,

Lily," and he lifted his head, holding her luminous gaze with a tender look. "That's what I really wanted to say a moment ago, but I was too chicken. I was afraid you'd think I was bs-ing you."

"I like being thought of as magic, Jake. It doesn't feel like you're handing me a line."

His mouth cut into a thinner line, withholding a lot of emotions. "I can't figure out how you're able to hold on and slowly get yourself back together when you strike me as being more fey than real."

She smiled a little. "Fey. That's a lovely word. I wish I felt like that inside."

"It will come with time," he soothed. "You're doing well, Lily. Coming along fast. That's a testament to your inner strength, your backbone. Whether you believe it or not, you have it. I see it every day."

"A magical being with a broken backbone," she amended wryly. "That's quite a visual, Murdoch."

He chuckled and said, "Best I could do on short notice."

"There's so much to talk about. Someday . . . soon . . . I want to hear your story of how you got PTSD. I've been edging toward telling you about what happened to me." She swallowed hard, looked away for a moment and then met his concerned gaze. "I . . . I'm afraid if I start talking about it, Jake, and I lose control, I don't know what I'll do. There are times when I want to scream." She twisted her hands in her lap.

He pushed his palms down his thighs. "It's not something you can force, Lily. You have to respect it and you'll know when it's right to let go. And it would be my honor to hear your story, to be there for you."

"You won't judge me. I know that."

He snorted. "Hell, no."

There was a lull in their conversation.

"Where does this leave us, Jake?" Her voice was soft with feeling, trepidation.

"I don't know. You're wrestling with the first year, which is bad enough. I sensed that, and it's why I never let on that I enjoyed your company, looked forward to coming home every night and seeing you. I like to hear what's on your mind and what's in your heart. The last two months have been better than I can remember in a long, long time."

Her heart melted as his voice went gruff with feeling. "You've gone through so much, Jake. You're my role model. I see you handling things I didn't think I could, but you've done so much in three years. Honest to God, you look and act normal. If someone told me that you had PTSD, I wouldn't have believed it."

He slanted her a glance. "Believe it. I've got a lot more years of build-up than you do by the very job I held. You, from what I can figure out, were a nurse at an Afghan village that got overrun in a night attack by the Taliban. That's different than in my case." His nostrils quivered as he released a long exhale. "Years, Lily. There are days when I'm not sure I can take one more hit, one more stress, if I can handle a situation correctly or not. Maud relies heavily on me to make mature, well-thought-out decisions. I'm responsible for nearly a hundred people on this ranch. I know their stories, and I know them. That's what helps me rein myself in, take a check on my overreactions and calm down inwardly before I make a decision. The people on this ranch are mostly vets. Twenty of them aren't. The vets help remind me of what's being asked of me on their behalf. They're team oriented and they know how to support me in my bad moments, as I support them when they start to unravel. For that, I'm grateful."

"I've never seen you like that."

"Come spend a day with me out in the field with my crews. You will."

She gave him a caring look. "In some ways? Fessing up to you? I feel better. Relieved. What about you?"

"The same." He watched Sage and her puppies, who were now finding places to go to sleep in little piles here and there, after getting full bellies of milk. Lifting his head, he studied her. "Whatever we have, Lily, it's good. That's what I feel."

"Yes, same here."

"We need to keep talking because it's important. I admit, I'm not the best at it. Sometimes, you'll have to drag it out of me, as Jenna will tell you." He gave her a sour smile filled with apology. "But I'll keep trying to open up, not stay closed down."

"Women are used to men burying their feelings and thoughts. As long as I know you're at ease with what's happening between us, that's good enough for now."

"Well, as they say, we have nowhere to go but up. We'll keep being the good team we are in supporting each other in ways that are comfortable for us. Okay?"

It was more than okay. Lily wanted to wrap her arms around Jake's broad shoulders and hold him because he'd unveiled a lot to her just now. He was being vulnerable in a way she'd seen few men become and it called powerfully to her. She could do no less. He trusted her. "I trust you with my life."

"Back at you," he said gruffly.

July 21

Jake missed Lily. It was nearly five p.m. on Saturday, and she was volunteering at the shelter in Wind River. He'd spent the afternoon catching up on a lot of grass-lease documents, but it was dry and boring. Lily was not. Their spontaneous talk several days before had pulled a

Band-Aid off his wounded heart. For the first time, he felt a change in his life, a good one. He was falling in love. Last night, he'd awakened at three in the morning, in the midst of a torrid dream, loving her passionately, she loving him in return. Was it really possible?

Turning off the computer in the office, he stood. He'd rather go play with Sage and her pups than work. It didn't surprise him how quickly she had become a part of their home's dynamic. At any given time, Lily was back at the cabin, checking up on them, playing with them, holding each puppy, placing kisses all over tiny, furry heads. And the pups loved it. When she came in the door and spoke, all seven pups and Sage immediately raised their ears in her direction. Lily *was* magic. Heat curled around his heart. He missed her.

Guess who was out, snuffling and blindly moving around? Little runt Athena. She was prettily marked, Jake thought, as he sat down on the rug near her. She was the only one in the litter with freckles on the white blaze of her nose, and she stood out despite her being the smallest. She had two chestnut-colored eyebrows and most of the mask on both sides of her face was black, but with that same brown tone on the lower third of her face. He spoke her name and she stopped and lifted her head, her ears perked up in his direction. Chuckling, he gently slid his large hand beneath her full tummy. As he lifted her up, his heart beat hard, once. Finally, her eyes were opening! Grinning, Jake settled her against his chest and she snuggled, making little grunting noises. Lily was going to be happy.

The door opened.

"Hey!" Lily called, breaking into a smile, "I thought you were going to be working this afternoon?" She closed the door and hung her purse on a peg. Pushing her hands down her jeans, she adjusted the pink tee with three-quarter sleeves.

"Taking a break. Athena was exploring. I saw her way out here. Come over here; take a look." He watched her tilt her head, her gaze riveted on Athena.

Jake lifted the pup into her hands. She sat down next to him, their arms almost touching. That was a good sign as far as he was concerned. He wasn't sure what to do, say or how to act after their intimate talk. It had been stilted and awkward afterward. That invisible connection between them, however, hadn't wavered at all. And Jake clung to that as proof their destiny was to be together. "Look at her eyes."

Gasping, Lily held Athena up. "Her eyes! They're beginning to open!"

A smile tugged at his mouth. "It's probably going to take two or three days more before they're fully open." He gestured to the wicker basket. "The others have their eyes about half open right now."

"Yes," she murmured, peering into Athena's face, "and they look gray, like the others. Their true color isn't revealed yet."

"I'll bet they're blue."

"I hope so." She nuzzled Athena's head, then nestled her between her breasts. "How was your day, Jake?"

"Same as always. Some ups, some downs." He saw Lily give him a searching look, feeling as if she wanted more than that. "Does that look mean you want more than two sentences?"

Laughing, she bobbed her head, sliding her fingers down Athena's plump little body. "You're telepathic, Murdoch."

"I like your spunk, Ms. Thompson."

"Is there a third sentence?"

He liked her pluck and determination. "We had an altercation with one of the Elson clan earlier today."

"Who are they?"

"They're a family that lives in the southern part of the valley, but sometimes we find them hanging around the ranch. They're never up to any good. They're drug runners."

She chewed on her lip. "What happened?"

He heard the low, frightened tone in her voice. "Nothing. We found Hiram and Kaen Elson on a back road on ranch property. I don't know where they were going, but we stopped them. That road does lead to the main highway, and there's a heavy gate that's locked. These two boys, we found out later, used a pair of bolt cutters to get through the chain and padlock and onto private property. They didn't get permission to be on Maud and Steve's ranch."

"What do you think they were doing?"

"There's gossip they have some drug stashes along the foot of the Salt River Range. Maud and Steve's ranch butts right up against those slopes. I think they were probably looking for another place to hide their drugs. I've talked to Sarah, our county sheriff, and she says they deal in all types of drugs. They're buyers and distributors for a new drug lord, Pablo Gonzalez, who's in Guatemala."

"Ugh," she muttered, "I didn't know any of this." She gave him a worried look. "Were they carrying guns?"

"By law, they can't. Both have been in federal prison and aren't allowed to have firearms."

"Even out here, drugs touch our lives. It's so removed, so rural . . ."

Jake felt her vulnerability. "Hey," he coaxed, "this is Wyoming. Most ranchers have rifles, and some have pistols. We know how to use them. Sheriff Carter, three years ago, invited all the ranch owners in the valley to a briefing on the Elsons' drug activities, as well as Gonzalez trying to move into the area and claim it. She works closely with everyone in Lincoln County. I called her after the incident and let her know what was going on. Druggies are always trying to find dirt roads either in the mountains or up to the slopes because they can hide their cache until it's sold." He reached over, grazing her cheek with his finger. "Don't worry."

Lily leaned into him, resting her head against his upper arm. "I wasn't always like this, Jake. I used to be able to deal with anything. I feel like that incident stripped me of the shield that gets me through everyday life. It's gone, and I wish I had it back."

"Come here," and he slid his arm around her shoulders, drawing her gently against him. She came without tensing, but he saw the rawness in her features. He knew that from now on, he wasn't going to upset her with things like this happening around the ranch. She would worry way too much, and it would cause her anxiety to spike. He had to protect her for a while.

He pressed a kiss to the curls of her hair as she rested fully against him, entrusting herself to him. She was warm, soft, and he leaned his cheek against her hair for a moment. "The first year, I felt like a crab who'd had its shell ripped off. I couldn't handle being touched, deal with loud noises, big crowds or being jostled. I ran as hard and fast as I could to escape that kind of environment." He gave her a sympathetic look. "You're not alone in this, Lily. Every time you open up to me, it helps me open up to you. I'm here to support you in any way you need."

She cupped her hands over Athena, who was asleep between her breasts, happy and safe. "You have no idea how nice it is to be able to count on you, Jake."

Nodding, he slid his fingers gently up and down her arm, hoping it soothed and calmed her alarm. "This is the first time I've opened up to anyone. It feels good. Right."

"Just come to me, then, when you want an arm around you, or you want to be held. That's something I can easily give you." Lily pressed her cheek against his shirt, and it felt damned good to him. Jake wanted to make love to her, tenderly, to feed her soul with his hands, his kisses, adore her, shore her up emotionally. He knew he could do it because the connection between them was growing stronger by the day. With trust, he knew it could happen, but he had to open up, too, which he was trying to do right now.

"Thanks," she whispered, turning, looking up into his eyes. "That's a two-way street."

"Good, because I'm sure I'm going to need holding sooner or later. Our days consist of nothing but sharp ups and downs. It wears us out. And it will be nice to know your arms are waiting and open to me."

Lifting her hand from Athena, she placed it over Jake's chest, feeling the thud of his heart through the palm of her hand. "You have no idea how much you calm me. Ever since I came here, when you would come home at night, my anxiety would lower, sometimes go away. It was nothing you said or did. It was just your presence. Being in your home, being with you and Jenna, has helped me so much, and so has Sage. I didn't realize how much of my calm was due to both of you until she left."

He gave her a small hug, inhaling the scent of her recently washed hair, the sugary lemony aroma infusing him. It was so soft and silky. Longing to run his fingers through those shining strands, to love her, he pushed the desire away because it had no place between them right now. "I didn't know that."

"I was afraid to admit it to you. I wasn't sure you even liked me beyond my being your employee."

He lifted his head, placed his finger beneath her chin and eased it upward until their eyes met. "I never wanted to treat you as 'just an employee,' Lily. Like you? I was afraid to voice what I felt, that I was drawn to you, that I was starving to hear what you thought, what you felt, how you saw everyday things." He saw her eyes widen, fringed with those thick, dark lashes. Wanting to drown himself in that lustrous look that was melting his heart, it took everything not to lean down and kiss her parted lips. She was so close . . . so close . . . The moisture of her breath grazed him. He'd lived years on his gut instinct, and now it was telling him to go no further, that the look in Lily's glistening gaze was good enough. She hadn't given him the signal that she wanted him to kiss her. Reluctantly, he removed his finger from beneath her chin and said, "What? You look stunned by what I just said." Wanting to put a bit of teasing into the tension vibrating between them, he saw what he thought was a bit of relief in her eyes. They wanted each other so badly, but each, in their own way, was afraid to initiate. Okay, he got that. And it fed him the patience he knew he'd need to convince Lily he was a risk worth taking.

Chapter Sixteen

August 4

Joy bubbled up through Lily as she kept her stride short and slow. Ahead of her and Jake was Sage and her galloping, romping, frisky pups. The grass in the long, oval, flower-studded meadow was halfway up her calves. Jake was chuckling, as she was, as the four-week-old pups bounded, leaped, fell and rolled in the thick, tall grass. All one could see was seven waving, stubby tails as they plowed through the grass wall like kangaroos on short legs, following their mother.

The sun was high in the sky, the temperature reaching the high seventies, puffy white clouds skidding off the Wilson Range to the west of them, the sky a turquoise blue. It was a perfect Saturday. Jake carried a large knapsack on his broad back. Inside it was a thin cotton blanket, food for the picnic and goodies for Sage and her troop.

"I'm so glad you suggested this," she said breathlessly, smiling up at Jake. She reached out, catching his right hand. Lily knew from their previous conversations that he wasn't going to take the lead. It was Lily who had to do that. He'd admitted he was afraid of doing something she might interpret the wrong way, sending her tumbling into an anxiety attack through his artless actions. For now, she was okay with that. In the month since their first talk, it had sometimes been awkward, both stumbling, making mistakes, learning how to talk without worrying how the other person might take it. She felt Jake's fingers wrap securely around hers, and she drowned in that glint in his green eyes, knowing he wanted her, body and soul. Every day, every night, the sexual tension built between them. She longed to let him know she felt the same way, but fear kept her silent.

"Look at Athena." Jake laughed, pointing his chin toward the pup as she bounded and leaped through the tangled grass.

Lily grinned, watching Athena take a different tack. She had seen the grass was shorter in the direction she'd chosen. Half as tall, as a matter of fact. Bounding like a graceful deer on her short little black, brown and white legs, she leaped through the grass, quickly paralleling her panting mother. Her little yips of triumph filled the air, as if congratulating herself on finding an easier route than the rest of the pack.

Then, all her sisters and brothers realized it was a lot easier in the shorter grass and they turned, en masse, to follow her lead.

However, Athena had arrived first. Sage then wisely moved to the shorter grass, and her smallest daughter galloped madly to keep up with her, nose up in the air, tail wagging like a metronome.

Sage knew where they were going. At the other end of the meadow was a small creek, and a few trees that threw shade over the area. Lily looked forward to the weekends, the summer ripe, the breeze filled with various scents of flowers and the camphor-scented pine trees. The pups were in that snoop-sniff-and-check-things-out mode and dearly loved rooting around the trees, tasting the bark and spitting it out, then cavorting with one another in an ongoing game of tag.

"I'm so glad you could come with us," she said, a little breathless, feeling love welling up through her, making her heart speed up. She felt Jake squeeze her hand.

"Me too."

"You work too hard," she muttered, frowning. "I didn't realize weekends weren't really yours."

"A foreman is responsible for everything and everyone. Animals get caught in wire on weekends, have to be freed and taken care of."

"I know," she huffed, lifting her feet high enough so she didn't trip in the grass.

"Why are you wondering about my schedule?" Jake asked, keeping his stride in check. The pups were getting their legs under them, becoming surer of their balance, scents making them wild with curiosity.

"Well, I like having you around two days a week. I know that's selfish . . ."

He released her hand, briefly slid his arm around her shoulders. "It's nice to be wanted."

Lily heard a lot of emotion behind his growled words. She loved when he spontaneously hugged her like this, not wanting him to release her, though he always did. Something was better than nothing.

"The pups love having you around on weekends because you're always on the floor playing with them. They adore you, Jake."

A rumble moved through his chest. "And I love them. It's a great relaxer. And it's fun watching them grow and play around." He liked when the strands of her hair glinted in the sunlight, her head bare. Now her cheeks were ruddy with good health because she was getting outdoors into the clean, fresh air.

"I so look forward to our weekly picnics."

"Things look pretty nice for us now."

Nodding, she licked her lower lip, giving him a sideways glance. "It feels like I'm in some kind of dream, Jake. A good one." She opened her hands. "I sleep at night now. I have fewer nightmares. I haven't had a flashback in three weeks."

"They'll come and go, Lily. But as time moves forward, there will be even fewer of them."

"I know part of it is that you're in my life." She saw his mouth soften. Jake's responsibilities were far and wide. Lily understood now why he'd come in late, usually after six on many nights, the demands of the ranch always looming or some emergency suddenly popping up. It wasn't a job for a weakling, that was for sure. She gazed at the broadness of his shoulders, wondering what his flesh would feel like beneath her fingertips. Of late, all she could think about was sensually exploring him. That always sent a wave of longing through her. She was starving for a man's touch, but not just any man. She wanted to feel Jake surround her, feel his tenderness, which was always close to the surface when they were together.

Lily was always amazed by how hard and stable Jake appeared as the foreman of the ranch when he wasn't at home with her and Sage. He melted over the puppies, and that made her wounded heart begin to heal. She knew what love was because her parents had shown her in large and small ways. Her father regarded her mother as an equal. They were a great team, like she and Jake were beginning to become. So many small things—a glance, a touch, a slight smile—made her see she had been falling for Jake without ever realizing it. Lily knew she'd been too absorbed in her symptoms to take stock of anything outside herself. Until recently.

The roughness of his fingers made hers tingle with

desire. The look burning in his eyes made her lower body ache. When would she overcome her fear? It was so hard to speak about it. Every time she tried, her anxiety would arc and she'd have that inner war going on, distracting her, making her shaky and unsure once again.

They had a favorite tree with long, spreading branches, where they stopped and Jake put the bright red cotton blanket on the ground. The puppies frolicked across it, yipping and grabbing the edges of it, yanking it and tugging it here and there. Lily laughed at their antics. Soon, the pups got tired of playing with the ragged-looking blanket and spread out in all directions, following new, interesting scents only they could smell. Sage made herself comfortable on one edge of the blanket, happily panting and watching her exploring brood with a mother's protective eye.

Lily knelt and took the knapsack Jake handed her. They had made beef sandwiches from a roast the night before, slathered in a mayonnaise-horseradish spread, lettuce and sliced tomatoes. There was a large thermos of hot coffee, two plastic cups and brownies for dessert.

Athena came bouncing over to where she knelt, leaping up on her thighs, yipping.

"I'm sure she can smell the sandwiches," she told Jake as he sat down opposite her, pouring the coffee into the waiting cups.

"Yeah. She's the runt, so she's going to smell out the food because she wants to find it first. She wants to get plenty of it. She's no dummy." He chuckled.

Sure enough, Athena stuck her freckled black-and-white nose up in the air, leaped off Lily and tumbled head over tail, ending up at the plastic container holding the sandwiches.

They burst out laughing.

Jake was so close. Lily felt an invisible string pull her forward. She eased up on her knees, placing her hands on his shoulders, holding his gaze. His green eyes grew stormy and she saw raw longing in them—for her. All her fear melted away as he sat very still, watching her, assessing where she was at. They had agreed she must take the lead.

And she did.

Her eyes closed as she leaned forward, placing her lips tentatively upon his. Hearing Jake groan, his hands lifting, coming to rest lightly on her shoulders, she felt her world change forever. His mouth parted and so did hers, and she moved her lips, tasting him for the first time. Feeling his power as a man, his hesitancy, his care for her, she glided her lips firmly against his, giving him a message he couldn't misinterpret.

His fingers dug into her shoulders, rocking her forward, holding her because she was off balance now, keeping her safe and steady with his male strength. It was his mouth, those wonderfully shaped lips of his, that took hers with breathtaking hunger. It matched her own, and Lily lost herself in the sureness, the taste and then the tenderness of the way he held her steady so they could continue to be one in this unexpected, joyous moment.

Somehow, Lily knew Jake would be a consummate lover, a man who had had many experiences with women before her. She wasn't as adept or experienced, but that didn't matter. The wetness and heat between their lips gliding against each other sent an arc of heat exploding into her belly, and she moaned softly as his fingers moved through her hair, holding her so he could gain maximum entrance to her.

The world slowed and stopped. All the sounds went away except for her heightened breathing, his growl of pleasure as they clung to each other's mouths, never wanting to let the other go.

Gradually, ever so gradually, Lily had to end the kiss

because her knees were hurting from being at such an odd angle on the blanket. Opening her eyes, feeling dazed by the beauty and tenderness of their kiss, Jake eased her back into a more comfortable position. She sat down. Athena immediately pounced on her and she laughed breathily, petting her as she wagged her tiny tail, lapping up the affection.

Lifting her chin, she held Jake's stormy gaze, saw all the masks he usually wore gone. "Wow," she uttered. "I wasn't expecting to do that. . . ."

He gave her a heated look. "Me neither. But I liked it. Did you?"

"Oh, yes," she managed, feeling giddy, feeling so light and happy. More so than she could ever remember. "I liked it a lot, Jake."

Nodding, he watched Athena popping up and down, leaping on her abdomen, wanting to climb her torso to wedge herself between her breasts. Lily smiled and cupped the pup's rear and she did just that. Now, Athena was happy. "I think it's your heartbeat that makes her want to be there," he said.

"I think you're right." She took a deep breath and forced herself to hold eye contact. "I've been wanting to kiss you for so long, Jake."

"What stopped you?"

"My fear," she admitted hoarsely, holding Athena, needing her right now because she represented stability to her.

"Fear of what, Lily?"

His voice was low, emotion behind his words. "Fear that I'm not well enough to be a true partner for you," she managed to get out. Each word was forced because it was so hard to be brutally honest. Lily was so afraid of his rejection. "I'm broken, Jake, in ways I could never fathom. I–I'm not whole. I doubt I'll ever be. I've spent a month, almost every night, lying in bed wondering if I could give you half of what you give to me. You're so patient; you support me, with no questions asked." She lifted her fingers from Athena and reached out, touching his hand resting on his long, hard thigh. "You deserve someone who is whole, who isn't a mess like me. . . ." Gulping, she saw his eyes change, narrow and she tried to gird herself for his rejection. Why would he want to take on someone like her? She had so far to go in her healing process. Lily accepted she'd probably never be fully healed. It broke her heart because Jake deserved someone who was perfect.

Picking up her hand, he held it, his voice deep with feeling. "Lily, I want you just the way you are. It doesn't matter to me if you're whole or not. I'm not either. We seem to be able to put up with each other's quirks and ups and downs, and we still want to be in each other's company. Don't you see that?"

Her fingers tightened around his. "Not always. I have such trouble putting things into words, much less saying them to you. I'm so scared you don't want me the way I am. I need you to keep telling me I'm okay as is. At least until I can find the confidence I lost."

He lifted her hand, kissing the back of it. "You're taking me as I am, aren't you, darlin'?"

She blossomed beneath the gruffly spoken endearment. It meant everything to Lily. "Yes . . . yes, I am. I see you as so far ahead of me, Jake. Despite your symptoms, you have the strength, or whatever it is, to overcome them, and you know how not to let them interfere with anything. I'm not there. . . . I want to be, and there are days when I think I might be. Then there are other days when I think I'm a complete basket case and nothing is ever going to get better. I'm not a whiner. I usually don't put these thoughts into words, but I can't let you think I'm farther along than I am."

He took her hand, opening it within his larger one, lightly tracing her palm.

The skitters of pleasure thrummed through her hand and arm. She saw the pensive look on Jake's face as he lifted his finger, then closed his other hand over hers.

"In time," he said gently, "you'll be where I am. I have no doubt of that, Lily, because you're a fighter. You have courage and you have more inborn strength than a lot of people. We have something special, something that I want to pursue with you. I like waking up every morning knowing you're in my house. It lifts me. It feeds the hope that you brought with you when you came. I can't imagine a day without that," and he held her tearful gaze.

Tears trailed down her cheeks. "Oh, Jake . . ."

He gave her a tender look. "I'd rather live with you than without you. We've spent months together under one roof, Lily. I know we can make this work."

The dam burst within her, a burning feeling exploding like a wildfire in her chest. There was no way she could stop the sob that tore out of her. She set Athena aside, and the puppy wandered off toward her mother. Closing her hand over her face, she shook with more sobs, so much terror, grief and loss shearing through her. The next thing she knew, Jake was at her side, lifting her across his thighs, bringing her tightly against his body, his arms enclosing her. It was exactly what she needed: his care, his love and his incredible ability to sense where she was in the storm that lived within her. This time, Lily didn't fight to stop crying. This time, as Jake held her, rocking her slowly, his arms like warm blankets surrounding her, she capitulated to all the trauma she'd fought to control since the incident.

All the anguish and agony came ripping out of her. She was lost within the storm that was finally making its way

up and out of her. All she felt was the comfort and security
Jake was providing, allowing her the loss of control, allowing her to stop carrying that tragic night within her any
longer. The scent of him, the sweat, the alfalfa sweetness,
surrounded her. It lulled her, cossetted her, and she surren-
dered herself completely to Jake. With him, her heart
knew she'd found a safe harbor. She loved him. Loved his
softer side that had not been destroyed by war and trauma.
And it was more than enough for Lily as she sank into his
arms to be held and protected.

Jake rubbed his cheek against Lily's hair, his heart
breaking over the animal-like sounds that were ripping out
of her shaking body. He knew those sounds. How many
times had he hid in his room, door and windows closed,
while those same horrible, wrenching sounds came out of
him? He'd lost count because it hit him at odd times. And
there was never a warning when that volcanic trauma
would erupt within him and come spewing out. He rocked
her gently, whispering soft, trembling words of comfort,
knowing no one could help her right now. He could provide a safety net of sorts for Lily, but that was all. The
animal that had come to be birthed within her, as it had
him, would have its way with both of them from time to
time. Today was no different. Today, it was Lily's turn.

Wishing with all his heart he could heal her, destroy the
monster that paced, snarled and roared within her, Jake
knew he couldn't. It was the most helpless damned feeling
of all, wanting to protect Lily as she struggled to get better,
wanting to remove the trauma so she'd never have to go
through this again. The sunlight was warm and consoling
as it surrounded them on the blanket. There was a slight
breeze to cool Lily's perspiration. And most of all, Sage and

her pups surrounded them, in touch with the anguish Lily was going through. The dogs sensed her suffering.

He gently moved his hand slowly up and down her back, her shoulders shaking, her head buried deep against his chest, as if to try to hide from the terror within her. "It's going to be all right, Lily . . ." The lump in his throat grew, and then he rasped, "I love you. We'll get through this together. Just hang on. I'm here for you. . . ."

There. It was finally out. Jake doubted she could hear his low, broken voice against the background of her terror-filled sobs, wrapped within her own grief. How he wished he knew about the night she'd lived through in that Afghan village. It would help him to help her. Whispering once more, "I love you, Lily. We'll handle this together. . . ."

He wanted a lifetime with this brave woman who didn't know her own strength or what she was capable of accomplishing after she got her footing back. But he did. Lily was open, easy to read, simple in the way she saw life. She wasn't a woman who lived in clutter or complexity. He was a person who saw a lot of gray areas, wishing he had more of her simplicity. Just being around her was helping him readjust positively in so many ways.

Leaning down as he heard the sobs dissolve, he used his fingers to wipe some of the wetness from her wan cheeks. Lily began hiccupping and pressed her hand against her mouth, embarrassed. He pressed a kiss to her brow.

"Relax. Just let things settle naturally," he rasped. Her dark lashes were beaded and barely raised.

"Hang on," he muttered, releasing one arm and pulling a white handkerchief from his back pocket. He pressed it into her hand and she took it.

"T-thanks, Jake," and she blotted her eyes, her hand trembling.

Jake groaned silently as she laid against his chest, her hand near his heart, gripping the handkerchief. Moving his fingers across her unruly hair, while the breeze played with the strands, he saw the gold glinting in the chestnut. Heartened by her trust in him—and that was what it was—made his own heart swell with fierce love for her. Curving his arm around her shoulders, he held her as she began to quiet. Eventually, the hiccups stopped, and he could feel her trying to gather the strewn emotions that had blown up on her.

"That sort of sneaked up on you?" he asked, his cheek against her hair.

"Yes . . ." She dragged in a ragged breath, pressing her cheek against his dampened cotton shirt. "I needed to hear what you said, and I felt so much of the shield I'd tried to build to protect myself against the world just dissolve."

"It should," he rasped. "I'll do my best to protect you, Lily, to keep you safe. I know how raw you are. I know how I used to wake up, facing the next day feeling unprepared. It was a terrible feeling and I can see you going through the same thing."

Giving a jerky nod, she whispered hoarsely, "I feel that way every day, Jake. It never goes away."

"Over time, it will," he promised, inhaling the sweet scent of her hair. It felt as if he were laying his cheek against silk. Lily was like that, too. Graceful, adaptable, but oh so strong.

"I hope you're right . . ."

He eased his arm away from her shoulders, helping her to sit up. She gave him a sheepish look after wiping her face. Jake caressed her shoulder. "I'm glad you let me hold you, Lily. We all need one another. That's the biggest realization I came to during my first year out of the Marine Corps. I told you about the psychologist they brought over at the Bar C, Libby Hilbert, who works with the vets twice a month on Friday evenings." He shook his head. "We were all so damned locked up, unable to say much of anything, much less let go of our emotions. Over the months, as we got to know one another, we all sort of relaxed." He caressed her damp cheek, her eyes wounded-looking holes. "Libby taught us how to cry, Lily. You were locked up just as we were. And thank God, you had the courage to let it go. That speaks volumes, don't you know that?"

Shaking her head, she sniffed, blew her nose and gripped the hanky. Athena came galloping over, leaping into her lap. Lily cupped her hands, bringing the pup to her breast. "I didn't see it coming. It just overwhelmed me, but I think I know why." She lifted her head and met his softened gaze. "I trusted someone outside myself for the first time since that night, Jake. I trusted you . . ."

Chapter Seventeen

August 4

Jake had watched Lily after her long, hard cry, and then when she retreated deeply within herself, pensive. He understood why, based on his own experience. While crying had helped him, it opened the valve that was like an IED, ready to go off inside him. Lily barely ate anything. Again, understandable. She wasn't talking very much either. But the pups, as if sensing her agony and grief, surrounded her like a little troop, playing with her, as if to pull her out of the depression that came with the symptoms. They were a loving distraction and she did respond.

Sage came to sit next to him and he fed her bits of his sandwich because he wasn't in a mood to eat either. Still, he wanted to keep Lily outside, to have sunlight, blue sky and beauty surround her because he knew it would help her stop that deep dive into the black hole that resided within them both.

An hour later, they packed up everything. Jake wasn't about to let Lily deal with the aftermath alone. He placed his arm around her waist, walking with her. To his relief, she acquiesced and leaned again him, her arm sliding around his waist. Sensing her inner turmoil, Jake didn't try to chat with her. That would have been foolish. Instead, he kept his pace slow, his stride short, allowing the puppies to follow their mom home down the trail they'd made coming out to their picnic spot. Sometimes, he'd slant his glance down in Lily's direction, heartened that by the time they reached the cabin, her wan cheeks were pinking up, telling him she was feeling a little better than before.

Opening the gate, Sage and her brood went to lap water from one of the many bowls, then lay exhausted and panting afterward. Jake closed the gate. Later, near nightfall, they would bring them in for the evening, the night temperature dipping to the forties or, sometimes, even lower. Lily worried because they were still so young.

"Why don't you go get a long, hot bath?" he asked her, opening the door to the cabin.

"Good idea."

"I'll take care of things."

She shared a grateful look with him and stepped into the living room.

Jake busied himself in the kitchen, putting things away. He was sure Lily thought she had ruined their outing, but she hadn't. She loved going on these weekly picnics and so did he, not to mention the dogs. These grief interruptions that came out of nowhere couldn't be planned ahead of time or be seen coming. They happened out of the blue and caught everyone by surprise. More than anything, Jake wanted to hold Lily, give her a sense of outer security even if she didn't feel it inwardly.

Jake was bringing in the brood from the yard when he saw Lily emerge from her bedroom. She had taken a hot bath and then gone to her room to nap. Her eyes were puffy with sleep, her hair tangled and in need of a combing. These kinds of blowouts always made him exhausted afterward as well. The pups spilled down the hall as she emerged, and he saw her stop, bend down, and pick up Athena, who was leading the pack, her tail wagging wildly, her tiny yips echoing off the walls.

Smiling to himself, he finished by shutting the back door after Sage trotted in. He liked having dogs in his life again. Glancing to the still-sleepy Lily, he asked, "Up to a cup of fresh coffee?"

"That sounds good," she said, picking up Athena, who licked her chin and jaw. "Thank you . . ."

"Come to the kitchen," he urged, heading in that direction. Jake wanted to stop, turn and pull her into his arms, give her that sense of safety once more, but he knew he couldn't enable her. Strength was born of bouts like this, and no one knew it better than he did. Still, he wanted to hold her because he loved her.

She placed Athena on the floor, and the pup scampered across the kitchen floor and leaped down into the living room, where the other pups were now playing. Pushing the hair from her eyes, Lily walked into the kitchen, where Jake was pouring two cups of coffee for them.

"I crashed and burned," she admitted, her voice hoarse as she came to a halt near him. He had showered and changed also. The scent of lime soap gave him away. Even in jeans, he looked sexy to her, the denim molding to his long, hard thighs. Jake usually favored blue or checked white and blue chambray shirts, and he had one now as well. The cotton fabric stretched across his broad shoulders and well-muscled back.

Handing her a mug, he said, "You needed it. Can't have a blowout like that and not feel exhausted afterward."

Wrinkling her nose, she brought the mug to her lips,

sipping the steaming brew. She followed Jake to the kitchen table. He pulled out a chair for her.

"Whatever you're cooking smells good."

Jake sat down at her elbow. "Leftovers." He held her bruised-looking gaze and saw how the corners of her mouth were still pulled inward. That told him she was still experiencing a lot of pain or depression, he wasn't sure which. "Are you hungry at all?"

"No . . . but I know I have to eat something, and I will."

"If nothing else, we have an acute sense of survival," he teased drily.

A bit of light came to her eyes. "I've never cried that hard, Jake. I didn't realize how it would total me. Afterward, I felt like someone had taken a bottle brush to the inside of me. I feel numb right now."

"Numbness always follows a cry like that," he agreed quietly, placing his hands around his warm cup. "It's how it always seems to go."

"How long does it take to recover from one of these sessions?"

Shrugging, he said, "From what I've experienced, sometimes hours. Sometimes a day or two. It depends on the person. I didn't get in touch with my emotions until I started going to the Bar C Friday-night therapy sessions."

"Do you still go to those sessions?"

"No, not anymore, because I got what I needed from Libby. I took the tools she taught us, and they worked. My life improved a lot from her suggestions and help."

"Does she still come to the Bar C?"

"Yes."

"Maybe I should attend some of those meetings, if Shay will let me."

"I'm sure she will. Give her a call tomorrow, if you feel up to it."

"I will." She tentatively sipped the coffee.

"I'll go with you, if you want company."

Giving him a warm look, she whispered, "I'd like that. Right now, I'm feeling pretty raw and unstable."

"It will pass. When I was in those funks, I would focus on something positive." He hitched a thumb toward the living room, where there were tussles and excited yips breaking out among the pups as they rolled and played and chased one another around the couch.

Her eyes narrowed slightly. "You've cried?"

Giving her a sheepish glance, he finally admitted, "Yes, I have . . . I still do sometimes. Odd moments. Hit me out of nowhere. I don't have any control over it. Libby explained it as being like a pocket of grief bubbling up to be released. She said it was a good thing, not to try to stop it or fight it."

"Did this ever happen out in public?"

"No, though some of my vet cowboys have had it happen to them. I leave them alone so they won't be embarrassed, and so do the other wrangler vets. We all understand."

"It's a lonely weeping," she said, her voice scratchy. "I was so glad when you held me, Jake. It helped so much. You gave me somewhere safe to land. I could give up and drown in my feelings and tears."

He reached out, placing his hand on her lower arm. "I wished I had someone to do that for me. Most of us don't. I knew what was happening to you, Lily, and I tried to do what I wanted done for me when I'd break down." His mouth thinned. "It's hard for me to admit this, but I want to try to be as open as I can with you. Better to hear it from me, and maybe my experiences can help you."

"I saw men cry in combat," she whispered, clearing her throat, looking up at the ceiling, fighting back fresh tears.

"That night?"

"Yes . . . Everyone I saw was crying. So was I."

Jake didn't press her with more questions. Lily would

tell him when she was ready; it wasn't something that could be squeezed out of her. "You're going to find in the next couple of days that you're wide open and raw. Everyday things are going to impact you a lot more emotionally than usual. You've been protecting yourself, and your shield has been torn away."

"Like right now," she wobbled, frowning. "I don't have any way to control it, Jake. It scares me to feel so out of control."

"I know. It did me, too, at first, until I got used to it and saw the 'pattern' of it, as Libby calls it. She called it a 'breakdown for a breakthrough,' and said it was a healthy response, a healing response, to what we went through." He moved his fingers down her arm and then squeezed her fingers. "After I had a major blowout one night, the next morning I was called early because one of our cows was having birthing difficulties. When the calf was born, I cried. Ann Sharp didn't look surprised at all. She'd seen this happen many times over the past five years she's been in the valley." He managed a twisted smile. "I was the one who was surprised. The birth, the calf being alive, not dead, triggered another episode in me."

"What did you do?"

"Turned around and walked away, sobbing. I stayed away from my crew until it had its way with me. Then, I tried to paste myself back together again, turned around and carried on. They acted as if nothing had happened because all of them had gone through the same thing themselves."

She turned her hand over, holding his. "This is so painful. I had no idea how this would impact my life every day and night. It's horrible."

Giving her a wry look, he growled, "It sucks. But at least we have each other, Lily. That helps so much."

"It sure didn't help the wives of the men, or the husbands

of the wives, coming back with PTSD, though. I've seen so many marriages break up because those traumas stood between them."

"There's that, too. Because we both have the same issue, I see it working for us, not against us. Is that how you see it?"

Nodding, she said, "Yes. You put yourself in my shoes."

"And because we're hypersensitive, we know when to come to or leave the other person alone."

Nodding, she grumbled, "It's a lot better than being alone, with no one to talk to about how you're feeling or what's going on inside."

"Misery loves company," and he shared an uneven grin with her. He saw her lips twitch, but her eyes were looking less muddy. Just getting to talk about this was helping her. "We'll get through this, Lily. You're stronger than you think. I've seen vets in far better shape than you and it broke them." He picked up her hand, kissing the back of it, then released it. "Keep fighting. You're winning this war, whether you feel you are or not."

August 5

Lily hesitated outside her bedroom, staring at Jake's closed door. It was three a.m. and she'd woken up, feeling panic. Knowing it was from the weeping session the day before, she padded barefoot into the living room. It was Sunday morning. There was a night-light on, and she could see Sage pop up her head from her large, comfy dog bed, watching her. All seven of her pups were nestled against her belly, sleeping deeply. Aiming herself at the couch, she sat down and pulled the dark green afghan Jenna had knitted for Jake around her shoulders. She huddled under it, laying in a fetal position, her head resting on the arm.

She felt so lonely. Wanting Jake so much, wanting him to hold her once again because it was healing to her.

A door opened in the hall.

Lily instantly sat up, her eyes widening as she saw the silhouette of Jake emerging from his room. She'd been quiet about opening her door and not making any noise. How could he know she'd come out here? Gulping, throat dry, she watched his silent progress toward her, feeling his unseen gaze upon her. Her heart began a slow beat. She needed him. As he drew nearer, she saw he was clothed in a pair of blue-and-white-vertical-striped PJ's, his upper body bare. The shadows made his masculinity stand out to her. It beckoned her.

"Want some company?" he asked, his voice low and gruff with drowsiness.

Her whole body burned as she caught the light in his darkened eyes. Lily wasn't sure who was hungrier for the other. "I want more than company, Jake."

Instantly, his eyes narrowed on her.

The silence lengthened, taut and sizzling.

"Tell me what you want, Lily."

It took every last shred of her courage to whisper brokenly, "You . . ."

He offered her his hand. "Come to bed with me?"

Feeling dazed and shocked by her own daring, she placed her cool, damp fingers into his hand. His flesh was warm, dry, and her fingertips tingled as she felt his calluses. He pulled her slowly to her feet. Turning, she pulled the afghan from her shoulders and allowed it to drop to the couch. "I won't be needing this." She was so brave! Maybe this was a part of her that wasn't wounded or broken, because she felt good, felt confident and stable as she lifted her chin, meeting Jake's shadowed gaze. His hand tightened around hers.

Without a word, she walked through the living room,

down the hall to the open door to his bedroom. With each step, Lily felt more and more of her old self begin to emerge, buried beneath her symptoms but alive, vibrant and wanting the man whose hand she held. It was liberating. Shocking in the best of ways. Freeing. As he quietly closed the door and turned toward her, she dropped his hand and slid her arms around his neck, pressing herself fully against him. There was no mistaking his wanting her.

"Jake? I need you." She clung to the look in his eyes, his hand coming to rest on her shoulders.

"Lily . . . Are you sure it isn't because of what happened yesterday?"

His fingers sent sparks down her shoulders and back, his touch light, searching.

"I don't know. I don't think so. This has been building for a long time." She studied his rugged features, saw the longing in his expression, his hair mussed, almost making him look boyish. But he wasn't a boy. He was a man. "I'm still rediscovering what parts of me are wounded and what aren't," she tried to explain, stumbling over her words, her mind racing with the beat of her heart. "Tonight I need you. Being around you has breathed new life into me. I can't explain it all. It's just you."

His hands stilled on the shoulders of her granny gown, purple cotton with white roses throughout the fabric. "I was afraid it was because of your finally crying, Lily."

Stubbornly, she shook her head. "No, not that. I woke up earlier knowing I wanted to love you." She lifted her hand, pointing toward his door. "I stood outside for a minute, waffling and wanting to knock and ask to come in. I chickened out."

He closed his eyes, his hand tightening momentarily. Opening them, he rasped, "I have a condom."

"I don't need one unless you do. I'm clean. And I just finished my period."

He leaned down, brushing her lips, framing her face and then making the kiss longer and deeper. As he pulled away, their noses almost touching, he growled, "You can stop me any time you want, Lily. Just tell me. I want to pleasure you, not scare you. All right?"

She understood that Jake knew how fragile she really was. And he wasn't a mind reader. He was asking for her to speak up. "I can do that. I don't feel you're going to hurt me. I feel if I love you, I'll somehow find another piece of myself, I'll find healing, as crazy as that sounds." She saw his eyes gleam, his beautifully shaped mouth barely lifting.

"I've been seen as many things, darling, but never before as a healer."

"Maybe because you hadn't met the right woman yet, hmmm?" and she reached up on her tiptoes, sealing her lips against his, not giving him time to think or talk anymore because she was starving for him. His rumbling groan vibrated through her, his arms coming around her, crushing her against him, his mouth hungry, clashing eagerly with hers. In no time, he'd guided her to the bed, lifted her up, settled her upon it. Lily wasn't shy. She moved to the center of the bed, pulling her gown over her head and dropping it onto the floor. He gave her a look of praise.

Untying the waist cord, his pajama bottoms fell downward.

Lily's gaze dropped, and she liked what she saw. Holding out her hand, she whispered, "Join me?"

Never had she wanted anyone like she wanted Jake. Glorying in herself, the fact that she wasn't completely damaged by the symptoms, all her hormones screamingly online, healthy, hungry and more than ready to have this man inside her.

Jake lay down, guiding her to him, his hand resting on her hip. "How long, Lily?"

"Over a year."

He cruised his fingers down her hip, following the length of her curved thigh. "Then let's go easy with each other. We have all night."

"Good idea. I want to be able to walk tomorrow morning, Murdoch."

Chuckling, Jake slid his fingers through her mussed hair, watching her lids lower, her lips part with invitation. How many times had he dreamed of this happening? How many times had he awakened in a sweat, a hard erection and in pain? Too many times. He leaned forward, cupping the back of her head, caressing her lips, wet, lush, the ache in his lower body growing harder by the moment. "I like meeting this woman," he murmured against her lips, feeling her smile beneath his. "I knew she existed."

"And it's nice to meet the real Jake Murdoch."

Her mouth was full, cushiony, and she tasted of the strawberry toothpaste she'd used before going to bed. The silk of her hair brushed against his cheek, catching in the growth of his beard here and there. As she pressed her belly against his rock-hard erection, he groaned. Firm, warm, her hands exploring him endlessly, Jake became lost in the heat of their moment together. He liked her boldness, unafraid to touch him, pleasure him and urge him on. The slick wetness on her inner thighs told him of how much she wanted him. Their breathing changed, became faster, more ragged as he turned over on his back, pulling her over his hips, settling her on the length of his erection.

The softened sound of pleasure tore from her lips and she barely opened her eyes, her hands coming to rest on his powerful chest sprinkled with dark hair.

Folding his hands around her flared hips, he ground her wet core against him, feeling her fingers dig into his chest, her eyes shuttering closed, a low moan rising in her throat. Lifting his hips, he moved slowly into her gate, allowing her time to get used to his size. A tremor went through her as she leaned forward, asking him to come further into her, a radiance in her face. A soaring triumph of joy rocked through him as she continued to introduce her smaller, tighter body to his. He lay very still, allowing her the time to introduce themselves to each other. It was a time of patience and enjoying her riding him with slow in-and-out movements. The wetness, the gliding against her tight, small walls made him groan as well.

When she leaned down, claiming his mouth, their breathing swift and her body tight, gripping him, he slowly raised his hips, lavishing her, letting her know how much he loved her. There was no hurry tonight, just the joy of coming together because Jake knew they had fallen in love with each other. It showed in small ways every day. Her hands crept upward, framing his face, her tongue touching his, making him tense. And when he did, she settled fully on him.

The moment was exquisite. Beautiful.

She lifted her face away from his, opening her eyes, staring deeply into his. "You are my everything," she quavered. "Everything . . ." and then she slowly sat up, curving her hands over his torso and began to slowly move forward and back, rocking into that ancient rhythm with him.

Jake lost his mind, the explosion of her orgasm gripping him, releasing him, gripping him once more as she screamed out in pleasure, frozen in place. Instantly, he cupped her hips, pulling her down on his erection, making that intense orgasm last and last until she uttered a little cry, collapsing against him. She quivered, her hand wrapping around his thick neck, breathing hard, sweat pooling between them. Giving her a few minutes, adoring her by gliding his hand across her naked, warm flesh, Jake coaxed her to sit back up when she was ready. And then he proceeded to bring her to another orgasm in no time. If she hadn't had any sex in over a year, she had a lot of built-up reserve, and he was determined to help her release all of it.

After several orgasms, Lily was spent, and Jake was happy to take her into his arms, their bodies pressed together. He knew that orgasm for men and women frequently had their PTSD symptoms erased for hours, sometimes days, afterward. Sex was a great antidote, but what he felt for her, his heart wide open with love, put their coming together on a plane far above just the physical connection.

After half an hour, she revived and urged him to lie on top of her. He followed her coaxing, feeling her long legs wrapping around his hips, offering herself to him. This time, he could ease into her, already wet and beckoning, a low growl tearing out of him as he rocked into her, feeling her efforts to support and now give him the ultimate pleasure. It felt as if someone had poured molten metal down his spinal column when he released within the tightness of her welcoming body. All he could do was rasp her name, his cheek pressed against hers, their bodies wrapped up with each other, his head exploding with light, stars and rainbows against his tightly shut eyes. Shortly after, he collapsed on her, spent and weak, their breath uneven, clinging to each other.

Jake was afraid of crushing Lily beneath him and eased off her, rolling to one side, bringing her alongside him, his hand splayed out across her lower back, keeping her near. She nestled her head into the crook of his shoulder, her arm twining across his rib cage, holding him with her woman's strength. And then he fell into the deepest, most healing sleep he'd ever experienced, and so did she.

Dawn crept up on the horizon and Jake slowly came awake. The scent of Lily filled his nostrils like a long-lost fragrance he'd been searching for all his life. Now, he had discovered it, and it was her. She slept languidly against him, her head nestled on his shoulder, arm limp across his belly. Not wanting to move, to break the magic of this moment he'd dreamed about for so long, he closed his eyes, feeling the soft rise and fall of her breasts against his chest. One of her legs was across one of his hairy ones and he imprinted the firm warmth of her curvy body against his harder, more angular one.

The first birds began singing in the dawn light and he felt euphoria quietly stealing through him. His arm was around her shoulders, holding her close to him even as they slept. Jake wanted Lily in his bed every night, if that was what she wanted. As wounded and broken as they were, they were right for each other. There was no question in his mind about that. Jake's thoughts ranged over their conversations, and her breaking the dam on those millions of gallons of tears she'd tried desperately to forget.

Lily made a snuffling sound, moved, her arm tightening momentarily around Jake's middle, as if to convince herself that he was still at her side. It was Sunday morning, the one day when his phone usually didn't ring. Cherishing this time with Lily, he branded it forever into his heart. He saw the struggles they were going to have ahead of them, but he could be her anchor while she righted herself from the PTSD. Those symptoms would never go away, but instead of medication, they could use each other. It was free, nonaddictive and had no side effects. A corner of his mouth quirked at that thought. He hated medication and had refused to use it from the get-go. And so had Lily. They were a lot alike in many ways. He wanted her to re-connect with her internal strength. She'd had it before or she'd never have joined the military. Wimps weren't drawn to the service, or else they got washed out in boot camp. Only someone with strong internal strength could do that job. She'd lost it during that Afghan attack, but it was still there, and he wanted to help her find it once more.

Moving his fingers lightly against her upper arm, not wanting to awaken her, Jake needed to absorb her physically. Already, his erection was stirring. He was sure Lily would be sore after the romp they'd had. He didn't want her pressured right now. More than ever, his logic to allow her to call the shots, to let him know what she needed and when, was working for them, not against him. He was patient in many ways and he knew he got that gene from his parents.

There was scratching at the bedroom door.

Scowling, he heard a couple of the puppies whining outside. The little rascals! Somehow, they'd figured out they were both in here. Grinning sourly, he tried to ease his arm from around Lily and allowed her to continue to sleep. She muttered something but didn't awaken.

Good.

Slipping out of bed, he pulled the covers over her, grabbed his pajama trousers and walked silently to the door. Leaning down as he opened it, Athena and another pup yipped happily, sitting and looking innocently up at him, their little tails thumping wildly with joy.

"You two," he muttered darkly, scooping them up, one in each hand. "Come on . . ." And he stepped into the hall, leaving the door open. He eased the two adventurers back into Sage's bed, where the rest of the pups were still sleeping. Then he hurried back toward his bedroom.

Athena yipped, leaping out of the dog bed, tumbling head over heels and righting herself, her four feet a blur, aiming for the hall again.

"You little pill," Jake growled, scooping her up halfway across the living room; he held her and quietly shut the bedroom door. "I know what will keep you from waking Lily." He smiled, heading first for the bathroom. Soon enough, he'd pour a tablespoon of half and half in the puppy food bowl in the kitchen and she'd get distracted from her target. As he looked toward the kitchen, he saw the eastern horizon growing pink with the coming dawn. Yes, it was going to be a good day. He just knew it.

Chapter Eighteen

August 6

Jake was waiting for Lily when she awoke near nine, a very late hour for her, but he knew she needed the sleep. She'd come from his room, walked naked down to hers and put on a robe. He'd been in the kitchen getting ready to make them some breakfast when she emerged. He'd heard her door open and turned, soaking in her tousled hair, her pink cheeks, her eyes half open and still drowsy-looking.

"Heading for the tub?" he asked.

"Yes."

"Hungry?" Jake thought she should be.

"Very much so. Are you going to make us something?"

"Yep. Dogs are already fed."

She smiled a little, watching the pups play, race and tumble around the living room. Athena spotted her and heard her voice, tearing across the room to where she stood. Scooping her up and kissing her soft, fuzzy head, she said, "I'll be out in about half an hour."

"Taking Athena with you?" he teased.

"When are you putting them out for the day?"

Jake looked out the kitchen window. "Probably in about half an hour. It's warming up quick outside."

"Good. I'll take Athena with me. She likes chewing on the fuzzy rug in front of the tub."

"She doesn't want to leave your side." And then he added in a lower tone, "Neither do I."

Her face grew soft with emotion. "I feel the same way, Jake."

"Get your bath. We'll talk over breakfast. Okay?"

"Okay."

Jake was busy putting the finishing touches on an omelet stuffed with mushrooms, fresh tomatoes, onions and steak he'd cut up into much smaller pieces. He heard a yip, recognizing it as Athena's sharp little bark, and twisted a look over his shoulder after turning the omelet in the big black iron skillet. Athena was racing madly across the living room, aimed straight at him. He laughed and shook his head, knowing full well the little female was going to crash into his legs, bounce off one of them, and then leap up, grab the edge of his Levi's with her sharp, tiny teeth and tug and tug and tug until she exhausted herself, plopping onto the floor, looking well satisfied she'd slain the dragon.

Yep, and that's exactly what happened. He heard Lily's laughter, which expanded his heart, his need for her rising all over again. She wore an apricot sleeveless tee, jeans outlining her body and tennis shoes. Her hair was washed, still drying, slightly curled around her temples. Most of all, he drowned in her shining blue eyes that were filled with love—for him. It was unmistakable, and Jake felt his whole world shifting into a better place because they'd found each other.

"Hey," she called, coming into the kitchen, "that smells so good! I'm starved!" She slid her arms around his waist, pressing her cheek against his strong back, giving him a powerful hug.

Jake turned off the gas burner, torn between saving their meal and turning around and kissing Lily until they melted together the way they had last night. Moving the skillet aside, he slowly turned and settled his arms around her shoulders. Lily lifted her chin, meeting his solemn expression, her lips parting. Without a word, he leaned down, taking her mouth with his, tasting the strawberry toothpaste, inhaling the lemon scent of the soap she'd bathed with. His whole world anchored to a heated stop.

Athena continued to growl, tugging and yanking on his pant leg after getting her second wind. She was merciless with that denim.

That little critter might be the runt of the litter, but she was the fiercest of them all, and never a quitter. Jake was careful not to step on her as Lily leaned bonelessly against him, her arms sliding around his neck, pressing herself wantonly against him. Her mouth was warm, welcoming, and Jake felt like they were already one, her breasts pressed to his chest, her hips moving suggestively against his. He liked her boldness. A lot. This was a priceless part of her that hadn't been bludgeoned by her PTSD. His heart soared with that realization.

Reluctantly, he broke their hot, hungry kiss. As he drew inches away, he grinned unevenly. "Bed or breakfast?"

"Both start with a *b*, Murdoch. Your call," she said breathlessly, smiling up at him.

Athena yipped, flipped over backward and landed on her back.

They looked down at the pup, laughing.

Rolling over, Athena scrambled to all fours and leaped on Lily's leg, begging to be held once more.

"I think we have our answer," Jake said wryly, releasing her. "Go sit down. I've got everything ready."

"Sounds good." She picked up Athena, who promptly started panting, her shining blue eyes on her affectionate mistress.

Chuckling, Jake took the coffeepot to the already set table. Next, two plates with half an omelet each on them. Lily had put two pieces of sourdough bread into the toaster. She set Athena down at her feet, where the pup promptly flopped down by her foot, happy to be near Lily.

"She's a fierce little tyke," Jake said, sitting down at her elbow.

"I love watching her develop, seeing more sides of her personality emerge."

Jake nodded, picking up the toast that had popped up, handing her one of them to be buttered. "She doesn't let her size determine her heart or courage. That's what I like about her."

"All the pups have that heart," Lily agreed. "Look at Sage. She was starving to death, almost ready to give birth and she kept on going. She's resilient in ways that stun me."

"It gives *dogged* a new meaning, doesn't it?" He dug into his fragrant omelet, glancing toward her. She, too, was hungry.

Between bites, Lily said, "It sure does. Jake? Have you thought what we should do when the puppies are six weeks old? We need to take Butterscotch to your mom. That leaves five puppies left who need a home. Shay and Reese said they wanted one of them. They have a wonderful, older golden retriever, Max, and Shay thinks he would love to have a younger companion."

"Maud and Steve want one," Jake added. "Roan and Shiloh Taggart heard about them, and he approached me weeks ago about taking one of the brood. Kira and Garret Fleming asked if we'd let them have one. I've been meaning to let you know, but other things happened, and I put it on a back burner."

"There's been a lot going on," Lily agreed.

"Oh, and the other day at the hay and feed store, I talked to Pixie and Charlie when I was in town. She'd just come in with some oatmeal cookies for everyone, and I found out their old dog, Muster, died a few months ago at the ripe old age of fifteen. They said they'd love to have one of the puppies. And, of course, you get Athena."

"What about Sage?" and she gave him a worried look. "Do we have room for two dogs in our lives, Jake?"

"Always. I would never try to take either her or Athena away from you, Lily. From what I can see, they're healing for both of us. I'd like them to be a part of our family, if that's okay with you."

Was it ever! She reached over, squeezing his hand. "Thank you. I've stayed up some nights worrying and wondering what would happen to Sage and her brood."

"Everyone who has asked for a puppy knows Border collies are herd animals and smart as hell, on a par with the Australian heelers and shepherds. They're all great at herding cattle, cats and anything else, not to mention crazy sheep and goats."

"I think once the puppies are gone, we should continue to give Sage time to recover from being a mom and get her full weight back. Then, have her spayed. She's gone through enough. We don't need her being made pregnant by a local dog and dealing with more puppies."

"I agree," he murmured.

"And Athena? I want her spayed when she's old enough. That's the right thing to do."

"Yes. They can both have happy lives with us."

"Sage has really taken to you. I wonder when the time is right for you to take her in the truck with you. I think she must have herded cattle. I watch her with her pups."

"We see the same thing. I've already been thinking of taking her with me around the ranch. She's a cattle dog, I'm sure. Roan works on the ranch, mainly with the cattle portion, and he'll want a male pup to ride around with him. He does a lot of herding of cattle, and sometimes buffalo from horseback. He could use a good herd dog as a helper."

"It's so nice to know every one of them will be finding happy, caring homes." Lily sighed, giving Athena, who was tuckered out, her eyes closed, sleeping across one of her shoes, a pat.

"I think we're going to have a happy home with each other, Lily," and he gave her a tender look.

She finished her omelet and set the dish aside. "Yes, and it's been a long time coming."

"Any regrets about last night?"

Shaking her head, she gave him a wistful look. "No . . . none." She picked up her mug of coffee. "You?"

He grinned. "Zip. Zilch. Zero."

Lily became serious. "Last night, I discovered something about myself. For so long, I believed all of me was destroyed. But it wasn't. I was so drawn to you, Jake, and I wanted to get to know the person behind your walls. Most of all, I loved that you entrusted me with knowing the real you." She pushed a curl away from her temple. "I questioned myself, my ability to love you like you deserved." She inhaled raggedly and released a breath. "You deserved a whole woman, not half of one. I was so scared when we came together. At the last minute, I realized how much I wanted to love you. How long it had been since I'd had an orgasm. And then, the rest of this incredible awareness flooded my being. I knew I loved you, Jake. I'd been falling in love with you almost from the moment I met you. At the time, I didn't know it. Last night, I knew it. I know the difference between sex and love. And while sex is great, we both know it's just a part of love, not the entirety of it."

Jake reached out, capturing her hand, her fingers warm because they had been wrapped around the coffee cup. "You weren't the same person I knew before last night, Lily. I figured out pretty quickly that even though you were wounded, you weren't shattered in every way. As a woman, you were incredible. There was no wounding to that part of you that I could see."

She smiled tentatively, a little nervous. "You were right. I felt whole. I felt like my old self, and that's the first time since Afghanistan the old me reappeared. It was shocking, but in a good way. It was then," and she held his amused gaze, "I knew you had the maturity to handle whatever I needed, and you'd accommodate me. And you did. I'm still floating from last night with you."

"I don't want to come down from it either," he admitted, drowning in the hope he saw building in her expression. For so long, Lily had fought to reclaim just a little bit of her old self. A scrap to hold on to, a foundation to regrow from. He relished her joy as it washed through him like bright, clean sunlight. Their coming together had given her a powerful new sense of confidence, and he thought that perhaps, for the first time, he was seeing Lily as she'd been before the PTSD happened.

"You didn't seem to have any issues in that department," she teased. "You loved me so well. Thank you," and she touched his shaven cheek. "I'm still in a good kind of shock this morning because it seems like a dream I've had and I'm afraid I'll wake up from it."

"It's no dream, Lily. It's real. When I got cut loose from the Marine Corps, I was lost, just like you have felt. Trauma destroys the reality we grew up with. We're cartwheeling and out of control, with no mooring, no anchor to hold us, support us or keep us grounded afterward. We were so used to combat; it was familiar to us. To step back into this other world, this other reality? I lost something so vital that once I'd consciously realized what it was, it made me feel like an alien living in this civilian world."

"What was that?"

"The love you have for your teammates, that you'd give your life for any of them just as they would give theirs for you. Being a civilian, I no longer had that love that bound us as brothers and sisters in war. I drifted that first year, trying to re-create that connection, but I never could."

Glumly, she looked away. "I had that with my Afghan team, as well as my patients in the villages we visited. I loved them even though we were in a war that raged around us all the time. And coming here, I felt incomplete. Abandoned. Alone. I never quantified it like you just have to me. I was aimless. No purpose. No goals. Just . . . survive. And even when I could get a job, it didn't fulfill me like it had when I'd been in Afghanistan. And then I met you. I trusted you right away, without ever knowing why."

"Just as I automatically trusted you, I suspect, in the same unspoken ways." He gave her a wry look. "Last night, I lay there thinking that I never wanted you to leave my bed, Lily. That I loved you." He reached over, grazing her cheek, holding her tearful gaze. "I love you just the way you are. Together, we have a kind of imperfect perfection that I feel strongly will only get deeper and better as time goes on. For me, it's powerful and healing. Having someone in your life who loves you and you love in return, and you understand what they're going through? It's a blessing in disguise for me."

"For me, too. Last night I discovered an old, healthy part of myself. I celebrated myself with you, Jake." She laid her hand over his. "And I want to be in the same bed with you every night, too. I feel as if we're on a journey together, a new one, but I'm not afraid like I was before."

"Our love has pulled us out of our soul-deep loneliness, Lily. First, we had friendship, and then it morphed and became love. I have good friends here in the valley who mean everything to me and have helped me not only to survive but to thrive. I guess in a sense, they're my new team, my new family, and we can allow our wounded hearts to open once more and love them in return. I know I'm always going to love you."

She sniffed and wiped the tears from her eyes with her other hand. "Jake, you've helped me discover a new home. A place where I feel safe enough to endure what's changed in me, that I can deal with it and still have a life—with you."

"We've found another way home, Lily. Through and with each other."

August 25

Lily tried to still her excitement. Today, everyone was coming over to choose their puppy from Sage's brood. At six weeks old, the pups were lively, curious, rambunctious, loving any attention they could get from her and Jake. She had sent photos of the five pups to everyone. And, amazingly, each family chose a different one. There had been no tug-of-war between two families wanting the same Border collie.

Maud and Steve were the first to arrive. They knocked on the screen door, and Maud gave Lily a huge plate of cookies wrapped in aluminum foil.

"For everyone." She laughed.

Jake came forward and shook Steve's hand and said, "Come on in. The pups are out in the backyard with their mom. Let's go this way."

Lily placed the cookie platter on the table. She watched with joy as they followed Jake down the hall to the back door. Athena was with them, of course, but she didn't have a little ribbon collar on her with a name tag.

Taking down mugs for coffee or ice tea, she made sure there was plenty for the arriving guests.

Another knock.

Turning, she saw Shay and Reese standing and grinning at the screen door.

"Hey, great to see you," Lily said, opening it.

"I brought a Boston cream pie for everyone," Shay said, handing it to her.

Reese reached over, giving Lily a warm hug. "Looks like everyone is going to bring dessert."

Laughing, Lily set the cake on the table and gestured to them. "Maud and Steve are out back with Jake. Go find your puppy!"

Pixie and Charlie were next. She gave Lily a huge amount of chocolate brownies filled with walnuts and slathered with a chocolate-marshmallow frosting. It was heartwarming to see how excited they were to get their puppy, and Lily had to fight back tears of happiness as she led them down the hall.

Roan and Shiloh came within minutes of her getting back into the house. Shiloh handed her a sponge cake with pink frosting. Thanking them, Lily hugged them, seeing the excitement in their eyes. Everyone needed a dog, for sure.

The last to arrive were Garret and Kira Fleming. Kira had made several loaves of fresh banana bread. They, too, were so excited.

At the backdoor, Lily saw everyone down on their knees, a puppy in their arms, smiling, laughing and talking with the others. Athena was playing excitedly, running from one group to another. Sage remained by Jake, slowly wagging her tail, her blue eyes shining. It was a happy day for everyone.

"Hey," Lily called, gesturing for all of them to come in. "We've got dessert coming out of our ears, coffee and ice tea. Let's leave the dogs outside and you all come in and sit down."

Like a well-timed dance, everyone rose, gently set their charges in the grass and walked toward the backdoor. In no time, Lily, Shay and Kira served from the kitchen. Pixie came and took the plates, passing them around to the happy troop sitting around in the living room. The noise and laughter were ongoing, and Lily had never felt happier than then. Each pup would be dearly loved and well taken care of.

After making sure everyone had a beverage, she joined Jake, who sat at one end of the couch. He gave her a tender look as she settled next to him, her plate of sliced banana bread in her hand, along with a fork.

"I just love our puppy!" Shay bubbled. "He's so pretty! He has one blue eye and one brown eye."

"Maybe we should call him Spot?" Reese teased her, grinning.

The crowd erupted in laughter.

Shay frowned. "No, something more . . . well, special."

"We love our puppy!" Pixie crowed. "She's just wonderful! And she's so colorful! We've been so lonely without Muster. We're so indebted to you and Jake for letting us have one of Sage's babies."

"They're all going to great homes," Lily said. "We know they'll be the best cared for and most loved dogs in Wyoming."

Lots of heads bobbled up and down in agreement.

"I just love ours," Kira gushed. "He's got the most beautiful brown-gold eyes and he's so smart."

"He'll make a good herd dog for us," Garret said. "I'm planning on taking him with me when we're out fixing fences."

Roan chuckled. "Makes two of us, for sure. We like that our pup is already glued to us. He seemed to know we were going to be a team. He'll learn how to herd buffalo and cattle."

Shiloh glowed. "I want him as a house dog, too, Roan."

"Oh, he can stay in the house. He'll just be with me during the day, is all."

"Good," Shiloh said with a happy smile.

"They make great watchdogs," Jake told the gathering. "Sage knows everyone who comes and goes from here. She barks when there's a truck coming in and is able to tell if it's me or a stranger. We often have wranglers driving up here to see me and she's at the front door, barking a warning. She knows the sound of my truck versus how other vehicles sound. That's pretty impressive."

"We had a Border collie when we first got married," Maud said, giving Steve a loving look. "It's so nice to have another one to fill our lives."

"Yes, and I think we'll have to figure out where he stays. Will he want to be in my architecture office or your ranch office? Or will he figure it out and divide his time between both?"

Laughing, Maud said between bites of cookie, "Listen, that pup will have a mind of his own. We'll let him decide where and when he wants to visit us."

"Wise words," Steve agreed.

"Does anyone have a name for their puppy yet?" Lily wondered. "Jake's mom fell in love with the only pup that was white and gold and named her Butterscotch. We'll be driving her over to Jenna pretty soon."

Roan whispered a name to his wife. Shiloh smiled. "Oh, I like that name!"

"What is it?" Lily asked, just as excited as Shiloh was.

"Ranger," she said. "He's a very confident little puppy. He seems fearless. I like the name Ranger," she told her husband.

"I was thinking more along the lines that the pup would be on the range, chasing and herding," Roan said, giving his wife a kiss on her hair.

"Being a wordsmith," Shiloh said pertly, "ranger means a dog that can bring law and order to those cattle and buffalo. You know? Like a Texas Ranger?"

Everyone clapped and agreed.

Shiloh's cheeks reddened. Roan nodded, pleased with her explanation.

"I know when not to step into a writer's territory with words," Roan deadpanned.

Laughter followed; Shiloh was a *New York Times* bestselling author.

"Anyone else think of a name for their pup?" Lily prodded, smiling.

"I need some time just to watch our little girl," Pixie said. "Muster got his name because when he was a pup, he always knew when food was being served at the table. Charlie, here, said the pup could muster not at the sound of a bugle in the old days of the cavalry, but when the smell of food was in the air. He mustered himself to our table! And of course, to the kitchen when I was baking. It was his favorite spot."

The crowd crowed and nodded.

"I need time, too," Shay admitted, giving Reese a look. He nodded.

"And you, Maud and Steve?" Lily asked.

"We're going to need time, too," Maud agreed.

"We could always call him Split, as in split between going to one office or another?" Steve baited good-naturedly.

"Oh, pooh!" Maud chastised him. "He needs a wonderful name. Not split."

"Banana split?" Jake wondered.

Everyone howled.

"No," Maud intoned with her well-known firmness, "not that either."

"Well," Lily said, "when you know the name, let us know? I'm sure everyone would love to know what each puppy ends up with."

There was finally agreement among all parties.

Jake helped Lily take all the empty plates back to the kitchen. Pixie came up and grabbed the ice tea and Roan picked up the coffeepot. Pretty soon, everyone was relaxed and chatting among themselves, catching up on everyday events in their lives.

"Everyone," Jake called, "can I have your attention? There's something else to celebrate today, and we're glad you're here to be a part of it."

Lily gave him a questioning look. What on earth was he talking about? Because Jake looked like a man with a secret he was about to spring on everyone.

Chapter Nineteen

Jake stood up, looking around the circle of friends he'd known since returning home. All vets, except for Pixie, of course. But she acted like a vet, always helping others without any expectation of a thank-you. He gave Lily a look and saw a question in her eyes. Managing a nervous smile, he said, "You're all family to me. And we've gone a long, hard road with one another. Over the past year or so, I've seen so many of you find a military vet partner and it's made your life so much better."

He cleared his throat, giving Lily a tender glance. "My life just got better when Lily walked into this cabin. I wasn't expecting to ever be lucky like the rest of you, to find love." His voice fell with emotion. "But I have. With her," and he touched her shoulder. "I thought today would be a good time to ask Lily if she'd marry me when she's good and ready . . ." and he gave her a loving look.

Lily gulped, blinked like an owl, her entire focus on Jake standing next to her, his large, warm hand on her shoulder.

The living room quieted.

Lily reached up, touching Jake's hip. "Yes, I love you. And I'm happy just to live with you, Jake."

"No," he said, shaking his head, "this has to be official,

darling." He lifted his hand from her shoulder and dug into his pocket. Producing a small black velvet box, he opened it. "This is my promise to you that I'll cherish and love you the rest of my life . . ." and he held the diamond engagement ring toward her to take.

His heart was beating heavily in his chest. Never had Jake wanted anything more than this brave woman. Lily's eyes grew huge at the beauty of the engagement ring he held out to her, and then her gaze flew to his. "Well? What's your decision?" he teased, his voice low with so much feeling.

She took the ring out of the box. "Slide it on my finger?"

Tears jammed into his eyes, and it took everything he had to force them back. His fingers were huge, and the ring platinum and delicate. Fumbling, he finally got the ring situated correctly so that, as Lily held out her long, slender hand, he eased it on her finger. It fit beautifully, and she blushed. But her eyes, those crystalline blue eyes of hers through which he could see to her soul, were shining with such love for him.

She stood up, giving everyone a nervous smile. "I didn't expect this . . ."

There were cheers and clapping all around them as everyone celebrated the good news.

Lily slipped her hands across Jake's broad shoulders, standing up on tiptoe, her mouth meeting his. All the boisterous sounds dissolved as she melted beneath his mouth, which moved so worshipfully across hers. Tears dribbled out of her shut eyes, down her cheeks, the salty warmth of them tasted between them. It was a forever kiss, so warm and welcoming, a new chapter in their lives—together.

Don't miss the next exciting book in the
WIND RIVER VALLEY series:

WIND RIVER PROTECTOR

by
Lindsay McKenna

Coming to your favorite retailers and e-retailers
in November 2019!

Connect with  Us

Visit us online at
KensingtonBooks.com
to read more from your favorite authors, see books
by series, view reading group guides, and more.

Join us on social media

for sneak peeks, chances to win books and prize packs,
and to share your thoughts with other readers.

facebook.com/kensingtonpublishing
twitter.com/kensingtonbooks

Tell us what you think!

To share your thoughts, submit a review,
or sign up for our eNewsletters, please visit:
KensingtonBooks.com/TellUs.

More by Bestselling Author
Hannah Howell

More from Bestselling Author
JANET DAILEY